PRAISE FOR *Altered*

"Within minutes, this medical-engineering thriller will have readers glued to their seats.... **Riveting**."
—*Kirkus Reviews*

"**Heart-racing** action complete with identity twists, mystery, and romance born from the core of the story make this unputdownable." —LISSA PRICE, international bestselling author of *Starters*

"**Action-packed**..." —*Publishers Weekly*

"**A rapid-fire thriller**.... Fans of the Hunger Games and Maze Runner series seeking more dystopian titles would likely enjoy this new adventure." —*Booklist*

"A thrill ride full of twists, secrets, and betrayals. **I loved it. More, please!**" —KIM HARRINGTON, author of *The Dead and Buried*

JENNIFER RUSH

REB

O R N

Little, Brown and Company

New York Boston

Little, Brown and Company

Hachette Book Group
1290 Avenue of the Americas, New York, NY 10104
Visit us at lb-teens.com

Little, Brown and Company is a division of Hachette Book Group, Inc.

First Paperback Edition: January 2016
First published in hardcover in January 2015 by Little, Brown and Company
"Played" first published as an ebook edition in February 2015 by
Little, Brown and Company

Library of Congress Cataloging-in-Publication Data

Rush, Jennifer (Jennifer Marie), 1983– author.
Reborn / Jennifer Rush. — First edition.
pages cm
Sequel to: Erased.
Summary: Racing against remnants of the Branch, genetically altered teenager Nick follows his scattered memories to find a mysterious girl who has been haunting his dreams.
ISBN 978-0-316-19706-9 (hc) — ISBN 978-0-316-32368-0 (ebook) —
ISBN 978-0-316-19707-6 (pb)
[1. Genetic engineering—Fiction. 2. Memory—Fiction.
3. Identity—Fiction. 4. Love—Fiction. 5. Science fiction.]
I. Title.
PZ7.R89535Re 2015
[Fic]—dc23
2014011346

10 9 8 7 6 5 4 3 2 1

RRD-H

Printed in the United States of America

To Lacy "Loose Cannon,"

for helping me keep the faith

1

NICK

I NEVER TOOK TO FIGHTING LIKE THE others. I could do it well enough. Maybe I was even good at it. But I didn't like it. Or maybe it was that I liked it too much.

Sam fought only when it meant something. Like escaping. Surviving. Protecting. Cas treated fighting like a dance—he always wanted to show off the best moves. Mostly because he's a jackass.

When I fought, I had a hard time pulling back.

I slammed a shot of whiskey, the cheap shit, and felt the muscles in my stomach tense. *Pull from the core*, that's what Sam always said. Or maybe it was something he used to say, back before we lost our memories to the Branch—the shadowy organization that had turned us into supersoldiers, and then tried to kill us when we didn't obey like dogs.

I have a hard time telling the difference between an old memory and a recent one.

"Did you hear me?" the man next to me said.

"I did." I felt the gloom of the bar settle over me. There'd always been something about dark, smoky bars. Something familiar.

"Well, what do you have to say, then?" the man said.

He was taller than me by a handful of inches. Bigger, too. Fatter, though, which meant he was slower. Speed always wins over brawn, if you ask me. Not that anyone ever does.

I turned to the man and wavered to give him the idea I was drunk, which I wasn't. Or at least, not entirely. I peered at him from beneath heavy lids, and then looked over his shoulder at his girlfriend or wife or sister or maybe it was his mom. "Your mom is pretty. I'm sorry I hit on her."

The woman frowned. The man scowled.

"That ain't what I'm talking about. My friend says he saw you steal my wallet back near the john. Did you?"

Yes. "No."

"Well, he said you did."

If I'd really been trying, there wouldn't have been witnesses to the lift. So I guess I'd been sloppy on purpose.

Maybe I did like fighting after all. There, I admitted it.

Anna's voice came back to me, from this morning. *Be honest with yourself. And if you can't, at least be honest with me.*

"Give it to me." The man took a step closer. My fingers itched to curl into fists.

Stop exploding so often, Anna said. *You'll be happier.*

The problem with Anna was that she saw things in me that weren't there. I was a lost cause.

"Hand it over and we'll forget this ever happened," the man went on. His girlfriend laid a hand on his shoulder and gave him a tug.

"Raymond, he's just a kid. I don't even know how he got in here." She scowled at the bartender, as if this was somehow his fault.

I was actually somewhere north of twenty, so I was most likely legal. I just looked younger. Genetic alterations will do that to you. And since none of us—me, Sam, Anna, and Cas—had any real, legal papers, we'd secured fake IDs through some guy Sam had used in the past.

Two of the man's friends stepped closer. The bartender set his towel down. "Come on, guys. You're not doing this in here. Take it outside."

Raymond set a hand on the bar and leaned in. His breath smelled like cigars and vodka. His eyes were bloodshot. He'd been here when I came in, so he'd probably been drinking longer than I had.

"Give me my goddamn wallet, son. Or you'll regret it."

I doubted that. Regret wasn't something I was familiar with.

"For God's sake, Raymond," his girlfriend said.

The friend on his left opened the fold of his down-filled vest to show off the handgun he had holstered to his belt. Like that was supposed to scare me. "Hand it over," he said. "We all saw you take it."

I blinked lazily. "I don't have whatever you're looking for."

Raymond took in a deep breath, and his chest puffed out. The veins in his neck fattened like a blow snake. He was ready to swing. He was the kind of man who had a tell so obvious, it was practically written across his forehead. That's no way to win a fight.

You keep your face straight. Your body loose. Your steps light. And if you do it right, they'll never know it's coming.

Raymond's face turned from ruddy to crimson right before he reached over and grabbed my wrist. He pulled my arm toward him, as if he meant to twist it behind my back.

I had already slid off the stool three seconds earlier, ready for this five seconds before that.

I kicked with my right foot, catching his knee. He howled and let go of my wrist, so I threw a backhanded fist, catching him across the temple. His friend, the one carrying the pistol, came at me.

I grabbed my empty shot glass and chucked it at him. It collided with his forehead with a resounding *crack*. His flesh split open, spewing blood down the bridge of his nose.

The third friend caught me off guard with a jab to my side, then a quick punch to the face. There wasn't much power behind it, though, and ignoring the pain was easy. I hit him across the jaw. He staggered back and rocked the table behind him, spilling drinks all over the place.

Someone shouted to call the cops.

Raymond recovered and barreled toward me, catching me in the wide span of his arms. He slammed me into the wall with his weight, and all the air left my lungs.

He punched with meaty knuckles, cracking my nose. Blood ran down the back of my throat with a hot, coppery tang.

I slid down the wall fast, hitting the floor in a second. Raymond brought his booted foot up when I grabbed the leg of the nearest chair, hauling it over me, using the seat as a shield.

The chair smashed into pieces, leaving me with nothing but a leg still in my hands.

I rocked forward onto a knee and whacked Raymond in the shin with the leg, and cracked him in the knee on the comeback. I rose to my feet, hitting him once, then twice in the head.

Raymond hit the floor with a satisfying *thud*.

The pistol-carrying friend made a grab for his gun when I rounded on him, the chair leg hanging loosely by my side.

"Don't," I said.

The entire bar was silent save for Raymond groaning at my feet and the *click-scratch* of the old jukebox switching records behind me.

I could hear the pounding of my heart in my head, and finally I felt alive.

I pulled Raymond's wallet from the inside pocket of my coat and tossed it toward him. It landed with a slap on his chest. His girlfriend just stared at me.

Everyone was staring at me. A toxic rush of power ran through my veins.

Sirens blared in the distance, so I hurried toward the back door, the chair leg still in my hand.

"This is the third time in a month you've come home looking like this."

I ignored Anna and made my way up the stairs. She followed.

"Nick. Talk to me, damn it."

I went into the bathroom and tried to shut the door, but she shot a foot into the doorway and pushed her way in. I groaned.

The upstairs bathroom wasn't much bigger than the downstairs bathroom, and two people in it was one too many.

I leaned back into the vanity, propping the heels of my hands on the sink. "I ran into a doorknob," I said. She smacked me in the side, and fresh pain chased the hit. I hunched over. "Fuck, Anna."

"The doorknob hit you in the ribs, too?"

I turned around, giving her my back, and leaned over the sink. I suddenly felt like I might puke.

"What happened?" She shut the door, making room for herself at the side of the vanity. "Was it someone from the Branch?"

The panic in her voice made the truth race out. "No."

She exhaled. "Thank God. I thought…" She trailed off and sighed.

Out of all of us, Anna was particularly edgy when it came to matters of the Branch. Her uncle, Will O'Brien, had created the organization to research and produce bio-weaponry, and he'd roped his family into participating in his programs in exchange for the things they needed most. For Anna's older sister, Dani, it was help for their pill-popping father.

And later, when Anna was near death after getting shot by that very same deadbeat dad, Dani made a deal with Will to save Anna's life. In exchange, Dani had given us all up. Sam, Cas, and me. I still wasn't sure how I felt about the whole thing. Dani's deception was the reason I'd been locked in a cell in a basement for five years, getting poked and prodded like an animal. It was also how Anna found herself mixed up with the Branch. But her life had been saved, and I thought that made my being a prisoner worth it, no matter how much it had sucked.

Five years later, when Anna's memories started to return and she realized the truth, she killed Will in a showdown, thereby destroying the head of the Branch. His second-in-command—Riley—was still out there, though. None of us would really be free until Riley was dead. We'd picked up on some leads, hoping to hunt him down and take him out, but all of them were dead ends. Wherever Riley was, he was keeping a low profile, and that worried us. He'd had plenty of time to reach out to old contacts and pull the Branch back together, provided he found the right funding.

Anna gave me a shove. "Sit so I can take a look at your injuries." All trace of her earlier panic was gone, leaving only exasperation and a driving need to take care of something that was broken. Unfortunately, that something was me.

"You don't have to—"

"I know I don't have to." Her jaw tensed. "Sit down."

I closed the toilet seat and sat, feeling the ache of the fight settling into my joints. I needed painkillers. Maybe something stronger than OTC.

"Where's Sam?" I asked.

"In town, filling the gas cans."

"Cas?"

She bent down to fish out the first-aid kit from beneath the sink. "He went running about a half hour ago." She unzipped the kit on the vanity top and started tearing into gauze packs. I caught her hand mid-tear, and she glared over at me.

"Stop," I said. "Don't waste the supplies. A rag will do."

She frowned, but didn't argue, and switched to a rag she dug out of the closet. She wetted it down and came over to me, hunching so we were face-to-face.

Her blond hair was braided, and it hung over her shoulder, tied off with a black rubber band. Dark shadows painted the skin beneath her eyes. She hadn't been sleeping well lately. Flashbacks and old demons haunted her out of bed. I could relate. None of us really slept well, except for Cas. Cas could sleep through an air raid.

Anna cleaned the blood from my face and the open wound on

the side of my eye, working with the methodic confidence of a professional, even though she wasn't.

"Why do you keep doing this?" she mumbled.

I scowled. "Why do you keep asking?"

Another frown. It was her default expression with me.

"What's going on, Nick? Is it more flashbacks?"

Yes.

I looked past her at the towel hanging from the towel rack. It used to be brown. Now it was a faded mud color.

I saw a flash of a girl. I kept seeing her. The same girl. And every time I did, she was shaking. No, not shaking. *Trembling.*

And there was always blood on her face, tears running through it. Blood pulsed out of a bullet wound in her chest, and she held her left side like it hurt.

I didn't know who she was. I didn't know how she'd been injured, or if it'd been me who did it. Sometimes I doubted the reliability of my head. Maybe she was an image left over from my life before the Branch. A girl I saw in a movie. A character I read about in a book.

If she was real, I couldn't stand to live with the idea that I'd hurt her. The only way I'd have gone that far was if she was trying to kill me first. If the girl was connected to the Branch, then she wasn't innocent. No one involved with them was ever innocent. Me included.

"In my files," I started, "did it say anything about a girl from any of my missions? She might have been about our age. Or maybe a bit younger."

Anna thought for a second. "I don't think so, but I could check again." She nudged my chin, forcing me to look at her, but I quickly shifted away.

Anna had always been the type of person who didn't hesitate when it came to touching. For her, touching was caring. For me though, touching always meant pain. That's what happens when your dad spends his free time beating the shit out of you. My life was crap even before I joined the Branch.

"Is that what all this is about?" Anna asked. "A girl?" There was a note of worry in her voice. Like she was afraid I'd fall down the rabbit hole of love and get myself shot. Fuck that.

I didn't answer the question. Instead I did what I do best. I scowled at her. "Just look, please?"

She frowned, but nodded.

"Thanks." I edged past her to the door to escape. This time she didn't follow.

2

ELIZABETH

I SCANNED THE SHELVES ABOVE MY DESK and ran a finger down the row of cobalt glass bottles labeled with peeling stickers that said things like THAT DAY THE POWER WENT OUT, SPRING, and CARNIVALS.

My memories were carefully chronicled in fragrant oils, mixed in cobalt bottles, labeled and shelved.

I stopped when I found the bottle—the label—that I'd been searching for.

GABRIEL.

I dreamed of him last night.

Upon waking this morning, I was reminded immediately of just how long it'd been since he'd disappeared from my life, as quickly and suddenly as he'd arrived.

It was hard to forget someone when he'd saved your life, regardless of how much—or how little—you valued it.

Gabriel's bottle was the oldest. The first. Tied to one defining moment in my life—the night that I was saved, the night that I escaped the people who had kidnapped my mother and me and held us captive for six long months.

I plucked the bottle from the shelf. Though the cork was still firmly lodged in the neck, I immediately recalled the way he smelled.

Musk. Pine. A drop of cinnamon. Bergamot. And finally, cedarwood.

The scar running from my left side all the way down to my hip bone flared, a phantom burning where a knife dragged across my flesh, slicing through tissue and muscle, nicking bone.

The second scar, the old bullet wound in my chest, pulsed.

I missed him. I missed him in a foreign way that I couldn't explain. I didn't really know him. I hadn't even spent much time with him. But every time I thought of him, there was this crushing ache in my head, like Gabriel's absence was a hole inside me, so deep and wide that nothing else would fill it. By saving my life, he'd taken a part of it with him.

Without opening the bottle, I put it back on the shelf and tucked it behind the one labeled WILDFLOWERS.

I couldn't revisit Gabriel today. Maybe not tomorrow, either.

His bottle—its contents—was the one I loved and hated and feared and tried desperately to forget.

But it was the one I couldn't forget even if I tried.

Pots and pans crashed together in the kitchen as I made my way downstairs. I found my foster mother, Aggie, digging in one of the bottom cupboards, her hair tied back with a bandanna. Various ingredients were spread out on the countertop.

"What are you looking for?" I asked.

Startled, she whacked her head on the edge of the cabinet door. She scooted back, rubbing the sore spot. "You scared me."

"Sorry." I went straight for the coffeepot. Aggie had my favorite mug waiting for me nearby, and I filled it to the top.

"I'm looking for my Bundt cake pan."

I gestured at the cabinet on the far left. "Check that one."

She frowned, but looked inside and pulled out the pan in question. "Well, how about that."

Out of all the foster parents I'd had, Aggie was by far my favorite. I'd been through five homes before settling down here.

Aggie was well into her sixties when she took me in. She was a single woman who had lost her only daughter to breast cancer many years back. Aggie understood loss like none of my other foster families had.

Our suffering wasn't the same, exactly, but it was suffering nonetheless. She'd been patient with me from the beginning. Kind. Soft-spoken. I wasn't sure where I'd be without her.

After I'd been rescued, I'd felt like a buoy lost out at sea. My mother had always been my rock—she was strong and determined and smart. In some ways, living without her was worse than being held captive.

A lot of my earlier anxiety attacks could be traced back to my mom's absence. Some tiny thing would remind me of her—a scented candle, her favorite brand of chocolate, an old sweater—and the pain would come crashing back.

I couldn't stop seeing her face, the panic in her eyes, when my captors threatened us both to secure my full cooperation. They didn't come right out and say it, but it was certainly implied that if I didn't do everything they asked, they'd kill my mother without hesitation.

"Do you work today?" Aggie asked as she handed me a banana. "Eat that up while I cook you some eggs."

Aggie was forever pushing food on me, fussing over how thin I was. Compared to her, I was small—she was a large woman, with wide shoulders and a substantial chest—but compared to Chloe, or any of the girls Chloe hung out with, I was average sized.

"I have today off," I answered, peeling back the banana's skin. "Are you busy? We could have a movie day."

"I have to be at the senior citizens' center this afternoon, otherwise I would love to spend the day with you. You'll be all right on your own?"

"Of course," I lied. Honestly, I didn't want to spend the day in the house by myself. When I was alone, I tended to disappear inside my own head, and my head was a landscape of horrors from the past.

Aggie gave me a sidelong glance before turning and busying herself at the stove. "Actually, you know what, I'm sure they can find another volunteer. I'll give them a call and let them know I can't make it."

"You don't have to do that."

"Nonsense. I want to." She waved the spatula in the air. "We were supposed to paint flowerpots today, and really, do I need more flowerpots?"

Her back deck was littered with them. Big pots on the floor, small pots lined up on the railings. More pots were placed around the house, and not all of them held plants. At least a half dozen of them held odds and ends. She was right, she didn't need more, but that wasn't the point. I hated asking her to change her plans for me.

But I couldn't bring myself to object, either. The past was creeping up on me today, suffocating me like a shroud.

"If you're sure," I said, and she nodded. "Thanks, Aggie."

She smiled. "Of course."

I closed my eyes once she turned away, and pressed my fingers to the bridge of my nose, feeling a headache growing beneath my skull.

I saw my mother in the darkness, screaming my name as my captors dragged her from me.

I'd escaped from where I was being held, but my mother hadn't been so fortunate.

If I'd fought a little harder the last time I'd seen her, I would have hugged her, hugged her tightly and told her how much I loved her.

3

NICK

I WOKE IN THE MIDDLE OF THE NIGHT, choking back a memory of dear old Dad that had found its way into my dreams. I lay in bed for a while, trying to force myself back to sleep. When that didn't happen, I tossed off the sheet, threw on some clothes, and headed downstairs.

Everyone was asleep, so the house was quiet and dark. I dodged a creaky floorboard between the stairs and the living room, and made my way to the fridge. Inside were all the necessities—leftovers and beer. After dinner, Anna had sliced up what was left of the chicken into bite-sized pieces. Easy enough to eat with my fingers.

I left just enough food for it to be a tease, not enough for a meal. Cas would whine like he always did when things came down to food. I smiled to myself as I plucked a beer from the fridge.

With a quick *pop* of the front door lock, I was outside, grateful for the cool air. The moon was nearly full, so I didn't need a flashlight to find my way to the edge of the woods, to the hollowed-out log that sat beneath a massive maple tree. I rooted around inside and pulled out the pack of cigarettes I'd hidden there along with a lighter.

Vice in hand, I went back to the porch, eased into one of the old lawn chairs, and propped my feet on the railing.

The night was noisy. Always with the goddamn crickets. Sometimes a coyote or two howled at each other.

Leaning back in the chair, the front legs rocking off the porch floor, I lit a cigarette and drew on it. Smoking was an old habit, one I'd obviously quit somewhere along the line, but I couldn't remember if I'd quit on purpose, or if I'd just forgotten I'd smoked once my memories were wiped.

Either way, I still craved cigarettes like I craved good whiskey, and sometimes drawing on nicotine helped to break up all the shit crowding my head.

I felt better already.

I took another pull off the beer and then set it on the porch floor. I dug in my pants pocket and withdrew a flattened paper crane. Cigarette still clutched between two fingers, I brought the crane up to my line of sight and stared at its pointed head.

My mother was the one who taught me how to fold paper cranes. I was only five, maybe six. At first, my cranes came out crooked, with more fold lines in the paper than were needed. But origami was one of the few things we did together, and I didn't care so much about the cranes as I did the attention.

The memories of my old life were still foggy and disjointed, but more and more of it was coming back—things I didn't want to remember, things I was angry at having forgotten. The paper cranes were one of the first things I remembered about my mom. Everything else about her came after.

My mom was a shitty parent.

When my memories started to resurface, I'd remembered my dad first, and that my mom had left us when I was young. I'd wanted to think she left for a good reason, maybe because she couldn't stand the shit and chaos my dad put her through.

Now I knew better.

Mom left because she was a junkie, and being a junkie had always been more important to her than being a mom.

She had good days, where she was just high enough to be happy, not too blitzed to be useless. Those were the days when we folded. It was the only creative thing she knew how to do, maybe because it didn't require a lot of clearheaded thinking once you knew the steps, and she knew them by heart.

On the rarest days, I had both parents. Dad used to take me fishing on Little Hood Creek, and Mom would curl up on the bank, a book in her hand, big, round sunglasses hiding her eyes. When she was baked from the sun, she'd toss the book, dip her feet in the water, and point out the minnows darting between her legs.

It was all so goddamn good.

And so goddamn breakable.

The good days burned into bad nights, and the bad nights bled into bad weeks. Eventually Mom left, and Dad started drinking more, and every day was a bad day until I forgot what it was like to have a good one.

The first time Dad hit me, I was eight. He was drunk on cheap tequila and harassed by old demons. I'd broken a window hitting a ball around the yard. It was the only time he ever apologized for hitting me. And it was the only time I believed he wouldn't do it again.

After a while, when I got bigger, I started fighting back. Sometimes I was as drunk as him. Two dark-haired guys, haunted and sneering, stumbling around with fists flailing. We must have looked like a joke.

The last night I saw him, he beat me so bad I couldn't walk. I hid in my room for three days, only coming out when he was in town at the bar or bumbling his way through his job at a factory.

On the fourth night, after he passed out, I stole his car keys off the kitchen counter and a six-pack of beer out of the fridge, and crept outside in the dark.

I never looked back.

But now, for some fucked-up reason, I *was* looking back. I couldn't stop thinking about him. And about me. And about whether or not I was just like him.

And sometimes, when I killed someone with my own hands, I

worried I was worse than him. Far as I knew, he'd never murdered anyone. But me, I'd killed so many times I couldn't count the bodies.

Maybe that's what was driving me to dig up the past now, to find out the details of the mission I'd been on when I'd met that girl.

I took another hit off the cigarette and ground it out beneath my boot.

If I found out I'd killed that girl—well, then maybe I'd finally accept my fate. Embrace the cursed blood in my veins.

But if she was still alive...

Maybe there was redemption for me after all.

4

NICK

I SOMEHOW MANAGED TO SLEEP A FEW more hours, and when I got up, Cas was staring at me from across the room.

I scrubbed at my eyes, trying to scrub away the dregs of last night. I had a headache so fucking huge, it felt like my eyeballs were trying to pop out of their sockets. "What the hell are you looking at?"

"You were growling in your sleep," he answered.

"Bullshit."

"I thought you were turning into a werewolf. 'Course, at least as a dog, you'd be easier to house-train."

I grabbed an empty beer bottle from the dresser and lobbed it at him. He deftly plucked it from the air and grinned. He was always so disgustingly pleased with himself.

"I'm so badass."

I ignored him as I made my way for the door.

"Put some clothes on!" he yelled. "Anna doesn't want to be assaulted by your junk."

I looked down at my boxers and turned back around, throwing on some pants before I headed downstairs. Anna and Sam were already up, dressed in their running clothes.

"You guys heading out, or just coming back?" I asked.

"Heading out," Sam said. "You want to come?"

One thing that helped clear my head was running.

"Give me five minutes?" I asked, and Sam nodded.

Exactly six minutes later, we were facing the woods behind our house. I'd thrown on a T-shirt and baggy sweatpants, along with my running shoes. I preferred training with as many disadvantages as I could come up with, so I always overdressed, and rarely wore sunglasses. The clothes were easy to run in, but in less than a quarter of a mile, I was sweating buckets. The day had promised to be a hot one, and zero cloud cover made the sun merciless. The more scenarios I was prepared for, the better.

When we rented this house in the woods, we'd gone out and mapped a running route that took us through dense forest for over seven miles. It was uneven terrain, the path barely worn enough to give us clear access to the forest. Every few feet, branches were clawing at my face and threatening to blast out an eye. Anna, the shortest out of all of us, had it easier. She raced through the forest like a ghost.

We came back to the house somewhere around ten AM. Anna called the shower first, so Sam and I hung out in the backyard to spar. We'd tossed our soaked T-shirts onto the porch to make it harder for either of us to get a grip on the other.

Sam swung with a left hook that I dodged easily enough. I caught him with a right to the ribs, and he hunched over, blowing out a breath.

"Fuck," he muttered, holding his side.

As much as I liked Anna, I liked Sam better without her. For one, he cursed more. And two, he was a lot more vicious.

"Come on, pretty boy," I said. "Is that all you got?"

He straightened and smiled, but his eyes were burning with a promise to do me bodily harm. I'd like to see him try. He was a better technical fighter, but I was more explosive, even hungover. When I hit, I hit hard, and although Sam hid it well, I could tell he was hurting.

We circled each other. Sam cut left, then switched at the last second, catching me off guard. He landed a blow to my face, cracking my jaw off-kilter, and I staggered back, spitting blood to the dirt.

His smile grew wider.

"All right," I said. "Now we're talking."

I didn't pause, didn't want him to catch his breath. I went in fast, threw one, two, three punches that Sam deftly blocked. He swung for my face again, and I ducked. When I came back up, he caught me in the nose.

"Son of a bitch," I said, feeling the blood already pouring down my throat.

"Come on, pretty boy," he mocked. "Is that all you got?"

I laughed. "You're such an asshole sometimes. If Anna only knew how ruthless you really are."

He threw an uppercut. I blocked.

"Anna isn't delusional," he said. "She knows I'll kick your ass just for fun."

I laughed again and rocked back for a kick to his knee, but he was gone before I could land it. A second later, his arm was around my neck, his other arm moving into place for a choke hold.

I grabbed both his wrists and flipped him over my back. He landed with a *thud* on the ground, and a ragged chuckle escaped him as he rolled onto all fours.

Being the considerate person I am, I gave him three seconds to recuperate before I kicked him in the kidneys. He flew back, but got his feet beneath him and charged before he'd barely landed.

He slammed me into a tree, and the breath rushed out of my lungs. I came up with a knee to his chest. He countered with an elbow to my face.

I was just about to kick him off me when a shot of cold water blasted both of us.

Anna stood ten feet away with the hose in her hands. "You guys never know when to call it quits. You keep going and you'll kill each other!"

Sam stalked toward her. "We just started. No one got hurt."

"Blood is running down your face," she pointed out. "And Nick's nose is bleeding. And your lip is split and—"

While Sam distracted her, I charged toward her, grabbed the hose, and yanked the sprayer out of her hand.

"Nick!" she screamed, and then I soaked her.

Sam threw his head back and let out a chest-deep laugh. Anna wasn't so amused. She stood there, soaking wet, glaring at me.

"I hate you both!" she screamed, and turned for the house, but Sam caught her, his arms around her waist, before she could escape. He kissed her neck, murmured something through her hair that made her blush.

"That's my cue to leave," I said.

Cas was leaning against the sink in the kitchen when I came inside, a hunk of steak in his hands.

I grabbed a towel out of the laundry room. "You look like a fucking barbarian."

"And you look like a dumbass."

I took the stairs up two at a time, and claimed the bathroom before anyone else could. After running seven miles, sparring with Sam, and then getting doused with bitingly cold water, the hot water felt good. I stayed beneath the showerhead longer than I should have—the hot water would run out before Sam got in here—but I didn't give a shit.

When I came up for a breath and swiped the water out of my eyes, a pulse started in the base of my neck and rocketed up my skull.

I slammed my eyelids shut.

I knew what that feeling meant. It was the precursor to a flashback.

Images flickered in the darkness beyond my closed eyes. Like the past was a movie slowly coming back in fits and starts.

There was the girl again—the one I'd seen in the forest—but she was somewhere else now. In a white room, with a white floor, dark hair wild around her face. She looked at me, through that wild hair, and said my name.

But it wasn't *Nick* she used.

It was Gabriel.

5

ELIZABETH

AS I WALKED IN THE SIDE DOOR OF Merv's Bar & Grill, I nearly ran into my best friend, Chloe.

"Heeeeeyyyy," she called, sliding her order pad into the apron tied around her waist. "I nearly knocked your face off."

"Sorry," I said, and made my way to the break room, Chloe trailing behind.

"What do you work tonight?" she asked, and hopped onto the table, swinging her legs.

"Umm... I think I work till eleven."

"Oh?"

Though my back was to her, I could hear the devious smile spreading across her face.

"Why?" I asked, turning.

"Evan works tonight," she sang, and waggled her eyebrows.

"I thought he had today off?"

"Well." She grabbed a pen from the table and twirled it between her fingers. "I may or may not have told John, who was supposed to work tonight, that we overscheduled, and then I may or may not have told Evan that we were shorthanded. Ergo..."

"Chloe!"

"What?" She shrugged. "Now you get an entire shift with Evan. Though"—she checked the clock—"he's, like, two minutes away from being late. Go figure."

I hung my bag in my locker and pulled out my apron, trying to pretend like I didn't care that Evan was working the same shift I did, like I wasn't thankful that Chloe had pulled all these strings to put us on the same shift.

I liked Evan. A lot. But I was also A-level dysfunctional, and having a real relationship seemed the least likely thing to ever happen to me. It didn't help that the entire town knew about the horrible things that had happened to me six years ago. The kidnapping. The trauma thereafter.

Three months after I'd been rescued, I'd had a meltdown in a grocery store that nearly made the local news. It didn't matter that it hadn't. Everyone had heard about it within a day anyway.

I'd started screaming in the toilet paper aisle, and then burrowed into the stacked packages shaking and sobbing. That was the first time I'd switched foster homes, and it wasn't the last.

"You shouldn't have gone to all that trouble," I said. "I mean, it's Evan. And it's me."

Chloe bit the end of the pen between her teeth. "Don't even feed me that line of bullshit about how you're unlovable."

She teased out another smile, this one wanton, as she added, "Evan asked about you yesterday."

My interest was piqued and it got the better of me. "He did? What did he say?"

"He asked what you were doing. Said we should call you up and invite you out after our shift was over." She twirled the pen. "I texted you, but you never answered."

My heart sank. She *had* texted me. And I'd ignored it because I'd been watching movies with Aggie. But if she'd told me in the first text that Evan wanted me to hang out with the group, I would have answered. All she'd said was, *Hey.* That was it. Chloe was the kind of person who would talk your ear off face-to-face, but her texts were sparse. One word. Sometimes two. Never strung together in a coherent sentence.

"Are you guys going out tonight?" I asked.

She nodded. "But we're hitting up Arrow."

"Oh." Arrow was a nightclub that was eighteen and over, and I wouldn't be eighteen for a few more months.

The back door opened and then slammed shut. Evan sauntered

into the break room a few seconds later, his eyes heavy and bloodshot. His Merv's Bar & Grill polo was wrinkled and untucked, and his blond hair was unkempt. He dropped into the chair next to Chloe and rested his head on his arms.

"Feeling good today?" Chloe asked him, to which he replied with merely a grunt.

I stared at the back of his head, at the long blond hair hanging over the collar of his polo.

"My fucking head is pounding," he said. "Whose idea was it to buy a fifth of Jäger last night?"

"Um, yours," Chloe said. "I tried talking you out of it."

"Well, you clearly didn't try hard enough." He sat up and glanced at me. "Hey, Lis. How come you didn't come out with us last night?"

I shrugged. "I fell asleep early."

Chloe arched a brow my way, but I ignored it.

Evan leaned back in his chair and stretched his legs out. "Maybe that was for the best. Considering I feel like shit today."

"You look like shit, too," Chloe said.

He narrowed his eyes at her. "Why are we friends? You're always so mean to me, *Emily*."

Chloe scowled in return. She hated being called by her first name. Chloe was her middle name, and she'd been using it as long as anyone could remember. I'd known of Chloe before I started working at Merv's. She was friends with some of my friends, but we hadn't been properly introduced.

I didn't get to know her until last year, when I'd nearly had a panic attack in the middle of Merv's while Aggie and I were there for dinner. Chloe had been the one to sweep me away to the bathroom where, by some miracle, she'd been able to talk me down.

We'd been close ever since. She was the one who convinced me it might be a good idea to apply at the restaurant. "When you can't stand being inside your own head, getting out, being around other people helps," she'd said. I hadn't believed her at the time, but I was a believer now. Though I was nowhere near mentally healthy, I'd been doing a lot better since starting a part-time job.

Merv, of "Bar & Grill" fame, came into the back room and clapped his hands. "Chop-chop, people!"

Evan winced. "Merv. God. Too loud."

Merv bent over and shouted into Evan's ear. "Is this better?"

Evan covered his eyes with one hand and his exposed ear with the other. "I'm calling in sick."

"Too late," Merv said. "You're already here."

Evan rose slowly out of the chair and made his way toward the front of the restaurant. Merv glanced at Chloe and me. "Ladies. That means you, too."

Chloe grinned as she breezed past Merv. "I'm off in five minutes anyway."

"Then make the most of them!"

I tied my apron on and slid my order pad into the front pocket along with a handful of pens. They had a tendency to disappear—probably because Chloe liked chewing on them. It was a good idea to have extras.

"Lissy," Merv said, and I slowed. "You all right today?"

I glanced up at him. Merv was six foot four, and slight as a rail. He had warm, kind eyes, and a nice smile, and dark brown hair that went every which way. He was also extremely good at reading people. Like, to the point that it seemed like a superpower.

Despite the fact that I was damaged, erratic, sullen most of the time, and sometimes so depressed I could barely get out of bed, Merv hired me six months ago on the spot. I didn't even have experience. I suspected Chloe had had something to do with that, but I wasn't complaining. And I wasn't about to let Merv down.

"I'm fine," I said. "Thanks."

"All right." He clapped his hands and grinned. "Chop-chop, then!"

I'd been overwhelmed by waiting tables my first week on the job. The second week wasn't much better, but Chloe helped bolster my self-confidence to the point that I felt like maybe I could function like a normal person, and have a normal job like every other seventeen-year-old in town.

Evan helped, too.

I went over to the bar with a new drink order. Since I was still a minor, I could only place drink orders, not serve them. And whenever a customer placed an order, I got a tiny little thrill in my belly, knowing I'd have an excuse to go talk to Evan.

He was Merv's best bartender. Quick. Precise. A good listener, too, which seemed a prerequisite to the job. Evan once told me he'd considered minoring in psychology at the small university in town just to up his bartending game. His exact words. But then he decided he liked welding better, because it required less thinking and more doing.

"Hey, good-looking," he said when I came around the bar.

A smile instantly spread across my face. Evan technically called every girl here *good-looking,* but it still made me feel something I hadn't felt in a long time—noticed, in a good way.

"Hey." I handed him the drink order, and he got to work. "So Chloe said you guys are going to Arrow tonight?"

Evan grabbed a shaker. "Are we? I hadn't heard."

I leaned against the counter. "I wish I was eighteen."

Where did that come from? I sounded a little too whiny and needy, two things I absolutely hated.

"Why?" He nodded at the cut lime wedges behind me, and I handed one over, stuck between the claws of the silver tongs. "Would you go out with us?"

I shrugged. "Probably. Maybe. I don't know."

He smiled as he shook the mixed drink. "That is three non-answers."

"Yes," I said. "The answer is yes."

"Then we can change our plans. Arrow will be there tomorrow night. And the night after that. There's plenty to do around here that doesn't require you to be eighteen."

I straightened. "I didn't mean you had to rearrange your night for me."

He handed Merv a tray with the finished drink and an open beer. "Table twelve," he said, and Merv nodded as he left.

Evan came closer. My face warmed. I couldn't help but wonder if my makeup had held up since I put it on, or if my pores were huge, or if my teeth were clean. I quickly ran over in my head what I'd eaten for lunch. Apple, peanut butter, string cheese. Nothing that should have been stuck in my teeth.

Someone called for Evan down the bar, but he ignored it.

"I *want* to rearrange my night for you." He leaned in even closer. "Besides, I go out with the same people every single night. It'd be nice to have someone else to hang out with."

He winked and turned away to wait on the customer who was nagging him at the other end of the bar.

I lingered for a few seconds longer, listening to Evan greet the customer with as much cheeriness as he greeted everyone, despite the fact that the older man was still scowling, clearly frustrated with being ignored.

When the bell dinged in the kitchen, signaling a finished order, I turned away and hurried to check if it was one of mine.

The smile on my face remained the rest of the night.

6

ELIZABETH

"YOU REALLY DON'T HAVE TO DO THIS," I told Chloe as she tore clothing free of its hangers and tossed it at me.

"Yes, I do. Because I'm your best friend and best friends do not let their friends go out with boys they like looking"—she turned to me and waved her hand in the air, gesturing wildly at me—"like that."

I glanced down at my Merv's uniform. "I just got off work. Besides, I had planned on changing."

Evan was right, Chloe *was* mean, but it wasn't the kind of mean that was born out of malice. At least not with me. Since we'd become friends, she'd been on a mission to improve my life. If it wasn't for her, I never would have had the courage to speak to Evan, let alone go out with him and his friends.

I owed her a lot.

But really, did I need a makeover?

"I know what you're thinking," she said as she handed me a tank dress with a silky polka-dot skirt.

"What?"

"You're thinking I'm thinking you need a makeover if you're to impress Evan."

I blanched. That was exactly what I'd been thinking. Or at least, something like that.

"But I'm not doing this for Evan," she said.

"You're not?"

"No, silly." She laid her hand on my shoulder and squeezed. "I'm doing this for you. I don't think you need a makeover, but you keep telling me how you're beneath Evan, so I figure the better you feel about your appearance, the better you'll feel in your own skin."

I hung my head and let out a strangled laugh. "I'm not sure I could ever feel comfortable in my own skin."

Chloe sighed and led me to the bed. "Sit." I did, and she went on. "I know what you went through must have been..." She trailed off, and when I glanced at her, her eyes were unfocused and watery. "Well"—she took a breath—"it must have been terrible."

She said it with such conviction, it was almost as if she knew everything I'd gone through and just how bad it'd been. As if she understood every broken part of me and didn't think less of me because of it.

But then she blinked and asked quietly, "What *was* it like?"

No one had ever expressly asked me that before. They'd asked me what had happened, and they wanted to know right down to the minute details. But they'd never asked what it was *like*. It was as if they wanted the experience pared down to a bulleted list without any of the emotion, as if they wanted the horrors that filled the spaces in between to be forgotten, never mentioned. Even my therapist skirted the conversation, focusing instead on the present, and how I was feeling *now*.

"I don't know," I said, my voice raw. I cleared my throat. "It was . . . scary."

Chloe nodded and took my hand in hers. Hers was warm and strong. Chloe always came off small and harmless and bubbly, like a chickadee chirping for no other reason than to chirp. But right now, the hardness in her eyes and the sure way she held herself, shoulders rigid, forearms tense, it was like she'd flipped a switch. I realized, suddenly, that there was nothing small about her, no matter what she looked like.

"Then this is what you do," she said. "You take that fear, you take those horrible experiences and you lay them at your feet, and you build yourself a throne on top of them. You survived. You lived. It makes you special, Lis. No one else in this godforsaken town is as strong as you."

I blushed, for a moment believing every word she said. That surviving did make me special. But then the horror of the experience rushed back in, and I remembered that I was nothing more than a victim who'd barely survived at all.

"If you hate this town so much," I said, "why do you stay?"

Chloe lived alone in a small studio apartment. She'd once told me she'd moved to Trademarr when she was thirteen, and that her parents had homeschooled her. I'd never met them though, and as far as I could tell, they no longer lived here.

If I had the resources to leave Trademarr, I would in a heartbeat. In fact, I dreamed about it, and sometimes it was the only thing keeping me going. I wasn't sure about my plans after high school—I still had one more year to complete before graduating—but if I was able to go to college, then I was going as far away as I could.

When I was young, my mother had always talked about moving to California. To the *land of permanent summer*, she'd called it, and sometimes, in my heart of hearts, I entertained the thought of escaping there, too.

Chloe stood up, still considering my question, and returned to the closet, giving me her back. "Let's just say I have a lot of history here and leaving it has been harder than I thought it'd be."

"Oh."

When she turned again, all traces of her earlier hardness had disappeared, replaced with her wide smile and glittering blue eyes. "Look at this! I forgot I had it. You should wear it."

She handed me a silky peach-colored dress. I was fairer skinned than Chloe, like bleached sand. The dress would disappear on me.

"That's the point," Chloe said when I mentioned it. "It'll look like you're naked without actually showing anything."

I frowned. "I'm not sure that's what I want."

She screwed up her mouth as she thought. "Okay, fine, then how about the dress with the polka dots?"

I grabbed it from the bed. "I do like this one."

"Good." Chloe set her hands on my shoulders and steered me toward the bathroom. "Now hurry. Evan said he'd be here to pick us up in less than twenty minutes."

My stomach thrilled at the idea of spending the night, outside of Merv's, with Evan. Twenty minutes seemed like an eternity, and like no time at all.

7

NICK

I THREW A FEW T-SHIRTS IN MY BAG AND went back to the closet for a pair of jeans.

"Let us come with you," Sam said.

I ignored him and grabbed the jeans from the floor of the closet, then tore a flannel from a hanger.

"Nick," Anna said. "Stop for a second and talk to us."

Cas dropped onto my bed, even though his was right across the room. Of course, it was hard to sit on his bed when it was piled so high with shit; you'd need a fucking shovel to clean it off.

I hated sharing a room with him. I needed to get out of this place. I needed to *go*. It'd been over twenty-four hours since I'd had the flashback where the girl had called me Gabriel, and it'd taken Anna and me over fourteen of those hours to find the information I needed in my files.

Now I had the name of a town—Trademarr, Illinois—and I wasn't going to sit around any longer. There was only five or so hours of driving between me and the answers I needed.

"I don't want you guys coming," I said, and stuffed a few more things in the bag before zipping it up.

"He's secretly running off to join the circus," Cas said. He propped himself against the headboard of my bed. "What's your act going to be, Nicky? Oh, wait, I got a good one. The Surly Man. You'll scowl the crowd to death."

Anna crossed her arms. "Stop it, Cas."

"What?" Cas said. "I'm being serious."

"You're never serious," she replied.

"Am, too."

"Out," Sam said to Cas. Cas groaned, but didn't argue. He was obedient like a dog.

Sam stared at Anna for a second, and she caught on. "Me, too?" she said. Sam didn't answer the question, which was answer enough.

Anna paused for a beat, as if she meant to challenge him, but finally gave in. "I'll be downstairs if you need me." She closed the door behind her when she left.

"I don't want a lecture," I said to Sam.

"I didn't plan on giving one."

He crossed the room, his boots thudding heavy on the floor before he sat on the edge of my bed. He balanced his elbows on his knees and folded his hands together as he looked over at me. His right eye was circled in deep red and purple from the punch I'd caught him with yesterday. I was still feeling the ache of the fight in my ribs.

"What are they about?" he asked.

"What are what about?"

"Nick." Sam gave me the look he always gave me when he knew I was being a dumbass on purpose.

He'd meant the flashbacks.

"What, Anna didn't tell you?"

"She didn't."

I sighed and leaned into the dresser behind me. "A girl."

"You know who she is?"

I'd been thinking about her for days. No, *weeks.* But the flashbacks never gave me anything important.

"I don't even have a name," I answered. "Nothing. She's like a ghost." I scrubbed at my face, closed my eyes, and saw her again. "I have to know if she's real. Or alive."

Sam glanced at me, catching what I didn't say. "She was part of a mission, wasn't she?" I didn't answer. He nodded, like he already knew anyway, like it all made perfect fucking sense. "What if you go there," he said, "and you find out you killed her? Or what if you find out she's nothing like you thought? You think filling in the blanks is somehow going to fix everything?"

"Maybe."

"It won't."

"This is starting to sound like a lecture."

He looked away and let out a half laugh. "You're right."

What I didn't tell him was that I needed to know if I'd killed some innocent girl only because the Branch had told me to. I needed to know once and for all if I was just as bad as my dad. Maybe I'd been following in his footsteps all along, hurting people because it was in my blood.

"If you won't stay for me or Cas or even yourself," Sam said, "stay for Anna. You have no idea what she's like when you're gone."

I frowned. "What's she like?"

He thought for a second. "Restless."

I pushed away from the dresser. "You never told me this before."

"That's because you always came back."

I let out a grunt. "I'm not leaving for good, you know. Anna's a big girl."

"Don't be a dick. You can't promise that. Not when you're messing with things that trace back to the Branch."

What he meant was, *You can't promise you won't be dead in a week.*

I pictured my body rotting in a shallow grave in the middle of nowhere, and Sam, Cas, and Anna waiting for me to come home, wondering if this was the time I wouldn't. The guilt nearly changed my mind. Nearly.

"I have to go," I said.

Sam cracked a knuckle and thought for a second. Finally, he stood up. "What'd you pack, then?"

He wasn't asking about the clothes.

"A couple of knives. A Glock."

He took a few steps toward me as he reached behind him, beneath his T-shirt, and pulled out the Browning. He dropped out the clip, checked the bullets, and slammed it back into place. "Take it." He handed it to me.

"I got the Glock."

His expression never wavered. "Take it. You're on your own, you'll need more guns. Just in case."

I gave in. The Browning was *his* gun. If he was offering it to me, then it meant something important. "Thanks."

"If you need us, call. We'll be there in a second."

"I will." I wouldn't.

He clapped my shoulder. "Don't do anything stupid."

"The shit I do can't be half as stupid as the shit Cas does."

Sam laughed and shook his head as he turned away. "I'm not going to reply to that."

"Because it's true."

He pulled the door open and disappeared into the darkened hallway.

I took his spot on the bed, staring at the gun in my hands. I pictured the next few days alone, without Anna or Sam or even Cas within shouting distance, and started to wonder if I was making one of the biggest mistakes of my life.

The three of them were all I knew. All I'd ever needed to know.

But living like this, wondering about the past, about the mistakes I might have made, was tearing away at my insides like a handful of pills.

I had to go.

No matter what I found.

8

ELIZABETH

JUST AS EVAN PROMISED, EVERYONE changed their plans for me. It was a testament to how much sway Evan had over the group. Everyone did what Evan wanted.

The group had decided to have a bonfire out by Walsh Lake instead of going to Arrow. Evan picked up Chloe and me right on time, and he made his friend Sean move to the backseat, so I could ride shotgun. Another car with five of Evan's friends inside trailed behind us on the road.

Walsh Lake was north of town, and though the drive usually took twenty-five minutes or so, Evan sped nearly the whole way, cutting it down to fifteen. He had a foreign sports car, one of those compact cars that rode close to the ground, with a rear spoiler that was nearly as tall as me. It was a manual transmission, and I couldn't help but watch Evan as he shifted through the gears, the muscles and tendons in his forearm twining in a weird sort of dance.

With the night dark around us, the headlights cutting through it, and the summer air filtering in through our open windows, I started to plan what oils I'd mix to remember this night.

Mentally, I flipped through my collection. Amber, definitely. Musk. Maybe one of my cleaner fragrances, something reminiscent of a lake or—

"Lissy?" Evan said.

"What?"

He pulled his cell phone away from his ear and said, "What do you feel like drinking?"

One of Evan's friends was old enough to buy alcohol and was taking requests before meeting us at the lake with the haul.

"Whatever you're having."

"Fifth of Morgan," he said through the phone. Then, "I don't care. Coke, I guess." He ended the call and slid the phone into the center console.

A streetlight winked to red, and Evan shifted. The car's engine went down an octave, but still rumbled as we waited for a green light.

"I'm glad you came out with us tonight," he said.

"Me, too," I answered, shoving my hands in my lap.

"We should do this more often."

"Yeah," Chloe said, and sat forward, sticking her head through the seats. "You need to get out more. You need to find a man, too." She turned her head just enough to wink at me without Evan seeing.

"I volunteer," Sean said. "I'm free tonight."

Evan laughed and shook his head. "She's too good for you, you idiot."

The light flicked to green, and Evan hit the gas. The thrill of the takeoff, and his words, turned my stomach over on itself.

The west shore of Walsh Lake was dotted with openings where several fire pits had been installed. Across the lake, large, expensive houses were outlined in the moonlight, a few windows glowing amber in the dark.

Once we found an open spot, Evan parked, and we all clambered out. Crickets chirped from the underbrush and tree frogs croaked in between. The moon was full and cast its light on the black water in ripples of silver.

Evan started the bonfire with hardly any trouble before grabbing a few camping chairs from the trunk of his car. He offered me one and I sat. He opened a chair next to me and settled in as the fire gained ground.

"Tom should be here soon," he told everyone, and they answered with cheers. Tom was the supplier of alcohol.

A car stereo had been cranked up, and the windows rolled down, so that rock music wound its way to us at the shore. The steady beats seemed to vibrate through my chest.

Chloe and another girl, named Madison, danced around the fire while a few guys gathered wood to keep the fire going. Evan leaned toward me.

"Having fun yet?"

I smiled and nodded. "It's nice getting out every once in a while."

He grew serious. "How come you don't come out with us more?"

What I wanted to say was, *You guys don't always invite me*, or, *Some nights I can't stand the thought of being in public.*

Instead I said, "I don't know."

"Well, you should," he answered. "You should come out with us every night from now on."

I laughed. "That would mean you couldn't go to Arrow. And that wouldn't be fair."

He waved his hand in the air. "Arrow is lame anyway. They've started playing mostly techno music, and while I like techno music as much as the next guy, I need a little more rock, you know?"

I said yes, as if I did, but really I didn't.

Headlights flickered through the trees as a vehicle wound its way up the narrow trail to our spot. Tom turned his truck around at the end of the road and backed up. When he climbed out, he said, "Booze is here!" and everyone cheered again.

"I'll go mix you a drink," Evan said, and hurried off.

Tom opened the truck's tailgate, and a drinks station was quickly assembled. Chloe grabbed a beer and crashed into Evan's abandoned chair.

She waggled her eyebrows. "How's it going?"

"It's going fine."

"Don't be coy. You want to jump his bones, don't you?"

"Chloe!" I shouted.

"It's fine if you do! Every girl here does." She tipped her head at Madison, who was very *very* close to Evan's side as she waited for the bottle of Coke. "Madison has had a crush on him for years. And Hanna"—she pointed at a petite girl across the fire from us, who was chatting with another guy but checking on Evan every few seconds—"hooked up with Evan last month and hasn't stopped talking about it since. She will somehow find a way to insert it into every conversation. It drives us all mad."

I looked from Hanna to Evan and wondered what had happened. I also wondered what that sour taste on the back of my tongue was and realized it was the taste of jealousy.

"So listen, kid," Chloe said. "I know you try to pretend like (a) you don't like Evan or (b) you're somehow a Spam sandwich or the worst, (c), you're invisible! But I think Evan likes you and I think you should have some fun and I think you should stop thinking about it so much and just do it."

I wasn't sure if she meant do it, as in *it*, or as in kiss, hold hands, whatever. I didn't ask for clarification, because Evan reappeared at my side and shooed Chloe away.

She grinned at me as she wandered off.

"Here," Evan said, and handed me a red plastic cup.

I gave it a cursory smell. It was a deep, rich smell, like amber and spices. I'd never had rum before. In fact, I'd only ever had a few glasses of wine. I wasn't supposed to drink with all the medication I was on, but one wouldn't hurt. Would it?

I thought about Aggie finding out. When I'd called her to tell her I'd be home late, she'd sounded positively ecstatic. She'd told me to stay out as long as I wanted, and that she wouldn't wait up. Chances were she wouldn't even find out I'd been drinking, but a sliver of shame twisted in my chest.

"Try it," Evan said, and I took a drink.

The rum mixed with the Coke wasn't so bad. It was good, even. I took another sip, and another.

Evan and I chatted while I finished my first cup. He made me another after I asked for more. Near the bottom of my second, my face grew warm and my head grew fuzzy. The fire shifted left, then right. Chloe skipped in front of me, chasing after Sean, and for a second I had a hard time focusing on her.

The more I drank, the lighter and fuzzier I felt. The more I laughed, the more Evan laughed. The more I felt like maybe I could *do it*, whatever *it* was.

A lot of my insecurities drifted away with the embers of the fire. I forgot about Gabriel, about losing my mother, the terrible things I'd gone through. I finally felt like a normal girl.

After I'd finished my second drink and half of my third, Evan asked if I'd go for a walk with him. I left my cup sitting on the ground near my chair, and Evan grabbed my hand as he pulled me into the woods.

I immediately missed the heat of the fire, but the warmth of Evan's body pressed close to my side helped. His fingers were threaded with mine, our arms intertwined. We ducked through the trees and followed a trail that had been worn into the forest over time.

"This goes down to a little inlet," Evan explained, his voice quieter now that we weren't talking over the noise of the group. "It's really pretty," he added.

I smiled, even though he couldn't see me. I couldn't stop smiling.

The path we were on was wide and clear, and the moonlight lit it pretty well. Still, I had a hard time following a straight line. I kept stumbling over roots that had broken through the dirt. Evan let go of my hand and wove his arm around me, his fingers settling on my waist. A thrill went up my spine.

"That better?" he asked, a bit of amusement in his voice.

"Yes, thanks."

"Maybe you drank a little bit too much."

I laughed. "I guess I did."

"Sorry," he said, tightening his hold on me. "I should have stopped you after one."

"It's all right. I'm fine."

Better than fine.

The walk took less than ten minutes, and when we reached the inlet, the path turned into a steep decline. Evan went first and helped me down. When the ground flattened out again, Evan guided me to a large rock that sat half onshore, half in the water. It was big enough for both of us, and Evan pulled me in to him, tucking me in the crook of his arm.

My stomach swam.

"Sometimes I come out here by myself," he said, his voice low and heavy. "No one comes out here, especially at night. It's quiet."

It was. Though I could still hear the voices of the others off in the distance, here, now, was muffled by darkness, and punctuated by the constant slapping of the water against the shore.

"What do you think?" Evan asked, turning to face me.

I looked up at him. His eyes were flecked with silver from the moonlight, his lips gleaming, too. Maybe it was the alcohol, or maybe it was how kind Evan was being, but I leaned closer and kissed him.

He hesitated one second and no more before matching the kiss. His hand came up, fingers lacing through my hair. I reached over, placing my hand on his chest, and felt the flexing of muscle beneath the thin material of his T-shirt. His tongue ran across my mouth, growing more fervent, and I answered back.

I didn't want him to stop. I didn't want this night to stop.

Something chirped. Evan pulled away and sighed. "Sorry," he said, and dug his cell out of his pocket. The screen read MOM. "I gotta take this. Give me a second?"

"Sure."

Evan answered. "Hey, Ma." He paused, then, "I'm out at the lake. What? No. Hold on." He held the phone to his chest and said to me,

"I don't have much of a signal. I'm going to see if I can find one. Wait here?"

I wanted to tell him I'd come with, I was afraid of being out here in the dark alone, but instead I nodded. Because I didn't want to reveal how fragile I really was.

Evan kissed me once more before scooting off the rock and heading back up the hill. I watched him wander away, holding his phone in the air. Within seconds, he was gone, swallowed up by the forest.

I folded my arms around myself and stared out at the lake. The water was black, the other side invisible in the dark. Something cracked behind me. I whirled around. "Evan?" I called.

Nothing.

I slid off the rock and went up on tiptoes to see to the top of the hill. "Evan?"

A shuffle.

My heart sped up.

A twig snapped.

Goose bumps rose on my arms. I hurried up the hill and scanned the forest. I couldn't see Evan, or the glow of his cell phone. Something rattled the bushes to my left and I ran.

My heart beat at the back of my throat. My breath came quickly. My feet couldn't seem to move fast enough.

The forest teetered, my vision still unsteady. I caught my foot on something and went down hard, palms slamming into the rocky dirt. All the air left my lungs, and when I sucked in the next breath, I caught the overwhelming scent of pine.

Pine trees. Gabriel. Gabriel's scent.

I squeezed my eyes shut, that old feeling of panic and despair blowing up inside me, eating away at what was real and rational.

The old bullet wound in my chest burned, and I saw the flicker of a gun pointed at me in the darkness behind my closed eyelids.

The last night of the six months I'd been kidnapped had ended in a forest just like this.

A choked sound escaped my closing throat. Tears blurred my vision.

The scar running along my left side pulsed, and I acutely remembered the pain that had taken hold when the knife had cut my flesh.

Terror squeezed my windpipe.

I couldn't catch my breath.

What if they were here again? What if they were here to finish the job?

Hands reached for me, fingers digging into my shoulders, and I screamed.

I screamed and screamed and screamed.

"Lissy!"

I was sobbing now, sobbing and shaking, and every part of my body ached.

I wanted to go home. I wanted my mom.

"Elizabeth!" Chloe shook me.

On an inhale, I looked up. Everyone from the bonfire had gathered around. Evan was crouched in front of me, his hands gripping my wrists. Chloe was to my left.

"What happened?" Evan asked.

I tried so hard to stop the tears running down my face, but couldn't.

"Take me home," I said, my voice racked with sobs. "Please."

He nodded and helped me to my feet. As he led me away, I felt their eyes on me, watching. When I was gone, they'd whisper, and theorize, and joke about the crazy girl.

Because I was the crazy girl.

9

ELIZABETH

I CALLED IN SICK THE NEXT DAY. Merv sounded so unsurprised, so quiet and sympathetic, that I wondered if Evan or Chloe had told him what happened. Merv even told me to take the next day off, and the next if I needed it.

Retreating to my bedroom, the place that had become my safe spot since moving in with Aggie, sounded like the best idea ever. But hiding wouldn't change anything, and my therapist had told me the more I was alone with my thoughts, the worse they'd become.

So I assured Merv I'd return the next day, and hoped no one even mentioned what had happened. Most of all Evan.

A knock sounded on my bedroom door. I called out, "Come in," but didn't bother moving from the spot I'd been glued to since waking.

There was probably a permanent indentation where I'd been lying in my bed, staring at the cobalt bottles lined up on my shelf, wanting Gabriel's bottle so badly it hurt. It wasn't that I found comfort in him. Rather, that night in the woods had haunted me so much in the past twenty-four hours that I wanted to relive it, acutely, so I could get it all over at once. Experience the flashback and be done with it.

Aggie pushed my door open and shuffled in, a tray in her hands. "Hey, sweetie," she said. She came over to the bed and eased down onto the edge. "I brought you some nourishment."

I propped myself on an elbow and surveyed the tray. Steam rose from a bowl of potato soup. Crackers lay in a ramekin next to it. There was also a package of chocolates and a bottle of water.

"Did you just make the soup?" I asked. As far as I knew, we were out of frozen portions of her homemade soup. She made the best potato soup I'd ever tasted, and she always made it for me when I was sick or feeling low.

"I had a bag of potatoes I was saving for pot roast," she explained, "but I figured they were better used for today." She smiled, and the deep wrinkles around her eyes grew deeper still.

I sat upright and Aggie set the tray over my lap. "Thanks for this."

She patted my leg. "Don't mention it. How are you feeling?"

I'd told her briefly what had happened last night, since I'd come home earlier than she'd expected, and not only that, but I'd arrived shaken and pale. She knew right away something had gone wrong.

"I'm . . . embarrassed."

"If they are your real friends, they'll understand."

"Not everyone wants to deal with a crazy person."

She tilted her head to give me a look over the frames of her glasses. "You're not crazy, dear."

Though I hadn't felt much like eating at all today, now that the soup was in front of me, my stomach growled. I dug right in.

"I'll let you enjoy that in peace," Aggie said as she slowly rose from the bed, her knees cracking when she finally made it upright. "Let me know if you need anything else, hmm?"

"I will."

She nodded and ambled off, closing the door behind her.

I ate the soup in record time and got out of bed only to set the tray aside. I stared at the bottles again, the glass glowing in the sunlight that poured through my parted curtains.

GABRIEL.

I read his label over and over until his name was nothing but a string of consonants and vowels, until it didn't even sound like a name anymore.

He hadn't looked like a Gabriel. In fact, when I'd asked him what his name was, when he was rushing me to the ER, he'd paused before answering, as if he wasn't sure. Or maybe he didn't want to tell me.

GABRIEL.

I hadn't seen him at all while I was held captive. The first time I saw him was the day I escaped, the day some girl opened my cell door and ushered me out, her face hidden in the shadows cast by a black hood.

"Go," the girl had said, so I went. Though I'd been released from my room countless times before then, I knew instantly that this time was different. Usually I was flanked by two men. Usually I was led, stumbling, to a lab. Usually the place where I was held was silent save for the distant humming and thrumming of machines and vents.

That night, the place had been in complete chaos. I could still recall the distant thumping of feet, the shouting of voices, and the constant wailing of an alarm.

There was a heady feeling of escape in the air, and for the first time in a long time, I'd felt like maybe the captivity was finally over.

And then a man rounded into the hallway and shot me.

The bullet had hit me in the chest. My rescuer hollered and shot back. The man dropped where he stood as I slid to the floor, all the air leaving my lungs.

My chest felt like it was on fire. Like someone had built a pyre in my lungs and set a match to it. When I'd looked down at my white T-shirt, it was painted black with my own blood. And I realized that my hand was stamped over the wound, my fingers shaking.

"Can you walk?" my rescuer asked.

I'd nodded, because while I couldn't feel the beating of my heart, I could feel the curling of my toes.

"Am I dying?" I'd asked her as she hauled me to my feet. "Am I finally dying?"

"No." She examined me with a quick brush of her fingers. "It hit high in the chest. Missed the vital organs."

I'd nodded again, like, *Okay that's good*, but really I couldn't think of anything else but the pain in my chest, the pulling of inflamed muscle, and the pulsating beat of singed nerves.

I'd been injured so many times before, but I'd never been shot. I didn't know if it was an injury I'd survive, and I worried, like I had so many times before, that I'd die in that place and no one would ever know what had happened to me.

We'd threaded through the main area of the building, a maze of gray office partition walls. My rescuer seemed to know where we were going, but I couldn't tell the difference between one hallway and the next.

We pressed ourselves against a wall when a line of black-clad guards thundered past, but we failed to watch our backside and a man grabbed me by the wrist, yanking me back.

I caught sight of a knife at the man's waist and pulled it from its sheath. I wasn't a fighter, but I would fight now, because there was no way I'd be shoved back in that cell.

In the struggle, I was cut, from breast to hip bone, and it took me nearly five seconds to realize I didn't feel anything at all.

My rescuer stole the knife from the man's hand and shoved it in his gut. Two people dead in less than ten minutes. I'd never seen anyone killed before, and I was numb from the sight.

We made it out of the maze to the other side of the building, and my rescuer led me to a supply closet. She nodded at a vent in the ceiling. "Climb up. Go straight, then right, then left, then up the ladder."

She turned to go. "Wait!" I'd called. "My mother is here somewhere."

"I'll get her," she'd said, her voice low and indistinct.

More shouting sounded from the recesses of the building, and the girl slipped out the door.

I'd crawled through the vent and up the ladder and came out in a forest. But I never did see my mother again.

Whoever had held me captive had used her twice to get me to cooperate. They'd threatened her life, and I'd done whatever they'd asked of me after that, but I worried now, like I always did, that they'd killed her as a punishment for my escape.

I pushed aside several glass bottles to get to the one labeled MOM. Her scent had been a difficult one for me to mix. It still wasn't quite right. I pulled out the cork and breathed in deeply. Roses, for the rose water she used to dab behind her ears. The scent of clean linen, for the hospital scrubs she wore to work, and a hint of lemon, because her breath always smelled like it, like lemon and tea.

My therapist said that hope was a powerful thing, and I'd been clinging to the hope that my mother was alive ever since I'd escaped. But the more years that stretched between now and then, the more the hope dwindled.

If she hadn't returned yet, then she wasn't going to return.

I set her bottle back on the shelf and buried it behind the others.

I reached out for Gabriel's bottle next but pulled back at the last second. I'd already relived enough of that night. I wasn't sure if I could relive much more.

I turned away and curled back into bed again. I fell asleep quickly.

10

NICK

THE DRIVE TO TRADEMARR, ILLINOIS, took me less than six hours. I arrived before the sun. The GPS system in the truck brought me to the center of town, so I parked behind a row of shops and got out to walk.

The streets were dead and dark, save for spots of light from the lampposts. Even though it was the middle of August, the air was cold, so I threw on a flannel. It made it easier to hide the gun tucked against my back.

I shoved my hands in my pockets and tried to look disinterested in case a cop drove by. But really, I was scanning the surroundings, not only for signs of the Branch, but for things that looked familiar.

When Anna had found the name of this town in my file, I'd

thought arriving here would dislodge whatever memories the Branch had buried. It didn't.

Nothing looked familiar.

It'd been over six years since I'd been here, but I should have recognized something.

I walked to the main street and cut left, crossing at an intersection marked Washington and Ash. The shops were pretty standard. A New Agey store. A bookstore. A coffee shop. A bakery. A bar. Another bar. Good to know. Just in case I needed a drink.

I always did.

Everything was closed at this time of night, which made it easier to examine and mark what was here.

I crossed the next street, the streetlights flashing yellow in the gloom. A neon sign hanging in a window cast harsh shadows over the sidewalk.

MERV'S BAR & GRILL, the sign read. I peeked in the windows as I passed. The restaurant was separated into two rooms. One side held the bar and booths. The other side had some booths, tables, and a pool-table area. Maybe I'd go there first. Less likely to get into trouble in a family restaurant. Anna would be proud.

I kept walking until the shops thinned out and residential houses picked up. Nothing looked run-down here. The lawns were cut. The hedges were trimmed. The windows and shutters of the houses were clean and freshly painted.

It was exactly the kind of place where I felt like I didn't fit in.

A lot of my life before the Branch was still a muddy mess, but I acutely remembered the house my dad and I had lived in. Run-down piece of shit in the middle of a bunch of pine trees. Our driveway was dust and dirt, with patches of grass on the perimeter. Nothing that ever needed to be mowed. And even if it had, my dad wouldn't have bothered.

We'd moved there after my mom left us because my dad didn't like living in the middle of town. Probably because his neighbors hated him.

At the end of Washington Street, I found a park. A fountain stood in the center. A huge playground took up the back corner. A fenced dog park spanned the opposite corner. A garden took up the front, with benches stuck in between the flower beds.

I picked a bench in the back of the garden, hidden in the shadows cast by an oak tree, and sat. I looked out on Trademarr and took a deep breath, the cool air filling my lungs.

I thought of the girl and wondered if she lived in one of those perfect houses with the cut lawns and red shutters and trimmed hedges.

Or maybe she was dead already, her house six feet in the ground. And maybe I'd been the one to put her there.

After a few hours' sleep in the truck, I went in search of food. I walked straight to the coffee shop I'd passed earlier, since it was big enough to disappear in and small enough that I could keep track of who came and went.

A bell dinged as I entered the place, and a few heads glanced up. My skin crawled at the attention, and I worried my reasons for being here were immediately clear. And then one of Anna's comments came back to me, reminding me not to panic.

"Women watch you everywhere you go," she said once when we were shopping together in a bookstore. "You could walk in here in a garbage bag and they'd still look at you."

At the time I thought it sounded like complete bullshit, but then I had a flashback of me in a club, before the Branch, talking a woman into fucking me in the bathroom before she even knew my name.

It was memories like that that made me want to keep the past buried. I didn't want to remember who I used to be.

I ordered a coffee and an egg sandwich and took a seat near the front windows. The streets were busy with foot traffic, but not a lot of vehicles. I liked that about this town already. The buildings were mostly one story, another good thing. It meant it was harder for people to hide on the rooftops.

As I ate, I watched the faces of the people passing by, looking for the one face that mattered. The girl would probably be eighteen or nineteen now. I remembered her eyes the most. Big green eyes. As round as quarters. And freckles on the bridge of her nose.

There hadn't been any mention of her in my file, only of someone or something called Target E. The case file itself was labeled TURROW and talked about a doctor developing some kind of serum. Anna had said she'd continue digging while I was gone, but I wasn't holding out hope.

My first stop today was the public library. I wanted to read the newspapers from the month when I was here six years ago.

I took my coffee with me as I checked my phone for the library's location. Just as the GPS brought it up, a new text came in.

How are you?

There was no name with the text, since I hadn't programmed it in, but I knew right away who it was. Anna.

Fine, was all I said.

Then, *I told you to text me the second you got into town.*

I sighed and took a gulp of the now lukewarm coffee. Anna was sometimes impossible to placate. And I wasn't used to people constantly worrying about me. It made me uneasy. And annoyed.

I arrived, I wrote back. *And I'm fine.*

Text me later to let me know you're not dead. Got it?

Yes, fine, I replied, and activated the GPS again. I memorized the directions and quickly put the phone away.

The Trademarr public library was four blocks to the east, so I crossed the street with purpose, head up, shoulders loose. I didn't want to stick out, even if I looked like a tourist.

When I left Washington Street behind me, the foot traffic disappeared. It made it easier to focus my thoughts, instead of scanning the faces I passed, looking for someone who might register as familiar.

The public library was another one-story building, and it was made of brick the color of old blood. A flyer taped to the front door announced an arts festival in the park the following weekend. More people in town meant more distractions, more ways for the Branch, or Riley, to hide if they were still around and looking for me.

Sam was convinced Riley wouldn't let the Branch die, and while I didn't always agree with him and his unchecked paranoia, I had to side with him on this one. Riley was a weaselly son of a bitch, and he'd always been 100 percent dedicated to the Branch. He wouldn't let it go so easily.

As soon as I stepped through the second set of doors of the library, a short girl with white-blond hair smiled at me from behind the front desk and called out hello. Another thing I'd learned about small towns was how obscenely friendly people were. Like they were trying to make up for the fact that their town sucked ass.

I liked bigger cities. It was easier to disappear. And there was always something to do.

"Hey," I said to her, and flashed a grin, wondering what she'd think if she knew there was a Browning Hi-Power stuffed in the back of my pants. It was a reassuring weight, the cold metal a reminder that I was only inches—seconds—away from a weapon. I felt safer with a gun.

"Can I help you locate anything?" the girl asked, tilting her head to look up at me as I approached.

I felt her scanning me appreciatively. "Well," I started, and leaned in to the waist-high counter, closer to her. "I don't come to the library very often, so I'm kinda an idiot about how to use the stuff around here."

When she laughed, her eyes lit up, and a fake smile spread across my face.

"It's okay," she said. "I can definitely help you out. What are you looking for?"

I told her the dates of the newspapers I was hoping to find, and she led me to a glass-walled room. The door was labeled RESEARCH.

"Everything is digital nowadays and much easier to find," she explained as she brought up an archive program. "You just type in the newspaper name here"—she pointed at the screen, at a search bar—"and add your dates and hit search."

In a matter of seconds, several selections popped up.

"Thanks," I said, and took the seat she'd just vacated. "You saved me."

She threaded her fingers together and shrugged her shoulders. She was cute. And nauseatingly innocent. "It's no biggie. If you need help, just call for me."

When she was back at her post, I started opening newspaper selections. The first two weeks of newspapers brought up zero info. Nothing about a girl being injured or killed.

Then, on the Thursday newspaper for the following week, the front headline pulled me upright.

MISSING GIRL DELIVERED TO ER

I selected the clip and started reading.

> Elizabeth Creed, who's been missing for the last six months, was brought into Hallowell General early this morning by an unknown man.
>
> When Creed arrived, she was covered in blood and barely conscious, but after the ER doctors performed an examination, she appeared to have no injuries. She remained unconscious through the night and the next day. When she woke, she had little to offer police as to the details of her disappearance.
>
> Creed's mother, who disappeared at the same time as her daughter, has not been located.
>
> Police are still looking into the identity of the young man who brought Elizabeth into Hallowell General. He's said to have been sixteen or seventeen years of age. Tall, dark-haired, muscular in build, and reported to have been wearing jeans, a black T-shirt, and a black jacket.
>
> If you or anyone you know has any information on the young man, please call the sheriff's department.

I read the article several more times, something cold creeping up my spine. The article said the girl hadn't been injured, but in my flashback, she'd been shot and cut up. Was this the wrong girl? Wrong article? Although the details didn't match up, something told me it *was* the right girl. But it still didn't explain any of the other shit.

So I'd shot her, then saved her months later? After her initial injuries had healed? I had no concept of time in the flashback.

For all I knew, the gunshot wound could have taken place *after* I saved her.

I scrubbed at my eyes. None of this made sense. And I wasn't as good at piecing together research clues as Anna. Even Trev, the lying bastard, was better at this stuff than I was. If he hadn't double-crossed us, I would have gladly taken his help right now.

I spent the rest of the afternoon reading every article I could find, starting a year prior to and leading up to the day I'd taken Elizabeth Creed to the ER.

There was an article about her and her mother going missing. Elizabeth hadn't shown up for school for three days straight, and when the principal called her mother and got no response, he called the police.

They found the house torn up, like it'd been robbed, but only a few things had been taken. There was an investigation into the disappearance, but nothing turned up. The whole thing reeked of the Branch. Three months after the Creeds disappeared, Elizabeth's father was found dead in his apartment. He'd shot himself.

I did a search on Jonathan Creed, Elizabeth's father, and found tons of shit about how he was the number one suspect, that the police were building a case against him, despite the fact that he wasn't even in town when the disappearance occurred, and that the little town of Trademarr had turned him into a pariah.

No wonder he shot himself.

Which left Elizabeth with no one after she'd been found.

I skimmed the newspapers after the date of Elizabeth's return, but she was never mentioned again.

The problem with the information I did have was that I didn't have any concrete dates to go off of. I had no idea how long I'd been in Trademarr. For all I knew, I could have been the one to kidnap Elizabeth on the Branch's orders, and she could have been injured in the process. Then, months later, maybe my moral compass started working again and I saved her. That would explain why she'd been found uninjured once she was delivered to the ER.

That made a lot more sense than anything else I could come up with.

When I was done in the research room, I headed back to the librarian—the blond girl—and asked her if she knew Elizabeth. She gave me this look like, *Who doesn't know Elizabeth Creed?* And then she went on for a good twenty minutes about Elizabeth's life after the rescue. How she hopped from foster home to foster home, had several mental breakdowns in public, and was later diagnosed with PTSD.

"Do you know where she lives?" I asked, because I hadn't found a current address listed for her, and it wouldn't surprise me if she'd eventually left town.

The girl grew wary at that point, and said she didn't feel comfortable telling me.

I gave a vague excuse, saying I was a distant cousin on her father's side, but she didn't budge.

By the time I left the library, it was just after six, and my eyes were wrecked from too much reading. I hit up the closest hotel I could find and rented the cheapest room they had. I just needed a few hours of sleep. Maybe when I woke—and after I had a drink or two—all the shit I'd found today would make more sense.

Maybe.

11

NICK

I WOKE AFTER DARK AND TOSSED BACK two shots of whiskey before leaving my room. Outside on the street, I headed north and walked for a while before catching the distant thumping of bass. I found a nightclub with a sign out front that read ARROW in big neon-green letters. The line was short, and my thirst for booze was large, so I decided the club was good enough.

Inside, the music was ratcheted up to toxic levels so that everyone had to shout to be heard. Colored lights circled the space, and a floor-to-ceiling projection screen behind the DJ flipped through random images.

The place was packed, which gave me the distinct impression this was the only club in Trademarr, therefore the only thing to do. The number of sweaty bodies packed into this place must have been half the town's population.

I went straight for the bar. The bartender, a thirty-something guy with a buzzed head, checked for the neon-green bracelet on my wrist that said I was old enough to get plastered. When I passed the test, he asked for my order.

"Tequila," I said. "The best you got."

When the shot glass was thrust in front of me, I slammed it back, and a female voice hollered behind me.

I turned as the girl slid onto the stool next to me. "Get straight to the nasty stuff, I see," she said.

I flicked a finger at the bartender for another round. "You don't like tequila?" I asked the girl.

She had a green bracelet on her wrist, too, so at least twenty-one, though she didn't look it. All her features were soft and rounded off, like she hadn't matured into herself yet. Her eyes were big and bright, and though her smoky voice had the upswing of a flirty vibe, her gaze said otherwise.

I knew a predator when I saw one. Which made me wonder—in what twisted world did I look like prey?

"I like tequila just fine," she said, and folded her hands on the bar top. "It's what comes after the tequila I don't like."

"You mean the blackouts? Or the hangover?"

She smiled. "Both. Obviously."

The tempo of the music picked up, and I could feel the thrumming of the electronic beat in my chest.

"You want a shot?" I asked her, and she quickly nodded. I amended the order for one more.

When I went straight for the booze, the mystery girl stopped me with a hand on my forearm. I looked down at her fingers spread over my skin and tamped down the urge to yank my arm away.

"What?" I said, as lazily as I could manage.

"You drink tequila, you drink it right." She handed me a shaker of salt, and I rolled my eyes.

"You've got to be kidding," I said.

"I never kid."

She licked her hand between her thumb and index finger, her eyes trained on me as she did. I held up the shaker with an arch of my brow, and she gave me her hand. I shook out some salt. I pulled back to do the same, but she snatched my hand in hers and licked it for me.

I grinned at her. She grinned back.

"Ready?" she said.

"I was ready five minutes ago."

She laughed. We raised the shot glasses, and I swigged the tequila back after the salt, finishing it off with a bite of the lime wedge. The booze was smooth, and burned all the way down my throat, setting fire to my gut.

The girl smiled. "Another round?"

"Always," I said.

A half hour later, the club started to teeter around me, and everything was so fucking funny, I couldn't stop laughing.

"Dance with me," the girl said.

I set down the shot glass hard. "I don't dance."

"Yes, you do." She grabbed my wrist and tugged me toward the floor.

The electronic music had been replaced with hip-hop three shots ago, and the heavy bass thumps rocketed up my legs. I got in close to the girl, our bodies pressed together so tightly, you'd need a knife to separate us.

When the song's hook slowed the beat, the girl moved against me in equally slow, sinuous movements. The heat of the tequila in my gut sank lower, until I couldn't think of anything else but the girl and me.

The blow of trumpets punctuated the air—what kind of hip-hop song was this?—and the girl ran her hands beneath my shirt. When she looked up at me, her head tilted back to make up the ten inches of height difference between us, I recognized that look in her eye, and who was I to ignore it?

I hunched forward and kissed her, my hands running up her body.

Hers found their way to my stomach—girls always went for the stomach.

When I pulled back, she was breathing heavily, her eyes half-lidded.

"Want to get out of here?" I asked.

She nodded, so I pulled her hand out of my shirt and tugged her toward the door.

On our way back to my hotel room, my cell rang, and I fished it out of my pocket. When I answered, I tried my hardest not to sound blasted out of my mind.

"Hello?" I said.

The mystery girl—I still didn't know her name—grabbed my hand and asked who it was.

"Where are you?" Sam asked.

He'd ignored the code we'd agreed on. "Where do you think I am?"

"Are you drunk?"

I snorted. "No."

"Nicholas!" he growled.

" 'S fine," I said.

We stopped for traffic at a street corner, and the girl danced circles around me.

"What do you want?" I asked Sam.

"I want you to not be drunk."

I laughed. "Too late, boss."

"For fuck's sake, Nick." Sam pulled in a settling breath, as if he were three seconds away from reaching through the phone and throttling me.

"I'm on my way back to my room," I said. "I'll stay there till morning. Promise."

"Like that'll stop anyone from busting through the door?"

"I'll lock it," I said, and chuckled as the girl pulled me through the intersection, the streetlights casting glowing halos around her head.

Sam made a choked sound. "I knew this was a mistake. I'm coming down there."

"No, you're not. I'mmm fine. Stop being so damn overbearing."

He growled again. "Sober up, Nick, and stop being so goddamn sloppy or I'll come down there and drag you back here myself." The line went dead. I shoved the phone back in my pocket.

"Who was it?" the girl asked.

"My older brother. He's a dick."

We made it back to the room after getting turned around twice. Doubt started to settle in. Sam was definitely right. But no way was I going to tell him that. If I couldn't find my way back to my own hotel room, there was no way I'd be able to fight off a Branch agent.

Inside the room, I busted out the whiskey, and the girl and I drank straight from the bottle.

"So I just realized I don't even know your name," I said to her.

She took a swig of booze. "I don't know yours, either."

"Is that irresponsible of us?" I challenged with a grin.

She waggled her eyebrows. "Definitely."

"So you first," I said.

"Belinda."

"You're lying."

"I am."

I liked this girl.

"What's yours?" she asked.

No way was I giving her my real name. Not even an alias I'd used before. I said the first thing that came to mind. "Elijah."

"You don't look like an Elijah."

"You don't look like a Belinda."

"It's Sarah."

"Mm-hmm."

She smiled and came closer, the bottle of whiskey still in her hand. She offered it to me, and I took a long pull on it. After, she reached up on her toes to kiss me. I set the bottle down and wrapped my arms around her, guiding her to the bed. But when she brought her hand up to my face, fingers trailing along my jawline, a pulse started in the base of my skull, and I tensed.

"What is it?" she asked.

I staggered away, giving her my back.

I heard the voices first, the low tenor of whispered orders followed by the *click* of guns.

"Elijah?" she said.

I collapsed in the chair near the window and propped my head in my hands as the flashback flickered to life. I was in a gray room. No, a gray hallway, but every sound echoed through the space, as if the ceiling was three dozen feet away.

"Kill her on sight," a voice ordered through an earpiece in my ear.

I was wearing black tactical gear, a gun in my hand, a gun strapped to my leg.

"She was last sighted near the holding cells," the voice said.

I moved through the maze like a black ghost. When I came to the wall of cells in the back, I saw a girl crouched on the floor inside the last cell on the right. A mass of dark hair covered her face.

I brought my gun up.

Kill her on sight.

My finger pressed at the trigger.

"Elijah!"

I lurched upright, grabbed the wrist of the hand on my shoulder, and swept the person's legs out from beneath them.

The girl—Sarah—gasped, and I snapped out of it, catching her before she thudded to the floor.

She hung there, one foot from the dingy carpet, bright eyes staring up at me.

"I'm sorry," I muttered. "I didn't—"

"I should go," she said.

"You should," I echoed.

I righted her, and she straightened her T-shirt.

"I'm sorry," I said. I wasn't sure how to explain the flashbacks, so I didn't even try.

"It's okay." She headed for the door. I walked her down the hall and outside to the sidewalk.

"You want me to walk you back to the club? Or call you a cab or something?"

She waved me off. "I'll be fine. It was nice meeting you, Elijah." She said *Elijah* like she knew it was a fake.

"You, too."

She came over and kissed my cheek, a smirk on her lips. And as she walked off, disappearing in the darkness, I realized something I should have realized back in the hotel room. Something I would have noticed immediately if I wasn't drunk off my ass.

It was the look on her face after I'd nearly dropped her to the floor. Not fear. Not panic. Not shock. Not any of the things she should have been feeling.

Her expression had been blank.

She hadn't been scared at all.

12

ELIZABETH

WHEN I WALKED INTO MERV'S THE NEXT day, two days after my meltdown, I had the prickly sensation that everyone was staring at me but also trying not to make eye contact.

Heat spread across my cheeks and down my neck, and I considered quitting on the spot. Merv had a stack of applications in his office. He could find someone to replace me.

But then I considered what it would feel like to spend the rest of the summer in my bedroom, worrying about what people thought of me, and decided that was a far worse fate than facing everyone.

When Chloe spotted me, she followed me to the break room. "I'm so glad you're back." She dropped into one of the metal folding chairs and massaged her temple. "I couldn't stand another day without you."

"You don't look that good," I said.

She waved me off. "It's just a headache. It's this place, I swear it."

"So." I turned to face her. "Is everyone talking about what happened the other night?"

"Does it matter?"

"Yes."

The chair squawked when she pushed it back and stood up to face me. "No, it doesn't. Just keep your chin up and remember that you are better than half of the losers who work here. Including me."

I laughed and instantly felt a million times better. "Thanks."

She patted my shoulder and pulled away. "I think you'll also be happy to hear we had a guy ask for one of your tables, specifically. And when I told him you weren't here yet, he said he'd wait." She waggled her eyebrows. "Might be a big tip for you!"

She bounced off, her chandelier earrings swinging.

After dropping my bag in my locker and tying on my apron, I went out front to see who'd asked for my section. I saw a dark-haired guy sitting in booth fourteen, his back to me.

My stomach sank.

I knew exactly who that was.

I went over to the table, order pad in hand. "Hello, Dr. Sedwick."

"Elizabeth!" He turned slightly in the booth to face me, his hands folded on the table. He wasn't in his usual therapist clothes. Instead he wore athletic shorts and a blue T-shirt. He was young for a therapist, I thought, but Aggie had recommended him, and I'd trusted her opinion. She'd been right. Dr. Sedwick didn't have that monotone voice the therapists I'd seen in the past had. He didn't nod and scribble, nod and scribble. Our sessions were more of a conversation, and I'd come to think of him as a friend over the past few months.

That didn't mean I was happy to see him. Especially not today, two days after a meltdown.

"Aggie called you, didn't she?" I asked.

Dr. Sedwick kept his expression easy, casual, as he unfolded his hands. "Can't a guy get lunch without there being a reason behind it other than hunger?"

I frowned, not buying it.

"Okay." He held up his hand, admitting defeat. "Yes, she called me. But I'm not here on official business. I'm just a concerned friend checking in. Also, I *do* happen to be craving a burger."

"Well," I started, smiling despite myself, "I recommend the bacon-wrapped burger. It's quite good."

He raised a brow. "Oh? Well, then I'll have that. With a Heineken, please."

"Beer before noon? My therapist would not approve of that."

He chuckled. "Tell your therapist I promise only to have one and no more."

I hurried off to the bar to place the drink order. My heart thudded against my ribs when I saw Evan behind the bar. He wasn't supposed to be working today. He'd had the next two days off, which was one of the reasons I'd decided to come back today.

I stood there, frozen in the middle of the restaurant for far too long, until Evan caught sight of me and his eyes softened. *Come here*, he mouthed, before sliding a drink down the bar top to a forty-something woman who whistled appreciatively in return.

I came to the corner of the bar and stopped. My stomach tossed and turned. Sweat welled on my fingertips.

"Hey," Evan said, and came closer. "How are you?"

Discomfort and embarrassment had me looking at the floor, at my white Converse, dirt smudged across the fronts. I wouldn't blame Evan for running away. I wanted to run away.

"Lissy?" he said.

"I'm okay," I answered quickly and cleared my throat, trying to dislodge the overwhelming lump rising higher and higher. "I'm good."

He cocked his head and frowned. "You sure? Was... what happened... was it something I did? I keep thinking about that night, and what I could have done to make you... I don't know. I shouldn't have left you alone in the middle of the woods in the first place. I'm sorry."

I looked up. The expression on Evan's face was one of genuine concern. There was no hint of mockery.

"It really had nothing to do with you," I answered. "I promise."

I'm the one screwed up.

"Still." He reached over and set a hand on my shoulder, squeezing lightly. "If you need to talk or whatever, I'm here. I'm not going anywhere."

I sucked in a breath. That hadn't been how I'd imagined this conversation going. Actually, I hadn't really expected us to have a conversation at all.

The tension in my back dissipated, and my shoulders slumped. "Thanks, Evan. Really. It means a lot."

The corner of his mouth quirked. "Nah. We're friends. That's what friends are supposed to do."

Are we, or will we ever be, more than friends? I wanted to ask so badly I could practically taste the words on the tip of my tongue, sweet but with a bite of salt, possibly the best words ever spoken, possibly the worst words ever spoken.

I clamped my mouth shut before the question escaped on its own.

Things were good with Evan. I didn't want to muddy the waters.

"I better get back to work," I said, and hurried away, wondering if this would be the beginning of a new life. A better life than my screwed-up one.

13

NICK

I WOKE THE NEXT DAY TO THE SOUND OF my cell going off. I rolled over, eyes still glued shut, and groped around for the phone.

"Hello?" I answered, my voice raw and groggy.

The person on the other end sighed, relieved. "You're alive," Sam said.

"I think that's debatable."

With a groan, I sat up and scrubbed at my face. Daylight spilled through the cracked curtains. The clock on the nightstand said it was nearly three in the afternoon.

"I've been calling you all morning," Sam said.

"Sorry. I was sleeping off the booze. Those were your instructions, weren't they?"

Sam sighed again. "If you do something that reckless again, I swear to God, Nick, I'm going to—"

"Yeah, yeah, I know. You're going to come down here and drag me back."

"No, I'll shoot you in the kneecap."

I blew out a breath. "You're brutal this morning."

"This afternoon," he corrected. "And I'm fucking serious."

I stumbled to the bathroom. "Yeah, I get it. Hold on, I have to piss." I set the phone down and did my business. I grabbed the phone again on my way out of the bathroom and dropped into one of the chairs by the front window. "So now that we got the petty shit out of the way, I have to tell you something."

"What?"

"I had another flashback last night."

"And?"

"And, I think someone was trying to escape the Branch, but I don't know if it was Elizabeth."

"Who's Elizabeth?"

I poured myself a shot of whiskey and slung it back. "The girl. The whole reason I came here?"

"You got a name. Good. Anna can cross-reference it with what we have in the files. Have you found this girl yet? She still alive?"

"She's here. Sounds like she's a fucking basket case. I haven't found her yet, though."

"Yeah, well, not everyone is lucky enough to escape the Branch with their sanity."

I knew that all too well.

"You going to look for her today?" Sam asked.

"Yeah. But first I need—" I cut myself off. I was about to say a proper drink. Instead I said, "I need to eat."

"Call me later and let me know what you found. I'll get Anna on the files again."

I ended the call and looked around my room. I had one more night here before checking out. I had enough cash to pay for another night, but I hated wasting money on a bed. I could sleep in the truck if I had to. Wouldn't be the first time I'd lived out of a vehicle.

A lot of what I did for the Branch was still buried in a pile of shit in my head, but the memories of my life before the Branch had started to come back a while ago. When I left my dad's house for the last time, long before the Branch, I'd lived in his car for months. I used to con women for money to get by. Sometimes they made it too easy. Sometimes I felt the old guilt of that life creep back into this one. And then I reminded myself that sometimes you do what you have to do to survive, and the guilt quickly went away.

After a long, hot shower, I left the hotel just after four and headed toward the restaurant-slash-bar I'd seen when I first got into town.

Merv's Bar & Grill was the type of place that went too far with the whole themed bit, and Irish was apparently Merv's theme of choice. Everything inside was covered in clovers or painted green. Irish music blasted through the sound system.

I already hated Merv's, and I hadn't even sat down.

I picked an empty stool at the end of the bar and pulled out my fake ID.

The bartender, a shorter guy with overgrown blond hair, came over. The pin on his polo shirt said his name was Evan.

"What can I get for you?" he asked.

"Whiskey," I said, and flicked him the ID. He poured a drink and set it in front of me before hurrying to the other end of the bar.

I sipped the drink as I thought. Elizabeth definitely lived in Trademarr, otherwise the librarian would have mentioned she'd left town. There wouldn't have been any harm in giving out that information.

Maybe the bartender knew her. Bartenders know everything.

I took another long sip and scanned the mirror over the bar, checking the windows and the exits behind me, when I noticed a row of pictures taped above the register. Some of them were of customers raising their drinks to whoever had snapped the photo. But there were some of the employees, too, and when I saw an image of a girl with dark brown hair and eyes as round as quarters, my mouth went dry.

"Hey," I called to the bartender, and he gave me a look like, *Wait a goddamn second*, but I needed to know who that girl was and I needed to know right now.

I tapped the bar top with a finger.

The guy finally ambled down and looked at my half-empty whiskey. "Something wrong with the drink?"

"Who's that girl?" I asked, and pointed at the picture. I had realized, the second time I looked at it, that she was standing next to Evan, his arm around her. "That girl who's with you."

"Who?" he said, and frowned. "Lissy?"

Lissy. Elizabeth.

"Yes," I said, quick and quiet. "Does she still work here?" I turned around and scanned the restaurant. "Is she on shift right now?"

Evan's frown deepened. "No, she just got off. I can give her a message—"

I threw a ten on the bar, slid off the stool, and hurried for the front door, the need to *go* overtaking all my other senses.

I scanned Washington Street and the faces of the people walking past.

Evan slammed through the door behind me. "Dude," he said. "Who the hell are you?"

When I didn't spot Elizabeth on the main strip, I cut to the corner of the building and slipped around to the south side where I figured the employee entrance was.

"Dude!" Evan said again.

There was no one there.

I went to the back parking lot.

Empty.

My hands tightened into fists at my sides.

Evan's footsteps thudded on the pavement behind me. I whirled around, grabbed the collar of his shirt, and pulled him to me. "Where is she? Which way did she go?"

Evan scowled, but didn't pull back. He was five inches shorter than me, but full of bravado. "You think I'm going to tell you? You're a friggin' space case."

"Evan?" someone called.

I looked up and over the top of Evan's head.

Something shattered against the pavement as it was dropped from a trembling hand.

She met my eyes. Her lips moved, but nothing came out. All the color drained from her face.

My heart stopped. The world bubbled around me.

"It's you," she said.

14

ELIZABETH

I SET MY HAND AGAINST THE BRICK exterior of Merv's and leaned into it.

Was it really him?

Gabriel.

I didn't want to tear my eyes away, afraid that if I did, he'd disappear again. As it was, I worried that he was a figment of my imagination, caused by my questionable sanity. Although the night I'd been rescued was a blur, I did remember Gabriel clearly. He was the person who'd saved me after all.

But my broken mind must have seen him as older than he really was back then, because he didn't look much older than me now. I would almost swear he hadn't aged a day since that night.

"Are you real?" I whispered.

Gabriel let go of Evan and took a step toward me. I staggered back, my fingers dragging across the brick.

He must have read the fear on my face because he stopped and froze and stared at me.

He didn't say anything.

I couldn't feel my feet, my legs, my knees, the air in my lungs. I was reduced to a jumble of thoughts.

The old bullet wound vibrated in my chest.

He tilted his head. "You know me."

It wasn't a question, but the look in his eyes said it partly was.

I inhaled. Swallowed. Exhaled. Nodded. "Gabriel?"

The corners of his eyes pinched, and his jaw tensed, full lips pursed.

"No. Yes." He sighed. "Yes. Gabriel. For now."

I wasn't sure what that meant, but it was all I needed to hear.

"You know him?" Evan asked.

A car zoomed past on the street, a bunch of girls singing to the radio. It was nothing but a *buzz*, like flies, in my ears.

"Yeah," I said to Evan. "I know him."

"Are you . . . I mean . . ." Evan looked at Gabriel, and then at me. He came closer and lowered his voice. "Should I stay? I kinda left the bar unattended and—"

"No," I said too quickly, and licked my lips. "You should go back in. I'll be fine."

"Are you sure?"

"I'm sure."

Evan looked at Gabriel, as if unsatisfied with my assurances. I wasn't even sure if I was sure. Was I safe, alone with Gabriel? Was I even safe in Trademarr?

I'd always wondered, after I escaped, if staying in the same town where I'd been held captive was a risk. If they'd wanted to find me again, it wouldn't have been hard. But I'd never had the resources to leave. I didn't have any family left, and child protective services wasn't in the position to move me out of town.

I was as trapped here as I'd been in that lab. And now my greatest fear might have been coming true: They'd returned to finish the job, and I'd made it so easy.

"I'm fine, Evan," I said again, and he finally went back inside, leaving me alone in the parking lot with Gabriel still staring at me and me staring at him and the silence between us growing taut like a rubber band.

I didn't know what to say. I didn't know who'd make the first move.

Turned out, it was Gabriel.

He took another step toward me, and I startled. He held up his hands.

"I'm not here to hurt you."

My breath was coming too quickly, so my response came out shaky. "I'm not sure if I believe you."

I glanced at my smashed cell phone on the pavement. I'd dropped it when I saw Gabriel. He scooped it up and handed it to me slowly, as if I were a skittish rabbit he didn't want to run away.

I took it from him and tried turning it on, but the screen stayed dark.

I backed up along the side of the building until I stood in front of the large windows that looked in on Merv's. So there were witnesses.

"What are you doing here?" I asked.

His eyes flicked away from me, to the intersection, to the cars passing through. So many cars and so many people with normal lives, doing their normal things. I wanted desperately to be one of those people.

"I have memories of you," he finally answered. "And I'm trying to figure out what they mean."

I frowned. "You say that like you don't know. Like you don't know what happened."

"I don't."

"How is that possible?"

As soon as the question was out, I immediately wanted to retract it and swallow it back down my throat. What a stupid question to ask when there was a very clear answer.

"Amnesia," he said.

"Sorry, I..." I looked at the ground, heat racing to my cheeks. "That should have been obvious."

He didn't say anything.

"How did it happen? The amnesia."

His jaw tensed. "Long story."

"So you're not here to"—a lump settled in my throat—"kill me?"

The sharp planes of his face softened, and he took another step. "I saved you back then, didn't I?"

I nodded.

"Then why would I come back six years later to kill you?"

"I don't know... I don't—"

"I'm not that person anymore."

A breath rushed out of me, and I turned, pressing my back against the building. Were we really having this conversation? No one should have to have such conversations on the sidewalk outside of an Irish family restaurant.

I scrubbed at my face, trying to realign my life into an order that made sense. But then again, nothing had made sense for a very long time.

"Can we talk somewhere?" he asked. He gestured to the coffee shop across the street, and I nodded. That's what I needed. Caffeine. A familiar place. A chair beneath me to keep me upright.

The stoplight at the intersection was green, so we had to wait together at the curb as traffic passed.

I was immediately aware of how tall Gabriel was next to me, how solid and real he was. How broad his shoulders were in the black T-shirt he wore, how the cut of his biceps could be seen even through his sleeves. How the veins stood up on his hands, how rough his knuckles were. Scars covered his right hand more than his left.

He smelled different.

Not exactly like the memory I'd chronicled in the glass bottle sitting on my shelf. The balance of scents had changed.

There was a very faint undertone of pine trees clinging to him, and musk and maybe a touch of lavender. Something floral. Maybe that was laundry detergent.

When the light switched, allowing us to cross, Gabriel kept in step with me. We didn't talk.

At Declater's, he held the door open for me. I went inside. The rich scent of roasted coffee beans made me relax. Just a little. It was a normal smell. A normal thing for me to do, buy coffee. But who I was with wasn't normal, none of this was normal.

I ordered an iced latte. Gabriel ordered a black coffee. He picked a table near the windows, near the exit, and I was thankful for that.

We sat.

My stomach turned.

"My name," he started, looking down at the steam rising from his cup, "my name is Nick. Not Gabriel."

I might have been surprised by the revelation had I not already decided long ago that he didn't seem anything like a Gabriel.

"Nick," I repeated. "Why Gabriel?"

"It was an alias." He turned the coffee cup a quarter of an inch and looked at me.

During the years that'd stretched between when I'd met him and now, I realized I'd forgotten a very important detail about him—his eyes. They were the iciest blue. Ringed with a faint trace of black. The kind of eyes that knew things.

His black hair was longer than I remembered, and curled around his ears. His face was clean shaven. His teeth white as sugar.

"Why are you here?" I asked. "Why now?"

I didn't see any reason to dance around the question. I wanted to know. I needed to know.

He shifted and looked out the window, the stark light of day making the blue of his eyes almost white.

"That's a complicated answer. A long one."

"I'm not going anywhere."

He gazed back at me. "A lot has happened since..."

He didn't finish the sentence, but I knew what he meant. Since that night.

"Are they..." I wetted my lips, my mouth bone dry, my heart ramming against the back of my throat. "Are they here?"

He shook his head quickly. "I don't work for them anymore, and from what I can tell, they aren't around."

Work for them. Like he was a stock boy at a grocery store. Or a plumber's assistant. There was nothing normal about what he did. Or used to do.

"Who are they?" I asked.

Ever since I'd been kidnapped, I'd asked myself that over and over again. Why had I been taken? What did they do to my mother? Why did they do the things they'd done to me?

I hadn't told anyone what had happened while I'd been missing. No one would have believed me if I had. But the silence, keeping the secret, meant that the longer it stayed with me, bottled up, the more it seemed like a nightmare, and the more I felt crazy for believing what had happened.

Maybe it hadn't.

"They're called the Branch."

"What are they?"

"A private organization known for creating bio-weaponry, usually for the government."

The café's door opened, and a girl walked in, a cell phone glued to her ear. She was talking loudly about a dress she'd just bought. When she got in line at the register, she twisted, catching sight of Nick. Her whole body changed, elongating, back arched, eyes heavy and appreciative.

He's a killer. I'm sitting across the table from a killer.

My throat constricted.

"What is bio-weaponry, exactly?" I asked.

"Turning the human body into a weapon. Genetic alterations. That kind of thing."

I straightened. Several things clicked into place. Nick caught my morphing expression, and he frowned my way. "What?" he asked. "What is it?"

I arranged my face into an expression that I hoped was innocent. "Nothing."

His frown deepened. "If you know something, tell me."

I'd never breathed the confession to a single soul. I wasn't going to start now.

"It's just..." I shrugged. "It's hard to believe, that's all. I feel like I'm in an action movie or something."

"No." He laughed, but there was no hint of humor in his voice. "That's just my life."

"You say you remember me, but how much *do* you remember?"

"Well..." He scanned the coffee shop. "Do you have somewhere we can talk without..." He trailed off.

Without people hearing.

My old wounds pulsed with warning. Gabriel—Nick—hadn't harmed me that night, but he was still tangled in those memories, and even though he'd saved me, I was still wary.

"The park?" I replied. "We could probably find a bench or something where we'd have some privacy."

He nodded, and a lock of hair fell across his forehead. He swiped it back. "You lead," he said, "and I will follow."

15

NICK

I KNEW WHERE THE PARK WAS, BUT I wanted Elizabeth to feel in control, so I pretended I didn't know the way. She was extremely wary of me, and for good reason. I was part of a memory she probably wanted to bury.

It took us only five minutes to reach the park. She picked the bench. We sat in the shade of a maple tree, the fountain rushing behind us. The playground was packed, and the sound of screaming kids put me on edge.

Despite that, I pressed my back against the bench and took a deep breath and tried to act like I had my shit together.

For the next twenty minutes, I told Elizabeth half truths. I told her about the flashback, the one in the woods, because that was something she'd already know anyway. I didn't tell her much about the Branch, only the barest of details. I made her think that I'd been out of the Branch for a few years, that I'd been piecing together my past since then. I wanted her to think she was a trivial memory on a long list of heavy shit.

I didn't want her to know too much about me until I figured out why she'd been involved with the Branch in the first place, and why she'd been injured that night in the flashback. If I really had been sent to kill her, I needed to know why. There would have been a very good reason for it—the Branch didn't go out of their way to kill inconsequential people.

When I was finished, Elizabeth stared at the grass glowing in the sunlight beyond the reach of the tree.

I cracked a knuckle. And another. I needed a drink.

"So this Branch," she said, "they were the ones who took me?"

I tried to get a read on her face, tried to gauge whether or not she was playing me. Did *she* know why she'd been taken? Was she playing dumb to fool me?

Her eyes were squinted against the sun, her mouth relaxed, lips wet, shoulders drooped. I couldn't read her very well, which was either an indication of my shitty-ass perception, or of her talent for hiding things.

"I don't know for sure," I said, "but they were involved. Especially at the end."

What I didn't tell her was that I'd been tasked with killing her. *Me*, specifically. Once I found out her name, it hadn't taken a lot of deduction to figure out that the Target E named in my file was Elizabeth.

I didn't plan on telling her that part. Ever. It didn't matter that I hadn't gone through with it. If I'd been given the order once, I could be given the order again. No matter what I told her, she'd never trust me. And I needed her to trust me.

"Was I the one who took you to the hospital when you escaped?" I asked her.

She nodded. "Yeah. You found me in the woods that night."

"Had you been shot?"

She drew her hands into her lap and rubbed at the knuckles on her right hand, over and over again.

She was fidgeting. That I could read.

"No," she answered. "I didn't have any injuries."

She was lying.

Son of a bitch.

"I could have sworn—" I started, but she cut me off.

"There was a lot of blood on me, but it wasn't mine."

"Oh." I nodded, like that made sense. "I thought I was the one who shot you."

"No," she said quickly. "You didn't hurt me. Ever. At all."

I ran a hand through my hair. She had no idea how relieved I was to hear that. I'd been ordered to kill her, and I'd gone against the order. Maybe there was some humanity left in me after all.

"You still haven't answered my first question," she said as she pulled her hand away. "Why are you suffering from amnesia?"

"The Branch. They altered my memories. I'm trying to fill in the blanks." Default answer. Might as well stick to it.

"They can do that?" she asked, frowning with disbelief.

"They can do a lot of things that seem improbable."

She sat upright and angled her body toward mine. I couldn't help but eye her, and not her face. I hadn't considered how different she'd be from my memories. How much older she'd be.

My body was reacting in the way it always reacted when I was talking to a pretty girl. And right now I considered it a fucking traitor.

"So you came here," she started, looking over at me, "to find me?"

I nodded.

"And now that you've found me?"

"I don't know," I told her. And that was the truth.

"Are you staying?"

That wasn't what she wanted to ask. What she wanted to know was if I was leaving. But what I couldn't tell was if she wanted me to.

"There are still a lot of missing pieces," I admitted. "I don't know why I was here in the first place. Back then."

Partial truth. I knew the why, but why her? What threat had she posed to the Branch?

"Where are you staying?" she asked.

"Nowhere yet."

She stood up quickly. "You'll stay with us."

I stood up, too, unable to hide the shock spreading across my face. "What? No. I'll be fine."

A woman walked past on the sidewalk, two kids trailing behind her. She was buried in her cell phone, ignoring the kids. But when she caught sight of me, she slowed and pulled the phone away from her face.

My shoulders tensed. I couldn't get through the day without suspecting everyone I passed of being part of the Branch.

But then I figured a Branch operative would not go undercover with two kids. Too many variables. And too much risk.

"You're staying with us," Elizabeth said again. "Because whatever answers you're looking for, they involve me, too. We can help each other."

I couldn't tell if this was a good idea or not. Sam would say not. But if I wanted to know who Elizabeth was, then I needed to keep her close. That seemed like a good enough reason to accept.

"All right," I finally said. "If you're sure."

"I'm sure."

16

ELIZABETH

WHAT WAS I DOING?

Every part of my brain said I was being reckless, that Nick's good looks had me seeing stars.

But that wasn't it. Was it?

I'd only been with him less than an hour, and already I was acutely aware of how often women, girls, even older women, checked him out. Something I'd forgotten about him in the years that had passed—he was gorgeous. The kind of gorgeous that was hard to ignore, that almost seemed unnatural.

You're doing the right thing, I told myself. *Nick has answers that you need. It's a good idea for both of you.*

A totally crazy, completely risky, good idea.

Or maybe a bad idea masquerading as a good idea.

Aggie's house was a fifteen-minute walk from downtown. Close enough to reach everything by foot, but far enough away that it was quiet. She lived in an authentic Victorian decorated in the traditional "painted lady" style. I loved her house. It was large and old and well preserved. Aggie had taken great pains to keep up with the house as it aged right along with her.

And even better, especially now, she'd kept the apartment above the carriage house (as she called it) functional. I hoped she would agree to let Nick stay with us.

When we reached the house, he kept two paces between us as I led him up the front steps, across the large porch, through the double front door, and down the hallway to the kitchen. That was where I could always find Aggie.

And she didn't let me down today.

I came through the doorway first. She looked up and over her glasses at me, and smiled. She was making something—she always was—and had a cup of flour in her hands.

"Hello, dear," she said, and then Nick walked in.

Aggie moved to set the cup of flour down, and as she did she rammed it against the bag of sugar, knocking it over. Sugar spilled across the counter and poured to the floor.

"I'll get the broom," I said, and moved toward the closet.

"No." Aggie waved me away. "I'll take care of it." She wiped her hands on the towel tied to her apron. "Who's this?"

In Aggie's house, in the bright white kitchen, among the cat paintings and the vintage rolling pins hanging on the wall, Nick looked extremely out of place. Like a brand-new truck trying to blend in on a used-car lot.

He was large and pretty and overwhelming.

"This is my friend Nick," I told her. "He needs a place to stay and I was wondering if he could sleep in the carriage house for a few days."

Aggie set her hands on her wide hips and looked from me to Nick. "Hmm," she said. "I haven't heard you talk about a Nick."

"That's because—"

"I used to go to school with Elizabeth," he cut in. "I transferred out in the ninth grade, but I'm back in town for a bit. Just visiting." He shoved his hands in his jeans pockets and hunched his shoulders. He seemed to shrink by five inches. Had he done that on purpose?

"I told Elizabeth I could stay in a hotel," he went on. "I don't want to trouble you."

I held my breath as I waited for Aggie to respond. I really wanted her to say yes. I was afraid that if I let Nick out of my sight again, he'd disappear. I couldn't go another six years wondering where he was, who he was, what answers he might have.

Please, Aggie, I thought.

"All right," she said, and nodded once. "We have plenty of room around here. No sense keeping it all to ourselves." She came around the counter and sized Nick up. "You related to the Vermont family? You look like Old Man Vermont."

The Vermont family? I didn't know anyone by the name of Vermont.

Nick shook his head. "No, ma'am."

"Hmm," she said again, and turned to me. "Can you get him settled in? I need to finish this batch of cookies for the fair this weekend."

"Yes." I went over to her and kissed her cheek. "Thanks, Aggie."

She smiled, and a bit of tension left her shoulders. "No need to thank me, dear. Now go on so I can get back to work."

Nick called good-bye to Aggie as I led him out the back door to the carriage house.

The stairs to the apartment started at the front of the building and twisted around to the back, where a small deck overlooked the garden and storage shed beyond. I grabbed the spare key from under the mat and unlocked the door.

It'd been a while since I'd been inside the apartment. Dust swirled in the sunlight pouring through the large windows. It was a studio, one big open space. A queen-sized bed sat between the two biggest windows, across from the entrance. In one corner was a kitchenette, with a rickety laminate-topped table and matching chairs.

To the far left was the living-room area, with a couch and an old traveling trunk used as a coffee table. The bathroom was tucked between the kitchenette and the "living room."

If I didn't love my room so much, and being near Aggie, I would have taken the apartment in a heartbeat. It had a good vibe.

"There are extra blankets in the closet," I said, and pointed at the closed door to our right. "I can get you shampoo and stuff if you need it."

"No," he answered. "I have everything I need."

I frowned. He didn't have anything with him. "Where?"

"In my truck. It's still in town."

"Oh. Why didn't you say something while we were there? We could have grabbed it before coming here."

He walked farther into the room, keeping his back to me. "I have to go into town anyway. I'll grab it then."

"Okay."

I thought about offering to go with him, but more than anything, I wanted him to want me to come with.

He didn't ask.

"If you need me, I'll be in the main house. I'm making dinner tonight." I fidgeted with the hem of my Merv's Bar & Grill polo, wanting to say more. Not knowing what to say. Why had I mentioned making dinner? "Is there anything in particular you'd like? I was going to make a casserole but—"

He turned to me. "I can get something in town."

"Oh. Okay. I guess I'll see you later, then?"

He nodded, and I started for the door.

"Elizabeth?"

I turned. "Yeah?"

"Thank you."

"You're welcome."

I left him, immediately wishing I could stay.

17

NICK

I WATCHED ELIZABETH RETURN TO THE main house, and as soon as the door shut behind her, I dug out the cell and called home.

Sam answered.

"Where's the dog?" First thing he said to me.

That was our code for, *Are you okay?* If the dog was in the house, I was good. If the dog was in the shed, the shit had hit the fan. Which meant, *Get the fuck over here.*

"It's in the house," I answered.

We all wore GPS tracking devices when we were separated, but I wasn't good about remembering mine. I'd left it—a necklace—in the truck since last night.

"You've been in the same place for over twelve hours," Sam said. "Or did you forget to put it on again?"

I groaned. "What do you think?"

"Put the damn thing on, Nicholas." Sam always used my full name when he was pissed.

"Let me talk to Anna."

A pause. Then, "Hold on." There was a rustle, a whisper, then Sam again. "Put on the tracking device, Nick."

Anna came on the phone a second after, as if she'd ripped it away from Sam. "Hey," she said. "How are you?"

I dropped onto the couch in the back corner of the apartment and all the tension left my body. I wasn't at home, but in this place I felt as safe as I'd ever felt. I couldn't explain it. Maybe it was the little old lady who owned it. Maybe it was Elizabeth.

Maybe it was Anna on the other end of the line.

"I'm okay," I answered.

"So what have you found?"

I went to the kitchen, pulled open the fridge. Nothing inside. Not a goddamn thing. I needed a bottle of something strong.

"Nick?" Anna said.

I returned to the couch. "I found the girl. The one from the flashback."

"Go on."

"And I'm staying in the apartment above her garage."

A long exhale.

My eyes burned as I waited for Anna to say something. She was processing, most likely. I went to the bathroom and stared at myself in the mirror. I looked like hell. I checked the cabinet—actually, the old pie cupboard pretending to be a cabinet—looking for eyedrops. Nothing.

"That was fast," Anna finally said. "What's she like? Does she remember you? How did you convince her to trust you? Wait," she cut in. "I already know the answer to that."

"I didn't sleep with her, if that's what you're thinking."

She laughed. "No, that's not what I was thinking. But really, what's she like?"

I went to the windows again and glanced at the main house. I scanned the second-story windows, hoping for a glimpse of her.

"She's . . . nice."

"Nice?" Another laugh. "That's all you can give me?"

"She's pretty," I added. "And quiet." I recalled all the shit the librarian had told me. That Elizabeth had had several public meltdowns since she'd been rescued. I didn't tell Anna that part. It wasn't my story to tell. Hell, it wasn't the librarian's, either.

"So," Anna said, "anything else?"

I debated telling her my doubts about Elizabeth, that I'd caught her in a lie about the injuries she'd had the night I'd taken her to the ER, but I knew what those suspicions implied, and I wasn't ready to put them out there yet.

"That's all I got," I said. "Stop pumping me for information."

Anna laughed again. "Glad to see you're still yourself."

"Yeah, me, too." I turned away from the main house and let the curtains fall back over the windows. "I need to ask you a favor and I need you to swear you won't tell Sam yet."

I could hear the shuffling of feet on the other end as Anna walked into another room. "I think that depends on what the favor is."

"I need to call Trev."

"What?" she screeched.

"Shh!" I said, knowing that the second she sounded alarmed, Sam would come running.

"Why would you"—she lowered her voice to a whisper—"call Trev? You hate him."

"He knows things about the Branch that we don't. And trust me, if I had another option, I'd take it, but he's the best I've got. Just give me his number."

Anna thought for a second. "Fine. But when Sam finds out about this, I'm going to be in so much trouble. You better back me up."

I snorted. "Sam's going to be more pissed at me than at you. *You* better back *me* up."

She rattled off the number, and I wrote it down on a piece of scrap paper I found shoved in a kitchen drawer.

"Thanks," I said.

"Yeah. I know. Just be careful, okay?"

"Aren't I always?"

"No." She sighed. "Anyway, in the meantime, I'll keep digging through your files and let you know if I find anything useful."

We hung up. I considered catching some sleep before going back into town, but I was still feeling restless, and being without the truck made it worse. I needed to have a quick escape, just in case.

When I left the apartment, I felt eyes on me as I walked down the driveway. I looked up at the house and saw a shadow pass across the front window. I thought about asking Elizabeth if she wanted to come with me, but decided maybe it was too soon.

I didn't want to run into Evan again at Merv's Bar & Grill, so I kept walking down Washington until I ran into another bar. Inside, the place was still and dark.

As much as I wanted another drink, I hadn't eaten in a while, and I still had to drive back to Elizabeth's. I ordered a sandwich along with a beer and picked at the food while I thought.

Anna was right. I hated Trev, but he was the only one of us who still had a line to the Branch. He'd helped us wipe them out, including leveling several of their buildings, but was he still a part of it? Whatever part remained of it, that was.

Maybe he knew about the place nearby that the Branch used to operate out of.

I bristled at the thought of calling him.

Every time I saw the guy, I wanted to punch him.

I drained my beer and ordered another. By the bottom of the second, I was feeling a lot better. And more than that, I was feeling a little looser with the forgiveness.

I pulled the cell from my pocket, punched in Trev's number, and waited for it to ring.

"Anna?"

That was the first thing Trev said when he picked up.

"Sorry to disappoint you," I replied.

Trev cursed. "What the hell do you want? Where's Anna?"

"She's home."

"Is she okay?"

"Yes. Is there anything else you want to know about her? You want to know what she was wearing yesterday? You want to know what she had for breakfast? You want to know how often I stumble on her and Sam going at it?"

The last one was a lie, but twisting the knife always felt good. Anna would smack me for it if she ever found out. A little sliver of guilt wedged in my chest.

"I'm hanging up now."

"Wait," I said. "I'm sorry. Mostly for Anna's sake. Not yours."

"What do you want, Nick?"

"I need your help."

"And I'm just supposed to jump?"

"There's a girl," I started, looking over my shoulder. It was always good to know who was within earshot. A couple sat at a table a good ten feet away. No one on either side of me at the bar.

" 'There's a girl,' " Trev echoed. "Oh no! Not a girl."

"You're such an asshole," I said, and started again. "There's a girl that I was sent here to... *you know*, before the farmhouse lab. And I need to know what the mission was, and why she was part of it."

"Where's 'here'?"

"Trademarr, Illinois."

Trev cursed.

"What?" I said.

"I can be there in less than an hour."

That was close. Closer than he should have been.

"Where can I meet you?" he asked.

I told him the name of the bar and where he could find it.

"Stay there. I'll be in town soon."

All the warning bells in my head were going off. It was like a fucking holy hour of bells.

Something wasn't right. Staying put was probably the last thing I should do.

'Course, if anyone was good at doing the exact opposite of what should be done, it was me.

18

ELIZABETH

I PULLED THE GABRIEL BOTTLE FROM the shelf and popped out the cork. I took in a deep breath, and that night came flooding back in disjointed images.

The woods. The moonlight. The branches snapping at my feet and snagging my hair. The log that tripped me. The dry leaves rustling as I rolled over.

And finally Gabriel.

Nick.

"Take care of it," someone shouted.

The gun was pointed at me.

In the dark woods, the barrel was darker. Black. Empty. Bottomless. It was like staring into an abyss.

Nick whispered, "Say nothing. Do you understa—"

He cut himself off, and I whimpered at his feet. We were in the middle of nowhere. There was no one but Nick and the man in the distance. No one would hear my screams, so there was no point wasting my energy.

Nick shot. I was squeezed so tightly into a ball when the gun went off, I couldn't breathe. A ragged, choked sound escaped me.

The bullet sailed over me. I wrapped my arms around my head. Every part of my body hurt. Fire in my veins. And fire in my lungs. My side was slick with blood. My chest, too. If Nick didn't kill me, I'd be dead anyway. I was dead if he left me here.

"Stay here," he whispered. "I'll be back."

His footfalls sounded like thunder in my head.

"Go," he told the man. "I'll take care of the body."

"Decapitation, remember? Carry her back to the warehouse," the man said. "Wrap her in this, so you don't leave a trail of blood."

The ground smelled like coming winter. Like the end of everything. Or maybe that was just me and my dying, bloodless body.

The word *decapitation* kept running through my head like a flashing red marquee.

The man made a call on his cell. "It's taken care of," he said, and left, the leaves rustling as he walked away.

Nick reappeared with a roll of plastic. "Wait until he's farther out," he told me. "No sound. None at all. Got it?"

I nodded.

I was shaking so bad by that point, I felt like gelatin.

Nick took his coat off and wrapped it around me. Pine and musk and cinnamon and something else woodsy and sweet. I focused on the smell of his coat, dreaming up another life, another scenario, where I wasn't this girl slowly dying on the forest floor.

We waited so long, I swear I saw the moon tick through the sky. Until it was nothing but a speck of silver far below the tops of the trees.

Without warning, Nick scooped me up, his arm tight around my waist, the other sturdy beneath my knees. I cried out. Tears leaked from my eyes. I wanted to die in that moment.

"It's going to be all right," he said. "I promise. I won't let anything happen to you."

I capped the glass bottle, and the images flashed away. The pain was a distant memory, but the hopelessness, the need for the whole ordeal to end, was with me still to this day.

In my closet, I ducked down and pulled out an empty bottle from the box Aggie bought me the last time we'd been at the New Age store. I grabbed my treasure trove of oils. Some high-grade essential oils, some cheaper fragrance oils.

The new bottle needed a base of musk. I filled it halfway and added the rest on top of it. A third of the bottle was vanilla. Then bergamot. Pine. And finally, lavender. I stirred it with my glass stick and took in a breath.

Perfect.

Last to go on the bottle was a label. I wrote Nick's name on it in cursive, then plugged the neck with a cork.

I set it on the shelf behind the GABRIEL bottle.

A knock sounded on my door. Aggie ambled in. "Brought you some cookies." She put a plate with three cookies on my desk.

"Thanks."

"They turned out better than the last batch. Nice and gooey in the center. Just how I like them."

She paused in the middle of my room, and I got the distinct feeling she wasn't here to share cookies.

"What is it?" I asked.

"This boy..."

"Nick."

"Nick." She sat on the edge of my bed. I leaned against the desk. "You don't really know him from school, do you?"

I shifted and looked at the floor. "No."

"He a good kid?" she asked in a way that said she already knew the answer, but wanted to hear my opinion. Aggie was a fan of letting me make my own decisions. Freedom to grow and make your own mistakes, she'd often said. At first, I'd felt constricted by the freedom, as if there were too much of it, too many choices, for it to actually mean something.

" 'A good kid'?" I echoed.

Hearing someone refer to Nick as a kid seemed silly. He might have been under twenty, but he seemed further from a kid than a house cat from a cougar.

"Yes," I answered, even though I didn't know if it was true.

She eased off the bed, wincing when she made it upright. Her hips had been bothering her for a long time. But she didn't like to complain about them. In fact, I couldn't recall Aggie ever complaining about anything.

"Just be careful, huh?" she said, and winked at me as she shuffled past. "Oh, and..." She turned around briefly, to wag a finger at me, "he's not allowed in your bedroom with the door shut."

Okay, so maybe she drew the line at *some* freedoms.

A giggle burst from my throat at the thought of what she was implying.

Aggie wagged her finger a second time, a smile on her face. "I'm serious!" she said.

"I know. Of course, Aggie. No closed-door escapades."

She shook her head as she left, chuckling to herself.

But when I was alone again, I couldn't help but picture Nick in my room, sitting on my bed, here among my things. The door closed. His ridiculously blue eyes on me and only me. What that might entail.

The fire in my face said it all.

19

NICK

I WATCHED TREV ENTER THE BAR FROM across the street, hidden in the shadow of an alcove. I didn't want to find myself cornered inside if he arrived with Riley or any other Branch agents. At least here I could keep an eye on the street.

Trev had arrived alone in the same black Jaguar he'd been driving a few months back. He'd done something weird to his hair, though. Half shaved, half long, like someone had started buzzing it from the bottom up and then quit before it was done.

He was wearing jeans and a short-sleeved henley. No combat gear. No stock Branch uniform. I didn't miss the bulge of a gun at his back, though.

He went inside, the door creaking closed behind him, sealing the noise of the bar with it. I waited. A few other vehicles drove past. A minivan. A Jeep. A motorcycle. Another minivan. I scanned the roofs of the buildings.

Nothing.

I jogged across the street, pressed my back against the bar's exterior, hands loose at my sides.

The door opened, and Trev came out.

I stepped into him, grabbed him by the arms, whirled him around the corner of the building, and slammed him into the darkness of the next street, into the brick wall of the bar.

Trev countered quickly with a gut punch. My lungs emptied in a gasp of air. He brought his left hand up, slamming my bottom jaw into my top, and my teeth clacked together. He kicked me in the knee. I went down, rolled, pulled my gun out from beneath my shirt, and pointed.

Trev already had his Glock on me.

"What is this?" he asked, cool, calm, as even as ever.

"Why were you so close?" I asked.

"If you'd given me five minutes, I could have told you."

I spat blood to the sidewalk, felt a split in my lip when I ran my tongue across it.

"Are you alone?" I asked.

"Yes. Are you?"

"Yes."

We remained that way for several long seconds, me on the sidewalk, aiming a gun, him standing two feet away, gun trained on my head.

"Fine." He turned the gun away, hands up. "Let's talk."

I got to my feet, glad he was the first to give in. "Want a drink?"

"No."

"Well, I do."

"Smells like you've had enough already."

I scowled at him as I passed.

Back inside the dimly lit bar, I ordered a beer, because Trev was probably right, but hell if I was going to admit it. We sat at the table farthest from anyone, the jukebox blaring a bluegrass song ten feet behind me. It was enough to give us privacy.

"I don't work for the Branch anymore," Trev said. "Let's just get that out there right now."

I took a draw from the beer and waited for him to go on.

"They knew I'd turned when I helped you guys escape. And, of course, they suspected I was the one who planted the bombs."

"How much is left?"

He didn't need clarification to know I meant the Branch.

"Riley, obviously. He's the one running whatever is left. He just got a big push from someone in the Department of Defense. I don't know what it was. Or why. But I'm guessing they're working on some new program."

I cursed and tightened my hold on the beer bottle, wanting to smash something so badly my fingers itched. "So if you don't work for them, then why are you here?"

"Because..." He glanced at the bar's entrance, then at the back door, before going on. "We got word that there was something here that Riley might want, something to kick-start the new program. I didn't know it was you."

"Who's *we*?"

"We call ourselves the Coats."

I cocked a brow. "The Coats?"

"Short for Turncoats. Remember Sura mentioning she was part of a group that opposed the Branch?"

I nodded. Sura had been Arthur's ex-wife—Arthur was the scientist who ran the program at the farmhouse lab. He had also posed as Anna's dad for five years, after the Branch wiped her memory and made her forget her real parents.

Despite all the shit Arthur had put us through, and the lies he'd force-fed Anna, he was all right.

"The group Sura was part of," Trev said, "was the Coats. They're all ex–Branch employees. They still have some people on the inside, who provide us info as it comes in."

"So you were already on your way here to check out what Riley might be interested in?"

Trev nodded.

"Is Riley on his way here now?"

"Not yet."

Was Riley coming to Trademarr for me? Or for something connected to Elizabeth? He had to know she was still alive—the news of her rescue had been plastered all over the place.

"Will you know when Riley is coming?" I asked.

Trev nodded. "They'll keep me up-to-date on his movements."

"Good. Because I have a few things to take care of before then." I stood and drained the rest of my beer, slamming it on the table when I was finished.

I moved for the door.

"Wait," Trev said. "There's more."

I paused, and glanced over a shoulder. "What?"

He leaned back in his chair, stared me right in the face. "There's an old lab here, too."

Trev drove south of town, taking an old highway lined with decrepit, barely functioning factories. The Jaguar's engine roared as Trev picked up speed.

"What did this thing cost you?" I asked.

"A lot of money."

I grunted. "The Branch must have paid you well."

He glanced at me for a second before turning away again. "I would give it all back if I could."

"You mean, instead of turning on us?"

"Yes."

"Still feeling the guilt of that decision, huh?"

" 'You may be deceived if you trust too much, but you will live in torment if you don't trust enough.' "

"Great. You're doing that thing again."

"I just mean..." He trailed off as he slowed to make a left turn. "I trusted the Branch too much, is what I mean. But I thought it was worth it. It wasn't."

The others had forgiven Trev, to an extent. We'd all been warped by the Branch. They were good at telling lies. Good at cracking open your head like a pumpkin and scooping out the guts. All the things that mattered. I think that's why Sam, Cas, and Anna had cut Trev a little bit of slack.

I was still having a hard time following suit.

You screw me over once, that's it. Didn't mean I couldn't use Trev, though. He owed me.

"Yeah, well," I said, cracking a knuckle, "you'll always be a fucking rat in my book."

His hands tightened on the leather steering wheel. "I don't have to help you, you know."

"Fine. Then don't." He slammed on the brakes. I braced myself with a hand on the dash. "Jesus Christ."

"Get out."

I glanced at him. "Come on. Don't be a dick."

"Get the hell out of my car, Nick." His freaky orange eyes flashed in the light.

A second ticked by. Then another. I tried getting a read on him, wondering how far he'd push.

"Get. Out. Of. The. Car."

"You're an asshole, you know it?"

He grabbed the back of my head and slammed my face into the dash. White dots exploded in my vision. A sharp pain radiated out from my forehead, across my skull, and down my neck.

While I tried shaking off the blow, Trev reached over, opened the passenger door, and shoved me out. I hit the pavement on my back, still half in the car.

Trev stomped on the gas, and my legs slipped out. He stopped to slam the door closed and took off again.

I crawled to my feet and watched the beads of the red taillights disappear around a bend in the road.

"Shit."

Cornfields surrounded me on both sides. Behind me was the road we'd come in on, and more cornfields. In the time we'd been arguing, the factories had disappeared, replaced with absolutely nothing. Except corn.

How long had we been driving? Ten minutes? Fifteen?

My head swam, either from the hit, or the booze, I couldn't tell which. The contents of my stomach sloshed around and then was coming up, eyes burning, bulging. I stumbled to the shoulder of the road, crashed to my knees, and hurled everything I had in me till my stomach muscles ached and my head pounded.

I lay back in the grass trying to catch my breath, and let the wooziness pass. Now I was well and truly screwed. Why did I have to go and open my big mouth? Trev was the best lead I had, not only on the lab, but on Riley, too.

Locating the lab would be a big step in finding out what had gone on here and why I'd been sent here in the first place.

Now Trev was going on his own, leaving me completely out of the loop.

I started walking in the direction we'd come from, hoping I'd make it home at least before midnight.

20

ELIZABETH

AGGIE AND I ATE DINNER WITHOUT NICK. Of course, he'd said he'd eat in town, but part of me had still hoped. Despite the fact that he'd been out of my life for six years, now that he was back, it felt like he'd never left.

I'd known him for only a few hours, six years ago, but it'd been enough to leave an imprint so large, I felt like he would forever be a part of me. Like he'd always been a part of me. He'd arrived in my life when I didn't feel like it was worth much. And he'd showed me that it was.

Sometimes, when I was with Chloe and Evan and the others at Merv's, my past seemed like a horror movie I'd watched one night when I was too young to tell the difference between fiction and reality. It seemed too terrible to be true. Chloe's and Evan's lives were so normal that when I was with them, I could pretend that mine was, too.

After Aggie went to bed, I washed the dinner dishes by hand, telling myself it was simply because there were so few, and running the dishwasher seemed like a waste. When really it was because the window over the kitchen sink afforded me a clear view of the carriage house.

I finished just after nine and still Nick hadn't returned. I scrubbed down the counters. The table. I swept. I emptied the trash. I returned to the window. I stared at the carriage house until my eyes burned.

By ten o'clock, I had convinced myself I'd imagined Nick.

By eleven o'clock, I'd gone to bed, only to get back up and tiptoe to Aggie's sewing room. I set a chair in front of the window that looked out over the backyard and resumed my post.

I stared at the carriage house.

I stared some more.

The windows were dark. Nothing moved.

My chest grew heavy with waiting.

The minutes turned into hours. The hours into agonizing days.

He would come back.

Please come back.

Why did I want him to come back?

What would I do if he didn't?

For the past six years, I'd been trying so hard to make sense of what had happened to me. How it had ended. How Nick fit into it.

I'd tried telling myself I'd heal from the wounds. The physical ones. The emotional ones. The wounds that didn't even have a label. But as the years went on, they still felt wide open and festering. I felt like I'd never be right again.

Nick's arrival was a stitch in the gash, and a little part of me felt real again.

He had to come back.

I pulled my legs up, propping my feet on the edge of the chair, my arms wrapped around my knees. I glanced at the clock hanging above Aggie's sewing desk, and the hands marked midnight.

He was never coming back.

Movement out of the corner of my eye pulled me to the window.

Nick crossed the pool of light cast by the carriage house's exterior light, his steps slow and unsteady. He paused at the bottom of the stairs and turned toward the house.

I drew back, into the shadows, my heart pressing hot against my ribs.

He had come back.

He was real.

I was real.

I was real.

Dr. Sedwick's office was above my favorite New Age shop and had the distinct smell of oils and burning incense that permeated the floors.

It was a small office, with heavy leather furniture and enough books stuffed in glass-fronted cabinets to start a library.

I'd been to several therapists over the years, and Dr. Sedwick's office was definitely my favorite. It was warm and cozy and felt like a father's study, or at least what I imagined a father's study to feel like.

Mine had never had one. In fact, my dad had never been around much at all. He and Mom had divorced when I was four, and then he dove into his work, traveling so much, I rarely saw him.

When I found out he'd killed himself while Mom and I had been held captive, I'd been numb to the news. I hadn't seen Dad for months before I'd disappeared. It was like his death was a secondhand story I'd heard from a friend—the loss theirs, not mine.

I still felt guilty about not missing him.

"Good morning, Elizabeth," Dr. Sedwick said when I stepped inside.

I'd been seeing Dr. Sedwick for over a year now, and though I always doubted the effectiveness of talking about my problems, I did feel lighter when I finished a session with him.

"Morning," I replied, and made my way for the leather couch. I always sat on the right-hand side, wedged in the crook of the arm, the plaid throw draped over the couch a comforting warmth behind me.

"Give me one second." He made a few more notes in his notebook before closing it and shutting the door. He came around the desk and sat in the leather chair across from me, a new notebook propped on his lap.

"How are you today?" he asked.

We started every session this way. My first time seeing him I'd said, "I'm fine." I'd learned that when people asked me how I was, *fine* was what they wanted to hear.

Dr. Sedwick had seen straight through my BS, and asked me again, with a quirk of his eyebrow, a flicker of a smile. And he kept asking until I told him how I really was.

Now I cut straight to the truth.

"Confused. Happier. Hopeful."

"Go on."

I shrugged. "For the first time in a long time I feel like what happened in the past might finally start to make sense."

He pursed his lips and nodded as he scribbled something in the notebook.

"So that's where the hope comes from?" he asked. "And the happiness?"

"Yeah. I think so."

"Hope is a powerful thing. It's like..." He trailed off and stared out the window, eyes narrowed against the sunlight. "Well, it's like the flame in the darkness. You know?"

"Yeah. I think so."

"So where does the confusion come in?"

I raked my teeth over my bottom lip. Should I bring up Nick?

Dr. Sedwick beat me to it, though.

"Does this have anything to do with the boy staying at your house?"

I raised my brows. "Did Aggie call you already?"

He smiled. "You know how she is. She's concerned."

A clock ticked above the fireplace.

"Yes," I answered. "All of the above has to do with him, actually."

"He's helping you figure out your past?"

"Yes."

"Who is he, exactly?"

I swallowed, licked my lips. Dr. Sedwick knew parts of what had happened to me. But only parts. And none of the important ones.

"He... he's from my past."

The pen raced across the notebook.

"Does he know what happened to you?"

"Yes. I mean, somewhat."

"How did you meet him?"

I shifted, tucking my feet beneath me. Should I tell him? Everything I said in here was supposed to be confidential, but secrets are powerful, and this was a pretty important one. The police had searched for clues to Nick's identity when I'd arrived in the ER in his arms. And they'd found nothing.

Was Dr. Sedwick required to report who Nick was if I told him? Did the law trump patient confidentiality?

"I met him through a friend," I answered.

"How do you feel about Nick now?"

"I want to be with him every second of the day. I can't really explain why, though."

"Does he feel the same way?"

"I don't know."

Dr. Sedwick scratched the back of his head as he thought, the pen still tucked between his index and middle finger. "Why has Nick reappeared in your life?"

"He's just visiting."

"Has he told you why he's here?"

I frowned. Dr. Sedwick had never pried so much into one person's place in my life. Never. And he knew how I felt about Evan, even.

"No," I answered. "Can we talk about something else?"

He shrugged. "If you'd like."

I did. I wanted to talk about anything other than Nick. But I also couldn't think of anything to talk about but him.

"Why don't you tell me what happened the other night. With Chloe and Evan."

A painful memory. Still so sharp it chafed. "We were in the woods, and I think Evan was actually going to tell me he liked me, but then I flipped out. I had, like, a flashback or something."

I explained how Evan had wandered off looking for cell reception, and what my mind had turned to in his absence, in the dark, how the pine trees had triggered the memory.

"Scent is a powerful trigger," Dr. Sedwick said. "Have you ever considered working through the flashbacks in a controlled setting?"

"What do you mean?"

"Determine which scents trigger which memories and use those scents to experience the flashbacks in a place that's safe, like your home. Once you've faced them, they'll hold less power over you."

I hadn't considered that, though I had been doing it on my own the past few days, to an extent. Like with my mother's bottle.

"I could try that," I said.

Dr. Sedwick nodded and made another note. "Try it and let me know how it goes. Go slow, though."

"I will."

"So let's get back to Evan. What was his reaction to your incident?"

"Well, he seemed okay with everything after, but now I'm worried I ruined any chance I had with him."

Dr. Sedwick crossed one leg over the other knee and glanced at me. "If you had to pick between Evan and Nick, who would you pick?"

"I don't know. I barely know Nick. I mean... I've spent more time with Evan, I guess. So it makes sense that I should pick him. But..."

A long, pregnant pause.

"But?" he coaxed.

"Evan's like... well, if he's a raindrop, then Nick is the sea."

"Ahh." Dr. Sedwick nodded emphatically.

"So... what do I do?"

He set the notebook down on the table next to him and leaned closer, his hands folded together. "Oceans are vast and almost bottomless. You play in the rain, Elizabeth. You drown in the sea."

After my therapy session was up, I went down to the store below and bought three new bottles of scent: lavender, bergamot, and a fragrance oil called China Rain.

Back at home, in my room, I readied a new glass bottle. I started with a base of China Rain, then added cucumber, for its cool, crisp scent. A few drops of cyclamen. Musk. Vanilla. Mandarin. Pine. And last, the lavender.

Once it was stirred, I pressed my finger over the neck of the bottle and upended it. I rubbed the oil on the underside of my wrist and breathed in.

All the bottles I'd mixed until now could be definitively traced back to a subject or experience. Carnivals. Summer. Christmas. Mom. Nick.

But none of them had ever been mixed for a feeling.

Dr. Sedwick was right—scents were a strong trigger. And I needed something to keep me sane, to remind me of the flame in the darkness.

Hope.

And hope, if it had a scent, would smell like spring, like the sea, like something new and alive. Like Nick.

So I'd taken my favorite spring and water scents, and mixed them with some of Nick's. Because if I was ever going to figure out what had happened to me, Nick was the path to it.

Nick was my flame in the darkness.

I grabbed a new label, and wrote *hope* in cursive letters.

Instead of putting the bottle with the others on the shelf, I set it on my bedside table so I could uncork it whenever I wanted.

Whenever I needed.

21

NICK

THE CLOCK ABOVE THE BED SAID IT WAS just after eleven in the morning, but it felt like six, like I'd gotten up too early. My eyes were burning. My head was pounding. And anytime I moved at a normal pace, my stomach seesawed and I had to clamp my mouth shut to stop from puking my guts out.

I hated puking.

Probably a lot of the suffering was due to the hangover, but I was blaming it on Trev's head slam. Everything was his fault.

After crawling my ass out of bed, I went straight for the bathroom and scrubbed my face with icy-cold water. When I looked up in the mirror, I wasn't surprised to see a massive black-and-purple bruise on my forehead.

In the kitchen, I found the fridge stocked with essentials. Some fruit. Milk. Bottles of water. Some lunch meat. A package of English muffins. And a bowl of leftovers.

Elizabeth must have come in after I went into town again yesterday.

I gave the apartment a quick glance, wondering if I'd left anything incriminating out in the open.

Didn't look like it. I hadn't had much on me to begin with.

After making my way back to town last night, I'd retrieved the truck with my bag inside it. At least now I had clean clothes.

I threw on a fresh T-shirt and a pair of jeans, and ran a hand through my hair. Good enough.

In the depths of a cupboard, I found a coffeemaker and then set out on the counter a bag of overpriced coffee. Hawaiian Sumatra, it was called. Whatever. Coffee was coffee, and it would do.

Once I had a fresh cup in hand, I sat at the squeaky kitchen table and pulled out my gun. I dropped out the clip, set it aside, and field-stripped the rest.

Sam had taught me how to use a gun, back when I first joined the Branch. Those memories were still gone—the ones where I entered the Branch, the missions I'd gone on—but the one that had returned, and that stood out like a thumbprint on glass, was the memory of Sam giving me my first Glock.

Guns do funny things to people. They make the weak feel powerful and the powerful feel vulnerable. I was in the first group. When

I'd first met Sam, I knew a thing or two about fighting with my hands, but I didn't know shit about weapons. If I had, I probably would have put a bullet in my dad a long time ago.

With that Glock in my hand, I didn't feel as worthless as my dad had made me feel. I felt like I finally had a sure way to defend myself.

Sam had taken me to do target practice in an abandoned train yard where we shot at empty pop cans. I was a crappy shot at first. I expected the gun to do everything for me. Point and shoot, kill whatever stands in your way. I was like a kid playing at being a thug.

After a while, after Sam showed me the technical side of aiming, the instinctual side of assessing your target, I hit every can I aimed at and the gun became a part of me, as deadly as my fists.

Sam's number-one rule about owning a gun, besides the obvious "Respect the weapon," was that you had to clean it after every firing.

I hadn't fired my Glock in over a week, since Cas and I did some target practice, but cleaning my gun was familiar, and right now that's what I needed. Something to keep my hands busy and my mind blank.

I was wiping down the recoil spring when a knock sounded on the door.

"Nick," Elizabeth called. "It's me."

"Hold on."

Shit.

I grabbed the frame, the clip, the barrel, and the slide and stuffed them in a drawer.

I still had oil on my hands and quickly wiped them on my black shirt before pulling open the door. "Hey," I said, a second before I laid eyes on her.

In the hours since I'd seen her last, she'd somehow gotten hotter. Her hair was down, for one, when yesterday it'd been wound up in a ponytail. It was longer than I'd thought, reaching to the middle of her back. It hung around her face in loose waves, and I had the sudden urge to run my hands through it.

Short white shorts gave me a good look at her legs. A tight-fitting tank top showed off her chest. I could see the faint outline of her bra through the shirt and saw a flash of black lace in my head. There was no way I could know what kind of bra she was wearing, but apparently I wanted her in black lace. And that observation made my body do shit I didn't want it to do. At least not right now at eleven in the fucking morning.

"What happened to you?" she asked, and gestured at the knot on my forehead, her eyes pinched with concern.

Without thinking, I ran a hand over the damage and winced in return. Dumbass.

"It's nothing. Really."

"Hmm." She frowned and tilted her head, causing her bangs to slide forward and hide her eyes. "Do you want some aspirin for it? Does it hurt? I could—"

"No." I shook my head. "I'm fine."

"Okay." She shuffled her feet, shifting her weight, her eyes doing the same noncommittal dance. Finally, she raised an arm to show me the deli bag clutched in her hand. "I brought you breakfast. Muffins. I hope you like muffins."

I didn't. I might have been borderline alcoholic, but I rarely ate shitty food. I liked my protein. A lot of it.

But I didn't tell Elizabeth that. I couldn't, not when she had that expectant look on her face. So instead I said, "Yeah, sure. I like muffins."

"Good." She stayed there at the top of the steps for several long seconds, until I realized she was waiting for an invitation.

"You can come in, you know." I opened the door wider. Her lips turned up at the corners.

"Thanks." She stepped over the threshold, her flip-flops slapping the hardwood. She brought with her a scent that was heavy on the flowers, but something clean, too, like rain. Smell was one of the senses I didn't give much thought to. I had to rely a little more on gut instinct. But something about Elizabeth I'd noticed, something that stuck out, was that she always smelled different, and whatever she smelled like, it was strong, like it'd leached into her skin. Usually people have one specific scent that's only theirs, sometimes diluted with perfume or cologne. Elizabeth didn't.

"Did you sleep okay?" she asked.

I shut the door and followed her farther inside. "Not really."

She glanced at me, mouth parted in an O. "Was it the bed? I keep telling Aggie she needs to replace the mattress in here. It's super-old. I'm sorry if it was hard as a rock. I could get you some extra blankets for padding or—"

"It wasn't the bed." I cracked a knuckle. "It was probably the hangover."

"Oh." Her eyes scanned the room, as if searching for the evidence. When she found nothing, she flicked again to me. "You came home late."

Her lips tightened with regret. She hadn't meant to admit she'd noticed when I'd returned.

"I ran into an old friend," I said.

"Who?"

"His name is Trev."

"Is he still in town? You could invite him over for dinner tonight."

I crossed my arms over my chest. "I'm not sure. I don't think so."

She gestured to the table. "Can I sit?"

"Sure." I hurried to the table and swiped the recoil spring I'd forgotten to put away. "You want some coffee?"

"I can get it."

She set the bag of food on the table and went to the cupboard above the drawer with my hidden gun. She knew what I used to do, she knew about the Branch, but how would she feel if she knew I had a gun with me now?

When her cup was full, she took the chair directly across from me, her hair falling forward on her shoulders. The morning sunlight pouring through the window behind her lit her hair, turning it amber.

I looked down at my own cup.

Elizabeth handed me a napkin and then a blueberry muffin. I rocked back on the chair on two legs and tugged open the silverware drawer to grab a fork. She gave me an odd look.

"You're going to eat a muffin with a fork?"

"Less mess," I said, which made her smile. Which almost made me smile.

We ate in silence for a beat.

"Do you have any plans for today?" she asked.

I did. I had a lot of plans. Unfortunately, they all hinged on Trev not being an asshole. "Not yet."

"I have to work, unfortunately." She sipped from her coffee, holding the cup with both hands. There were rings on her middle and pointer fingers on one hand, and one on her thumb on the other. I wasn't close enough to make out the details, but the ring on her pointer finger looked like a feather.

"What's your shift?" I asked.

"Two to eight."

I bit my bottom lip, debating. But the question came out before I could squash it. "Do you want to do something tonight? Together?"

She lifted her chin to look me straight on. The move elongated her neck, exposing the soft skin just below her ear. I thought about kissing her there. I thought about doing other things with her.

"Yeah," she answered, and for a second, I totally forgot what I'd asked her. "Do you have anything in mind?"

I shrugged and tore my gaze away from her neck. "You're the Trademarr expert. Have any suggestions?"

Hitting on girls was my superpower, but I was having one hell of a time sounding competent at it. It was probably my conscience telling me to back off. Not this girl. And definitely not right now.

"Let me think about it." The corner of her mouth quirked into a half grin. "I'll try to come up with something not totally lame. Though I'm not making any promises."

"I won't hold you to it."

The grin widened. She set her cup down. "Can I tell you something?"

"Sure."

"I . . ." She spun the feather ring around her finger. Over and over again. "This is going to sound silly, but I feel like you've never left. Like you've always been here."

The apartment grew sticky with the silence that followed. I didn't know how to respond to that without sounding like a total jackass.

"I'm sorry," she added quickly. "I know that sounds dumb."

"It doesn't."

She pulled the ring up over her knuckle, then shoved it back down again. "Where have you been all this time?"

I debated telling her about the lab, about the Altered program, but decided against it. It was old news, and it didn't have anything to do with her.

"I was tied up for a long time." Almost literally.

"Mmm."

She did that a lot, made a noise that was part hum, part moan. Like a sound was better than a word, like a sound was all she could manage.

"How did you get out?" I asked suddenly. "Wherever they were keeping you. How did you escape?"

I'd been wondering about this for a while, since I read the news article, since I realized she'd escaped before I'd even met her in the forest.

"Someone let me out," she said, and hung her head, staring at her coffee trapped between her hands. "They opened the cell door and led me to an air vent and told me which way to go to crawl out."

I leaned forward over the table. "Did you see who it was?"

She shook her head quickly. "I never saw a face. It was a woman, that's all I know."

"Did she follow you out?"

"No. She said she would get my mother, but..." The open-ended sentence said enough.

"That kind of thing happens a lot with the Branch," I said. "People dying. People you care about."

She bit at her bottom lip and nodded. "Anyway... enough about me. What about you? How did *you* get out? I mean, how are you no longer working for this... Branch?"

"The guy who ran the program I was in is dead."

Her hands tightened on the coffee cup. "Did you . . . you know—"

"Kill him? No. But I would have, if I'd been given the chance."

"You can't mean that."

I didn't say anything.

She drew her shoulders back, and her shirt tightened across her chest. She met my eyes. I knew what my eyes could do to girls—sometimes they were obvious about it, twittering on and on about how blue they were, how unnatural they were—but Elizabeth didn't seem unnerved by them. If anything, it seemed like she saw right past the color, right into the blackness of my soul beyond them. And she didn't turn away.

She pursed her lips and the gesture made them plump, made her cheekbones carve severe lines across her face.

My heart shuddered one foot away from my mouth, and both wanted to haul Elizabeth closer and taste the blueberry on her tongue.

Shit.

I got up, whirled around, set my hands on the edge of the counter. All the muscles in my body convulsed, wanting to move, wanting to do something other than this dance that wasn't getting us anywhere.

What was it about this girl?

I'd only known her a day, and already I couldn't stop thinking about her.

No, that wasn't true.

I'd known her a lot longer than a day.

Elizabeth had always been there, haunting me even when the memories were buried.

"Nick?" she said, so quiet I barely heard her over the stomping of my heart.

"Yeah?"

"Did I... I mean... do you want me to leave?"

I inhaled so deep, I felt my lungs press against my ribs. I turned around. "I should probably take a shower."

A cold one.

"Okay." She pushed the chair back and stood. "Will you meet me in town later? After my shift?"

"Yeah. Eight, right?"

She nodded.

"I'll be there," I said.

She grabbed the trash from our breakfast. "I'll see you later, then."

I didn't relax until the door shut behind her.

22

ELIZABETH

EVAN, CHLOE, AND I TOOK OUR BREAK together since it was dead and Chloe didn't have any tables. We ordered fried pickles—one of Merv's most popular appetizers—and a round of sodas.

I got to sit next to Evan thanks to Chloe. She complained that her feet hurt, and that she wanted to stretch out sideways and put them up on the seat beside her.

Evan and I bumped shoulders when he scooted in beside me.

"So what's the plan for tonight?" Evan asked.

Chloe raised a brow at me and winked. "We get off at the same time, right?"

I dug around in my bag for the cell phone I'd bought earlier to replace the broken one and checked the messages. Zero new messages. Not surprising. "I get off at eight."

"Me too," Evan said.

"Let's all do something, then," Chloe suggested.

"I would, but..." I trailed off, torn between wanting to spend time with Nick and wanting to be with the group again. Even though Nick was ungodly good-looking, I still had a major crush on Evan. Evan would always be here, and Evan was safe. Nick would leave again, before too long, and he was most definitely *not* safe.

"But what?" Chloe coaxed.

"I promised Nick I'd hang out with him."

Evan tensed next to me.

Chloe dipped a pickle spear in her puddle of ranch dressing. "Bring him with."

"I don't know about that," Evan said. "I don't like the guy."

Chloe snorted. "You don't like him because he's probably better-looking than you."

Evan grumbled and slid out of the booth. "I should get back to work."

His break wasn't even half over.

"Oh, he's pouting," Chloe said, and waved a pickle spear in the air at me. "Pouting is good."

"Maybe I shouldn't bring Nick." I took a drink of soda. "After all, the first time I saw him, he had Evan by the collar of his shirt."

"That's because Evan can be a dick sometimes."

"Chloe!"

"Well, it's true. It's just male posturing. Don't worry about it." She pulled a compact mirror out of her purse and examined herself, picking at her hair. "I need to get my roots dyed again. I look like hell."

That was so far from the truth. Chloe was gorgeous, and dark roots showing through her sunny blond hair wouldn't change that.

We finished off the rest of the pickles in record time and grabbed our dishes.

"You want my opinion?" Chloe said as we walked back to the kitchen. "Bring Nick along. If anything, it'll make Evan jealous. And a jealous man is a motivated man."

"I don't know if he'd come anyway. He seems to like to keep to himself."

"Oh, girlie, if he likes you at all, he'll come."

She pushed through the kitchen door, her blond ponytail swinging behind her.

A few minutes after eight, Evan came back to the kitchen, where I was putting in one last order. "Nick is here," he said. "He's at the bar."

"The bar?" I echoed. I'd thought he was eighteen, nineteen at the most. But if he was at the bar, then that made him at least twenty-one.

"The bar," Evan repeated, hardening his eyes. "I'm not sure about this guy, Lis. How well do you even know him?"

I slipped my pen into my apron. "I don't. Not really. I mean, I owe him. I trust him, I think."

"You *think*?"

"Just give him a chance tonight?" I tried. "Please? He's a friend and I don't want anyone to be mean to him."

Evan softened. "Yeah, all right." He smiled. "Anything for our Lissy."

I blushed. "Thanks."

With my order placed and a few minutes to spare, I went out front. Nick's back was to the kitchen, but as soon as I entered the bar area, he straightened, shoulders leveling, as if he sensed me. And then I realized he was watching me through the mirror behind the bar. He turned as I walked up.

"Hey," he said. There was a tumbler in his left hand, a couple of inches of brown liquid inside.

Everyone carded here. Merv was strict about that kind of thing. So Nick definitely was over twenty-one. Or had a very good fake ID.

"I'm almost done," I said. "Give me a few more minutes?"

"Sure." He brought the tumbler to his lips and drained the glass. He waved at the bartender for another.

Out of the corner of my eye, I saw a tiny blond-headed girl weaving quickly through the tables as if on a mission. Chloe. She was grinning at me like a fool, her eyebrows waggling. When she bounded up, Nick went stiff as a cutting board.

"Hi," Chloe said, and held out her hand to Nick. "I'm Elizabeth's best friend. Her coolest friend."

Nick stared at her hand, his face impressively blank. But then he blinked, smiled, and shook her hand. "Hey," he said.

"Did Elizabeth talk to you about tonight yet?"

I cleared my throat and made shut-up eyes at Chloe. "Not yet. He just got here."

"What's tonight?" Nick asked, glancing between Chloe and me.

I told him about the group, and about the lake. After our break, Chloe, Evan, and I had decided it'd be fun to have another fire. It was supposed to be nice tonight.

"You don't have to come if you don't want to," I added when I'd finished.

"I'll come," he said without giving it a second thought. "Something tells me there isn't much else to do here anyway."

Chloe slid onto the bar stool next to him. "You got that right."

"Well," I started, "I should go check on my order, and then I'll be out. Chloe?"

She raised the line of her brow. "Yes, dear?"

"Be nice to Nick while I'm gone."

She glanced at him, and a large smile spread across her face. "Never fear, Lis. I'll be on my best behavior."

I wasn't sure I believed her, but the sooner I got my last order out, the sooner I could rescue Nick.

23

NICK

"WHAT THE FUCK?" I SAID IN A RUSH, once Elizabeth was out of earshot.

The smile on Chloe's face disappeared like a snuffed-out flame. "Calm down. I'm not going to say anything."

She was the girl. The girl I'd picked up at Arrow two nights ago. The girl who told me her name was Sarah.

Sarah/Chloe was Elizabeth's best friend?

The whiskey in my gut turned sour and cold. It wasn't just the connection between the two girls—there had been something off about Chloe. She hadn't blinked an eye when I'd come out of my flashback and nearly knocked her on her ass.

I twisted around on my bar stool and propped my elbows on the bar top, burying my hands in my hair.

Chloe leaned in to me and lowered her voice. "Lis doesn't need to know. Nothing happened between us anyway. Remember? You went ape-shit before anything could."

"Ape-shit." I snorted and shifted so that I could look at her through the gap of my bent arm. "How the hell does something like this happen? You of all people! Her best friend?"

She frowned and rested her chin in the palm of her hand. "Something tells me you pick up a lot of girls. And something tells me that the likelihood of this happening is actually pretty damn high considering how cute I am."

I scowled her way. "You are unbelievable."

"Me?" Her free hand fluttered at her chest. "I should be the one worried here. I'm Lis's best friend, and you are clearly, somehow, questionably important to her. And, if I had to guess, *you* don't place much importance on *anyone* you meet." She pulled herself upright. "Just what are your intentions with Lissy, anyway?"

I mirrored her, pulling back from the bar top. The stool creaked beneath me. "My intentions? Well, I don't plan on courting her, if that's what you mean."

A hoarse laugh escaped her throat. "Despite my better judgment, I actually like you. You're not a pussy."

She had no idea, and I was grateful for the flashback that'd interrupted us. If it hadn't, what else might have happened between us? What else might she have figured out about me? Elizabeth knew some of my past, but she didn't know the scary parts. And if she did, then she'd push me away and this whole mission would turn to ash.

Chloe narrowed her eyes, as if she sensed the horrible things I was hiding.

"What *did* happen the other night?" she asked. "What happened to you?"

"Migraine," I said quickly, too quickly.

"Sure." The look on her face said she knew it was bullshit, but she didn't press, and I wasn't about to elaborate.

Elizabeth came up behind me, her uniform apron gone, her purse slung over her body. "Ready?"

Chloe and I shared a look. If she could keep her mouth shut about the other night, then so could I. I just wasn't sure if I could hide the growing elephant in the room.

"Ready," I said.

Elizabeth led the way out.

Chloe shot a look over her shoulder at me and winked as she walked away.

We followed Evan in his puny little sports car north of Trademarr.

Evan had offered to give Elizabeth a ride to the lake, but she'd said she'd ride with me. Part of me was glad (smug) that she'd turned him down. The other part didn't know what to say to her now that we were trapped in the truck's cab together.

We slowed for a stop sign, and the truck idled as Evan waited for a car to pass through the intersection.

"Are you sure you're okay with going out with my friends?" Elizabeth asked.

"Yeah. It's fine."

More silence. Evan hit the gas, pulling away from me in just a few seconds. The truck I'd picked out earlier this spring had a V8, and I'd picked it out for that reason. I caught up to Evan fast.

Jackass.

Truth was, I didn't really feel like hanging out with Evan for the night, but I did want to stick close to Elizabeth. If she was hiding something, I needed to find out what. If she was drinking tonight—and from the sound of it, there'd be booze—then she might let something slip. And the more time I spent with her, the more opportunity I'd have to gain her trust.

There was something she wasn't telling me—or anyone for that matter—about what had happened during her captivity. And it was aggravating, because the more I could learn about her captivity, the more I'd know about the program and what the Branch was up to when they were here six years ago. In my experience, the Branch changed people in screwed-up ways, and if I had to guess, they'd altered Elizabeth, too.

The biggest question was—had they made her into a weapon like they had me? And if so, what was she capable of?

We left the main road, turning left down a dirt two-track that cut through the woods. The lake came into view when we rounded a thick grove of trees.

I parked the truck on the passenger side of Evan's car and got out. We still had some daylight left, but out here, away from the city lights, it felt duskier.

It was quieter, too.

Another few cars pulled in behind us. More of Evan's friends, from the looks of it.

A tall, skinny guy went straight for the fire pit and started stacking wood inside. There were several rickety lawn chairs around the pit, and a few logs that had been used for seats. From the looks of the trash lying around—empty beer cans, plastic cups—this was their favorite party spot.

I scanned the surrounding woods. The two-track we'd used to get here was the only viable way out. We were cornered, with the woods on either side and the lake at our backs. It left me on edge. If the Branch attacked, I could run to escape, but could Elizabeth?

The lake was probably the best route out. There was a house about two miles east of the party spot, with a boat tied to the dock. Mentally, I tagged it as my escape route, should I need one. Swim to the boat, steal it, and take it across to the other side. The Branch would need a lot more ground time to cut me off on the other side than I would to boat across it. By then, I'd be long gone.

Another of Evan's friends showed up with beer and liquor a few minutes after we arrived.

"Hey, Nick!" Evan called. "Want a beer?"

I glanced at the girls. Elizabeth was sitting between Chloe and me. "You guys want anything?"

"Beer, please," Chloe said. "I had a ton of tequila the other night and I'm still paying for it."

Elizabeth was watching me, so she missed the teasing look Chloe shot my way.

Was she trying to piss me off? Because it was working.

"A Coke, if they have some," Elizabeth said.

While I wasn't one to get a girl drunk if she didn't want to drink, I'd been counting on her getting a little bit sloppy. "Want me to throw in some rum?"

"Umm." She thought for a second and glanced at Chloe. Chloe nudged her knee with a smirk. "All right. But just a little."

The booze had been set up on the back of some guy's truck, the tailgate used like a table. There were cases of beer, some vodka, Red Bull, rum.

I grabbed the bottle of vodka and poured enough for a shot into one of the red plastic cups. I gulped it down, the alcohol lighting a fire in my gut. " 'Liquor before beer,' " I said, when Evan looked at me sideways. It was an old saying I'd learned from my dad. One of the many gems handed down from father to son.

Evan grabbed a cup and did the same. "Good thinking." He smiled, but it was tight against his teeth. If Evan and I got through the night without punching each other in the face, it'd be a goddamn miracle.

I poured Elizabeth a drink, grabbed beers for Chloe and me, and sat back down. Chloe was talking Elizabeth's ear off about some customer at the restaurant. I was pretending to listen, laughing when it seemed appropriate. I'd got through two beers by the time Chloe came up for air. She hadn't touched her beer, I noticed. Elizabeth had been nursing her drink, but at least half of it was gone.

A tall, blond girl came up and stood in front of me. At first, she chatted with Chloe and Elizabeth, but then she turned to me.

"Hi," she said, leaning toward me, affording me a clear view down her low-cut shirt. Not that I was looking. "I'm Heather."

"Hi."

"Where has Elizabeth been hiding you?"

"I haven't been hiding him," Elizabeth argued, but Heather ignored her.

Over the course of the next hour, all the girls in the group wandered away from the guys and gathered around me.

I caught sight of Evan seething across the clearing. It was a wonder his head didn't catch fire.

"So, like, where do you live?" a girl in a short skirt asked. I couldn't remember her name.

"Michigan," I answered. I thought about lying, but where I lived didn't matter. Especially not to these people.

"That's cool," Heather said. "Like, literally." She'd managed to squeeze her way in on the other side of me, on the log. She was sitting so close to me now that our legs were pressed together.

"Do you go to school there?" another girl asked.

"No. I'm taking a year off." If only school was the least of my worries. 'Course, even without the Branch, I still wouldn't go to school. From what I could remember, before the Branch, I'd dropped out when I was sixteen. I'd never had a plan beyond getting drunk for the day. Just like dear old dad.

"Do you have any brothers?" Chloe asked.

It was the first question she'd asked me since I'd become the focus of the girls' attention. It put me on guard for some reason. Like she was trying to rattle me, even though the question was innocent enough.

Sam had taught me a long time ago that if I was going to lie, to lie as close to the truth as I could. In my life before the Branch, I'd been an only child, but that life didn't count as far as I was concerned. Sam, Cas, and Anna were as close to family as I was ever going to get. "Two brothers and a sister," I answered.

A redhead took a sip of her drink and asked, "How old are your brothers?"

"One older, one younger."

"Ohhh," Chloe said, and flashed a smile that was all teeth. "Are they coming here? New meat gets snatched up quickly in Trademarr."

"No."

The group murmured their disappointment.

Chloe got up and went over to the boys. I got the sense they were bullshitting about me.

"Will you walk with me?" Heather asked, threading her fingers through mine. "There's a really cool cliff just over there." She pointed over her shoulder. "I could show you."

I turned to Elizabeth, but she was already pushing me away. "Go ahead. If you want. The view up there is great."

"Come on." Heather tugged on my arm.

I wasn't sure if "cliff" was code for "stick your tongue down my throat," but either way, it didn't matter. I *did* want to be alone with Heather, if only to get out some of this pent-up tension. Being so close to Elizabeth set me on edge and made me think things about her that I didn't want to think.

"Are you sure?" I asked Elizabeth. "I came here with you."

She smiled and shook her head. "It's all right. Really. I need to refill my drink anyway. Go."

"Come on," Heather said again. I got to my feet as Elizabeth turned away and Evan grinned at her.

Suddenly, I didn't want to leave.

Heather led me to a path in the woods that ran close to the lakeshore. We followed it through some dense pine, then right along the shore, then back through the woods again, where maple and oak trees lined the path.

Heather stopped at the top of a hill and pulled me beneath

the overhanging branches of a maple tree. She grinned and pressed her back against the tree's trunk, her hand still intertwined with mine.

"What about the cliff?" I asked in a voice that said I didn't really care about the cliff.

"Do you really want to see it? Because it's not as great as I made it sound."

I got in close to her. "I've seen a lot of cliffs. Missing one won't hurt, I suppose."

She giggled and wrapped her arms around my waist. Good thing I'd left the gun in the truck. "So are you and Elizabeth, like, together?"

"No. She's just a friend."

"Good." She went up on the tips of her toes and brought her lips to mine. All the shit filling my head disappeared. Her mouth tasted like beer, and she smelled like fruit.

I slipped my hand beneath her shirt, and she practically purred, arching her back. I lowered my other hand to her ass, pulling her closer.

"God, you're so hot," she whispered against my lips.

I responded with a laugh and kissed her again. A fire built in my gut and raced lower, between my legs.

"When I first saw you with Elizabeth, I was, like, 'What a waste of such a fine ass.'"

I pulled away. "What do you mean?"

"She's, like, crazy. You know?" She kissed me again, then let her lips trail along my jaw. I barely noticed. The fire had all but burned out.

"You have no idea what Elizabeth went through," I said.

Heather drew back but kept her hands on me, running them up and down my sides. "You're right. I'm sorry. Anyway, let's not talk about Elizabeth." She leaned in again, pushing her chest into me. "In fact, let's not talk at all."

I stepped away and turned toward the bonfire and the clearing.

"Hey! Where are you going?"

I didn't answer.

"Nick!"

She trailed me all the way back to the clearing, cursing at me as she did. When we hit the group again, she was downright pissed, and she stomped away.

Evan frowned. "What happened?"

"Nothing," Heather said. "Except that guy is a jerk."

Elizabeth came over to me. "Everything okay?"

"She was…" I trailed off and ran my hand through my hair. I didn't know how to talk my way out of this one. I couldn't stand the thought of embarrassing Elizabeth here, in front of her friends, so I decided staying silent was better than explaining.

Except Evan wouldn't let it go.

His fingers dug into the sides of his plastic cup, denting it as he came over.

I had at least five inches on him. And easily thirty pounds. Not to mention everything else I had that he didn't.

"What did you do to Heather?" His breath smelled like beer, vodka, and rum. Booze gave you bravado, but it wouldn't give you shit in a fight.

"I didn't *do* anything to Heather." I eyed her across the bonfire, the flames distorting the anger on her face, and now the color of her shame.

She knew damn well what had happened, but she wasn't going to spill. And neither was I.

"You know," Evan started, "from the moment I met you, I knew you were trouble. Lissy would be better off without you. Before you take her down with you."

I turned back to him. "You don't know shit about Elizabeth."

"And you do?"

I glanced at her. I didn't know everything. I didn't know what kind of person she was before the Branch showed up. I didn't know what they'd done to her, but I did know her better than Evan did. Or at least I understood what it was like to be at the hands of someone who did terrible things to you.

All of these people here, they had no fucking idea.

"I think it's time for me to go," I said to Elizabeth. "Do you want a ride back into town?"

I couldn't let this escalate into a fight. I wasn't sure if I could hold back enough not to murder Evan with my bare hands.

Elizabeth stood up. Chloe stood next to her and took her hand.

"Elizabeth?" I tried again. I wanted her to come with me. I didn't want to storm out of here and leave her with Evan. Who knew what kind of shit he'd put in her head once I was gone.

"She doesn't want to come with you," Evan said, and pushed me.

The push sent me two paces back, and in that time my body shifted into fighter mode, narrowing the world around me until it was just me and Evan in that clearing.

The air crackled.

I could hear the beating of my heart in my head and the pounding of it in my chest.

I could smell the burning of the wood in the fire pit, and the dirt beneath my feet.

But everyone else... everyone else disappeared.

My shoulders leveled out. The muscles in my forearms tightened and bunched as my hands pulled into fists.

My fingers itched for a gun and again I was glad I'd left it in the truck. Otherwise it'd already be in my hand.

Evan bit his bottom lip—an obvious tell. His right shoulder rose up, the fabric of his shirt rustled as he moved, and I saw the punch coming days before it did.

I ducked. Evan swung again. Another dodge. Another.

Evan rocked back, practically spitting with frustration after a fourth swing and miss.

"What's the matter, Evan?" I taunted. "I'm not even moving."

He lunged at me. I stepped aside, and he went down in the dirt on all fours. I kicked him in the stomach. He spun over from the blow, landing on his side.

One of his friends came at me with a broken branch. He swung at me, and I caught it, bent it down, and smashed it in half with a boot. I took my half and whacked him in the knee, just enough to leave a bruise and send him flat on his ass.

Another friend jumped on my back and tried winding me up in a choke hold. I grabbed his wrist and bent forward, flipping him over me. He landed on the ground.

A shorter guy whipped the bottle of rum at me, and I ducked two seconds before it made contact. The bottle hit a low-hanging tree branch and shattered into a million pieces. The girls screamed as the shards blew back their way.

Evan was up again, charging at me with fists cocked. I caught the punch in my left hand and grabbed him around the throat with my right. I whirled him around, slamming him into a tree.

A puff of air burst out of him, and he gasped. I tightened my hold, felt the frantic beating of his heart beneath my fingers.

"Give in," I said, my teeth grinding out the words. I could fight him all day long, but the longer I fought, the less control I had.

Evan growled, "You're an asshole." I squeezed tighter.

He made a sloppy choked sound. "Fine," he croaked. "Now let me go."

When I released him, he collapsed against the tree, sucking up air.

I turned to Elizabeth. She was surrounded by girls who were panicked and pale and shoving napkins at her face.

That's when I saw it, the blood, trickling down the bridge of her nose.

"She was hit with a piece of glass," Chloe said.

I surged toward her, and the group parted like I had a disease. I took Elizabeth's hand and pulled her in the direction of the truck. I couldn't find the right words to apologize, so all I said was, "I'm taking you to the hospital." She didn't argue.

24

ELIZABETH

"NICK?" I TRIED TO KEEP MY VOICE level and calm.

The speedometer said he was going fifty miles an hour and we were still in the woods, on the two-track, the trees crowded around us. It felt like we were going a hundred.

"Nick."

He glanced at me, and my heart leapt into my throat. His face was hardened to a razor's edge, his eyes burning fire blue.

"I'm okay," I said. "Please slow down."

"You're not okay." His hands tightened on the steering wheel. "None of this is okay."

I pulled the napkin away from my face. It was red with blood, my blood, but the pain was already gone and I couldn't let him take me to the hospital.

"Stop the truck for a second. Just look."

He slowed and checked me. Finally, he stomped on the brake, and I had to brace myself against the dash. I'd forgotten to put my seat belt on.

Nick threw the truck into park.

"Cuts to the face usually need stitches," he said. "They'll keep bleeding and bleeding and—"

"It's not bleeding anymore. And I think the glass must have hit somewhere in my hairline, because I can't find the cut."

He frowned and scooted closer, taking my face in his hands. Even though he'd just finished fighting, leaving the boys in the clearing sweating and panting, his hands were cold and dry.

He examined me with a quick swipe of his fingers. I knew he'd find nothing there.

A frown narrowed his eyes. He parted my hair, searching for the cut, and I had to bury a shiver that threatened to race up my spine.

"Really," I said. "I'm okay."

The frown deepened, and a look of suspicion followed closely behind.

That was exactly what I'd been worried about.

"It was probably supersmall," I tried explaining. "It probably just looked worse than it was."

"Blood was pouring down your face."

"Right. But now it's not. So you don't have to drive so fast."

His mouth turned down at the corners. He pulled his hands away, but stayed in close proximity.

"You sure you're okay?" he asked, and I nodded.

"Maybe you could just take me home?"

He slid behind the wheel, and like a magnet, I felt compelled to close the distance between us again. I buckled my seat belt to keep me in place.

Nick put the truck in drive. This time he kept the speedometer needle below forty, and I was thankful for it.

"Where did you learn how to fight like that?" I asked.

The line of his jaw tensed. "The Branch."

"You could have killed them, couldn't you?"

He flicked his eyes to me for a second, a look that was meant as a warning. A warning not to ask that question, because I wouldn't like his answer.

Was *I* safe with Nick?

God, I didn't even know. I didn't know anything anymore.

Evan had provoked the fight. I couldn't blame Nick for that. Of course, if he hadn't gone off with Heather, none of this would have happened in the first place. I didn't know why I'd even pushed him to go. Maybe because I didn't want him to, and I wanted to see what his reaction would be. It was the wrong one.

When we pulled into Aggie's driveway after a long, silent ride, Nick shut the engine off. Neither of us moved.

"What really happened?" I asked, crumpling the bloody napkins in my lap. "With Heather, I mean?"

Heather had a reputation around town. Everyone called her a slut. I didn't like defaulting to labels, considering all the ones attached to me. But she did tend to throw herself at anyone and everyone, so I didn't think Heather had reacted the way she had because of Nick's advances. It'd been her idea to go up to the cliff anyway. And I didn't think she'd ever intended to take him up there for the view.

"She wasn't very nice," Nick said.

"To you?"

"To you."

My face warmed, and I looked away, out the passenger-side window. Heather wasn't a close friend of mine. She never had been. I could only imagine all the things she'd whispered in Nick's ear. The stories of how I'd had panic attacks in public. How I'd been tossed around between foster homes because of them. How I'd been found once in school, cowering in the bathroom, nearly hysterical after smelling the sterile smell of bleach. Bleach always reminded me of the place where I'd been held captive. The scent unnerved me.

"What did she say about me?" My voice squeaked.

"It doesn't matter. And I didn't believe it."

"It's probably true."

He turned in his seat. "Don't let them get to you. They have no idea what it's like to be you. They have no idea the things you went through. The things you've seen. They can pretend they know. They can dream up the worst-case scenario, but chances are, it doesn't even come close. You are stronger than they are."

Tears burned in the depths of my eyes, and I covered my mouth when I felt a sob race to get out.

"Elizabeth?" he said.

I looked at him.

A horrified expression crossed his face.

"Don't," he said.

And then I did.

I started crying right there in the cab of Nick's truck and couldn't stop. I buried my face in my hands, embarrassed and upset that I *had* let them get to me, Heather most of all. Why did I care what she said about me?

"Elizabeth," Nick tried again.

I heard his door squeak open and then shut a second later.

Great. He was leaving me. Because who wanted to deal with a hysterical crazy person?

But then my door opened, and Nick leaned in, drawing me into his chest. He put his arms around my shoulders, and I folded, the tears falling harder now, faster.

He tucked me into the crook of his neck. He didn't say anything. He just let me cry.

I felt completely out of control of my own body, unable to stop the flow of tears or the heavy, racking sobs.

After forever, after I'd soaked Nick's black T-shirt and the tears had dried up, I said, my voice muffled against his chest, "I don't feel strong."

"You are," he said. "Because you survived."

If only he knew I hadn't had a choice.

Nick followed me inside the main house. Aggie wasn't home, thank God. I found a note from her stuck to the fridge saying she'd gone to the hospital for a volunteer night shift.

"I think I need to lie down," I told Nick.

"You need anything?"

"A glass of water?" I said.

"I'll bring it up to you."

"My room is the second door on the left."

He nodded and disappeared into the kitchen. I heard him opening and shutting cupboards as I trudged up the stairs. While I had a few moments alone, I changed into a pair of black leggings and an oversized T-shirt.

Nick came in a few minutes later with the glass of ice water in his hand.

"Thanks." I took it from him and grabbed my bottle of meds from the desk. I shook out two and swallowed both with a gulp of water.

"What are those for?" he asked quietly, as if he was unsure whether he should ask.

For some reason, with him, I didn't feel like I had to hide anything. "Anxiety."

He nodded at the cobalt glass bottles. "And these?"

Crap. When I'd asked him to bring me a glass of water, I'd forgotten all about those.

"Memory bottles," I said. "Scent is strongly tied to memories. And sometimes I just need a happy one."

Don't look at the end of the row, I thought. *Don't look.*

But he did.

He found the GABRIEL bottle easily enough—I'd forgotten to tuck it back behind the CARNIVALS bottle—and pulled it down. That exposed the NICK bottle, and he grabbed that one too.

"I have a bottle?" he asked. "Two bottles?" He seemed amused by this.

"It's weird, I know."

"It's not. Scent *is* a powerful trigger. But I wouldn't think my place in your past was a good one."

It's good and bad. It's many things.

"Can I smell them?" he asked.

I shrugged, trying to hide my dismay.

The cork came out with a *pop*. He took in a breath. "Cinnamon," he said. Another breath. "Pine?"

"Yes."

"And something else woodsy."

"Cedarwood. And musk."

He replaced the cork and smiled. "I smell good."

I laughed. "Well, I'm not in the habit of making terrible scents."

"And the other bottle?" he asked.

"Brand-new."

He replaced the GABRIEL bottle on the shelf and tried the NICK bottle. "The same, but with something new. Something"—another sniff—"flowery?" He looked slightly horrified by this.

"Lavender."

"I smell like lavender?"

"It could be your laundry detergent."

He nodded and smiled, like that made sense. "Anna likes the flowery shit."

"Anna?"

He paused for a second, then said, "My sister."

"Where is she now?"

"Home. Michigan."

"Do you still talk to her?"

He nodded. "I live with her. With her—and Sam and Cas."

"Your brothers?"

Another nod. He thought for a beat, then shook his head. "Actually, no. They're not related to me. They were a part of my group, with the Branch. But they're like my family."

"Oh."

The way he'd said that, quiet and husky, made me think these were details he hadn't wanted to share. More of the truth he wanted to keep buried. And if he was sharing these things with me, what did that mean?

He put the NICK bottle back and leaned into my desk, crossing his arms over his chest. I tried so hard not to look at the massive bulk of muscle on his upper arms. Tried and failed. I was not immune to the sight of a good-looking boy. In my room, of all places.

"What's Anna like? Do you get along with her?" I asked.

"I didn't use to. I do now. She's... strong, and smart. And forgiving." He ran a hand over his face, a very human gesture that I didn't see him do often. "Like you, she's been through a lot."

"Are you and her, like, you know..." I trailed off, wondering why in the hell I'd broached that subject in the first place.

"No," he said quickly. "She's with Sam."

I exhaled with relief. "So you're not—"

"With anyone?" he asked, his voice laced with mirth. His eyes always seemed brighter when he was amused. "No."

The heat returned to my cheeks. "It's not really any of my business anyway."

"I don't mind you asking." A pause. "Are you with anyone? Evan seems really protective of you."

I brought my legs up and folded them beneath me on the bed. "I'm not with Evan. He's just a friend. I'm not with anyone. Not a lot of people would feel like dealing with the crazy girl."

He scoffed. "First of all, you're not crazy. Second of all, Evan, as much as he is a jackass, does legitimately seem to like you."

I looked away, feeling a smile tug at my lips. I'd liked Evan for the greater part of the past year. I would have given anything to know he felt the same way about me.

But now I wasn't so sure what I wanted.

Nick changed everything.

He pushed away from the desk. "Will you be all right if I leave for a little while?"

"Yeah." I could already feel the anxiety meds kicking in. I fought back a yawn. They always left me sleepy. "When will you be back?"

"Not for a while."

I nodded. "Do you want me to bring breakfast again tomorrow?"

I wanted him to say yes more than I'd ever wanted anything.

"Sure. If you want."

He started for the door, but paused halfway there and glanced at me over a shoulder. "You're sure you're okay? I can stay."

"I'm fine."

He nodded, as if relieved I'd declined. I didn't blame him. No one wanted to take care of someone who was in a miserable mood. "I'll see you tomorrow morning."

I smiled. "I'll be there bright and early."

"Not too early," he said. "I'm not a morning person."

"Why am I not surprised?"

I caught the barest hint of a smile on his face as he pulled the door closed.

I curled up on the bed, hugging a pillow close to my chest. The sooner tomorrow morning came, the better.

25

NICK

AS SOON AS I GOT BACK TO THE APARTMENT, I stripped off my shirt and tossed it in the corner. It was still wet at the chest.

I sucked at consoling people. In fact, I was terrible at it. A shirt soaked with tears was about all I could manage.

After finding a clean shirt in my bag, I tried Trev's cell for the third time that day. It went straight to voice mail. I brought up the text screen and typed in, *Call me back, asshole,* then deleted *asshole* and hit send. The last bit was probably implied.

Now more than ever I had to get inside that lab. Chances were, it was the place Elizabeth had been held, and if so, there could be clues there as to what the program had been.

I had my suspicions, but I needed concrete proof.

As I waited for Trev to reply, I grabbed a bite to eat. After downing a turkey sandwich, I cleaned an apple and ate it as I stared out the front windows, zoning out, trying to put together a reliable theory about Elizabeth's treatments.

When Trev didn't immediately call me back, I went to plan B.

I called Anna.

"Hey," she answered. "Everything all right?"

"You forgot the code," I pointed out.

"If you're reminding me of the code, then clearly Riley isn't standing over your shoulder."

I laughed. "That's true."

Anna was silent for a beat. "You laughed."

I had.

"You never laugh," she said.

"Are you going to give me shit or are you going to help me?"

She groaned. "What's up?"

"I need you to call Trev and tell him I said sorry like seven times and that he needs to stop being such a pussy."

"You talked to Trev?" she asked, ignoring the rest.

"Yes, and now he won't talk to me."

She sighed. "What did you do?"

"Why is it always my fault?"

"Because it usually is."

"You're starting to sound like Cas."

"Nick."

"I need you to call him. Please."

Another sigh. "Why?"

"Because there's a lab here, and he knows where it is."

She relayed the news to someone in the room with her.

The phone exchanged hands. Sam came on the line. "We're coming down. Don't do anything until we get there."

"I don't need you here. I can handle it myself."

"Nicholas."

"Samuel."

"I'd rather we go together, instead of you going alone with Trev."

"We can trust Trev," Anna said in the background.

"No we can't," Sam argued.

"Despite my obvious hatred for the guy," I said, "I do think we can trust him. I just need him to talk to me."

Sam was silent, then said, "Fine. But first sign of trouble, call. I don't like you being down there without backup."

"You're like a broken record, you know that? I said I could take care of myself. I don't need you to hold my hand."

"Stop being so damn defensive. You know what I mean."

"Yeah, I got it, boss. I'll send out a bat signal if shit gets real. Now, is Anna going to call Trev or not?"

"She's calling him now on the other cell."

I waited. Sam waited. I could hear Anna talking in the background, but I couldn't make out what she was saying.

After a few minutes, she came back on the line. "He said to tell you to stop being so obstinate."

I didn't even know what that meant. "Fine."

She went back to Trev to tell him he'd gotten his way, then said good-bye. To me she said, "He's coming to pick you up right now."

"He doesn't even know where I'm staying."

"It's Trev," she said. "Of course he knows."

Trev and I didn't talk much on the way out to the lab. Fine by me. It took us nearly twenty minutes to reach it. It was an old dairy farm, stuck in the middle of nowhere. There was a run-down house on the property, the windows boarded shut. The barn was in good shape though, and had clearly been kept up.

That must have been where the lab was hidden.

Trev parked just outside the double barn doors with the Jag pointed outward, for a quick escape.

"Did you go in the other night?" I asked him. "After you dumped me on the side of the road?"

"No." He shut the car off. "I just drove past, then parked about a half mile away and walked back. I wanted to do some surveillance before I broke in."

"And?" I asked.

"Nothing. No activity. None whatsoever."

At least I hadn't missed any fun.

There was a chain on the barn doors, padlocked with a commercial-grade lock. Thankfully, Trev had thought to bring bolt cutters, and we were through in less than a minute.

The doors shuddered as we opened them, the tracks corroded from neglect. Inside, the place was pitch-black and smelled faintly of hay and wet animals.

Trev clicked on a flashlight and shot the beam across the space. There were several rooms on the left where the horses would have been kept. Another room on the right, probably for supplies. There was a hayloft fully intact above us. Bats flickered in the beam of light.

"So how do we get in?" I said.

"Good question."

I was the first one inside, and I used the light cast from Trev's flashlight to guide me. I checked the horse stalls and didn't find anything suspicious. Trev checked the supply room. Nothing there, either. There was one more room, on the right, in the way back. That, too, was empty.

"Shit," I muttered. "Why do they have to hide their hidden lab so well?"

"It's gotta be here somewhere." Trev returned to the main part of the barn. "I'll check the hayloft just in case."

Seemed unlikely they'd hide a lab in a hayloft, but whatever. Gave me a chance to snoop alone.

Using my boot, I cleared away dry hay from the concrete floor of the back room. No embedded door handles. No obvious seams in the concrete. I went back out to the main room and did a circle as my eyes adjusted to the darkness.

Something wasn't right about this place. I just couldn't tell what yet. I went to the back wall of the barn and ran my hand along it, feeling for anything that stuck out from the raw wood. There was another door there, but it led straight to the outside.

I glanced at the empty back room again. Then at the back wall.

"Trev," I called.

He hung his head over the edge of the loft. "Yeah?"

"Get down here."

He joined me a few seconds later.

"Look," I said, and pointed at the back room. "If that room met the back wall of the barn, its square footage should be one hundred or so. Maybe a hundred and twenty."

He looked at me in the gloom, and his eyes flashed. "That room is too narrow for that. It's sixty square feet at the most."

I nodded. "Exactly."

We hurried into the room again and examined the wall that should have met up with the barn's back wall. Ten seconds in, I found a loose board, and when I gave it a tug it swung out, revealing a door handle.

"Bingo," Trev said.

I tried it, but it didn't budge. There was a keypad, like all the labs had, embedded in the wall.

"Move over," Trev said. Since I was playing nice, I did. He

punched in a series of numbers, and the door hissed open, finishing with a *pop*.

I narrowed my eyes. "How'd you know the code?"

"All the labs have an override code. Most likely they were changed after I blew up several of the buildings, but I bet this one hadn't been, since it looks like no one has been here in years."

Stairs appeared beyond the door, leading down into total darkness.

When Trev didn't make a move to go, I snorted and went down first, but not before pilfering the flashlight from his pussy hands.

The stairs seemed to go on forever, winding around on themselves, until finally we reached a steel door. It opened without complaint.

This lab was nothing like the farmhouse lab.

For one, we'd entered onto a metal stairwell that looked down on one wide-open space, like a factory, and two, it went on and on as far as our flashlight would reach.

Trev felt along the wall, grunted, and flipped an old power switch. Fluorescent lights flickered on by rows with a *whir* and *click*.

"Holy shit," Trev said, his voice echoing.

Definitely a lot bigger than the farmhouse lab.

This place was easily the length of a football field, and the width of two. There were sectioned-off labs, some with nothing more than cubicle walls, others fully enclosed.

"I've been here before," I said. Trev gave me a look, so I elaborated because I was still feeling nice. "I had a flashback about this place. Someone had escaped, and I was hunting them down."

"Par for the course when it comes to the Branch. They're always holding people prisoner, and people are always trying to break free."

Trev went first, and the *clang* of our steps filled the room, bouncing off the back walls and hitting us on the comeback. Once on the floor, we stopped, unable to see across the span of space with the partition walls towering over us. We were mice in a maze.

"You know your way around?" Trev asked me.

"Not really."

"Well, whatever data remains will be on the system. We just need to find a computer."

We checked out the nearest exam room first. This one was enclosed, but the two metal exam chairs faced a wall of windows that looked out over a bank of workstations. No computers. The room was completely empty. There wasn't even a used bandage in the garbage.

We kept looking and checked out a few more exam rooms. Finally we found a computer in a cubicle somewhere midway through the maze. It booted up quickly, but we were immediately blocked with a password screen.

"Tell me you know an override code for this, too," I said.

Trev sat in the desk chair and ran a hand through his hair. "Unfortunately, no. But... there are a few things I can try."

I watched over his shoulder for a good fifteen minutes, and everything he tried got him nowhere.

"I'm going exploring," I said, feeling restless and impatient. "Yell if you get something."

He grunted as I left.

Every exam room I checked out was almost exactly the same as the last. Some rooms had one exam chair, others two. Never more than that.

I made a right turn down one aisle of cubicles, then a left, and found myself in the back of the lab where a row of rooms had been installed against the concrete wall. Each room had a window that looked in on it. In the third room on the left, I paused, and an image flickered in my head.

A girl. A gun. And me.

I stepped over the threshold, and a feeling of déjà vu gripped me by the head and shook me till my vision tunneled.

There'd been a girl here, crouched on the floor, wavy dark hair hiding her face.

I slammed my eyes shut and tried to remember more.

She was sobbing. "Please don't kill me," she said.

My finger was already on the trigger.

I had orders. And the order was to kill.

"Please, Gabriel! I'm not what they say I am."

"What do they say you are?" I asked.

She shifted, and her hair parted an inch. One gray-blue eye looked up at me. "They say I'm a monster."

And then she was moving, moving so fast I barely blinked before a cloud of white snapped at my face, leaving split flesh in its wake. Blood trickled down my cheek.

She'd snapped the bedsheet at me, turning it into a whip. She snapped it again, breaking the skin above my eye. Blood clotted my vision. And then she kicked me in the balls.

My head hit the tiled floor with a whack, *and everything went dark.*

I braced myself on the doorjamb, sucking in air. It'd been a long time since I'd had a flashback that strong. I could still feel the blood running down my face, and I brought a hand up to check.

Nothing.

"Nick!" Trev called.

"Yeah?"

"I got in."

I tried to shake off the ghost of the flashback as I stumbled through the maze toward his voice. I kept checking over my shoulder, the hair at the back of my neck standing on end, like the girl from the past was stalking me in the present.

Who was she? She had Elizabeth's dark hair, but all I'd gotten of her face was one eye, and that hadn't been enough.

When I found Trev ten minutes later—after a few wrong turns—he gave me a look like I really did have whip cuts on my face.

"What happened to you?"

"Nothing. What'd you find?"

"Got into the system and dug up the lead scientist's logs. She made audios."

"She got a name?"

"Dr. Turrow."

That name had been mentioned in my files. Trev cued up a recording marked AUGUST 12. A female voice with a cold, clinical edge sounded through the speakers.

"Patient 2124 is reacting better to the Angel Serum than I ever could have imagined. We continue to monitor her progress. So far, there appear to be no adverse side effects. We have a test scheduled for August 16. It is my sincerest hope that she survives."

The recording cut out, and Trev selected the one labeled AUGUST 16.

"The test was a success! Patient 2124's results were everything I'd hoped for. Zero activity phase lasted six minutes. We'll perform another test in one week, and increase the time frame."

We listened to three more recordings, and in every one, Patient 2124 continued to outperform Dr. Turrow's expectations. Her last zero activity phase—whatever that was—lasted thirty-two minutes. The doctor nearly squealed with excitement.

On the sixth audio, though, the doctor's voice cracked and wavered. Trev and I looked at each other. Something had changed.

"Patient 2124 has grown uncontrollable. Defensive. Stubborn.

Rebellious. I worry that there is a shelf life to the Angel Serum. I can see her degeneration with every test, as if her body is healing, but her mind is not."

On the last clip, Dr. Turrow had a hard time speaking without sobbing. "Patient 2124, during today's test, stole Agent Riker's gun and shot herself in the head."

Static filled the rest of the recording. That was the last one.

"Fucking hell," I said. If Patient 2124 was dead, then it ruled out the possibility of Elizabeth being her. But why hadn't Elizabeth been mentioned in the logs? Based on my files, I'd come here in October. Which meant she would have been in the lab in August.

"We have to find out what this Angel Serum is," Trev said.

"No shit."

And, more important, I had to find out who that girl from the flashback was, and whether or not she was Elizabeth.

Anna and Sam had us on speakerphone, and Trev did the same on our end. We'd already filled them in on what we'd found in the lab, and Anna had some new information from my files.

"Target E," Anna said, "was to be killed by decapitation, the body incinerated thereafter."

I dropped onto the bed in Trev's hotel room and lay back. Trev was on the couch near the phone. I still had a raging headache from the flashback. The more vivid they were, the worse the aftereffects.

"Why go to such lengths?" Trev said. "The Branch is brutal, but decapitating someone just seems like one too many extra steps for them."

"You decapitate vampires," I said, my eyes covered with a hand. The light was too damn bright.

"What the hell are you talking about?" Trev said.

"Think about it." I sat up. "Why do you decapitate someone? And then burn them?"

"To make sure they're dead," Sam said.

I nodded at Trev. "What was it the doctor kept saying in the logs? 'Zero activity phase.'"

Trev's face went as white as the sheets beneath me. "Shit," he muttered, and started to pace the room.

"Fill us in," Anna said.

"I think they were killing Patient 2124 repeatedly," I said. "'Zero activity phase' was code for 'dead'—and then they were bringing her back to life. Over and over again. And keeping her dead longer each time. How long was the last test?" I asked Trev.

"She was dead thirty-two minutes."

"That's impossible," Sam said. "The brain would lose function after that long."

Trev stopped pacing. "Unless the Angel Serum was essentially putting them on ice, and then healing and reanimating them."

"This is how the zombie apocalypse starts," Cas said. "You don't screw with death."

"Cas," Trev said, "I've missed you."

"Yeah, well, you can suck an egg," Cas said.

Trev smiled anyway. The guy really did want to be part of the group again. I could see it on his pathetic little face.

"So," I started, "how does Elizabeth fit into all this?"

I'd finally broken down and told Trev about her. I'd wanted to keep her a secret just in case he was still part of the Branch. They'd wanted her dead once; they'd want her dead again. But I was pretty sure he was on our side now. Call it gut instinct.

"She was obviously one of the test subjects," Anna said. "And when they shut down the program, they called you in to terminate her."

I winced, hearing *terminate* associated with Elizabeth. Trev caught it and frowned at me.

I flipped him off and he frowned harder.

"That still doesn't explain why the Branch let her live. Once I brought her to the ER, her rescue was all over the news. They would have known she was still alive."

"True," Anna said. "Unless they didn't think she posed much of a threat after all."

"Or the lab was shut down," Sam said, "and all Branch employees left the area because—"

"They would have been worried about the media attention," Trev cut in. "And killing Elizabeth at that point, after she'd been rescued, would have drawn too much heat."

"No," I said, "there's got to be more to it than that. I just don't know what yet."

And that also didn't explain who the dark-haired girl was from the flashback I'd had in the lab. Was she Elizabeth? Was she another test subject?

"Any other targets mentioned in the files?" I asked Anna.

"No. Just the one. But we'll keep digging. If there's more here, we'll find it."

"Thanks, Anna," Trev said. I noticed he didn't thank Sam or Cas.

"We'll check in later," I said.

"Sounds good."

"Love you, Nicky," Cas said. "Hate you, Trev."

Trev laughed as he called out good-bye.

"Take me home?" I asked Trev, once we'd hung up the phone.

"Only if you ask nicely."

"Take me home, asshole."

He sighed. "Good enough."

26

ELIZABETH

I GOT UP EARLY THE NEXT MORNING, even though Nick had said he'd prefer breakfast later. I hadn't been sleeping well anyway, so I figured I'd get a jump on the day.

After I showered, I spent a ridiculous amount of time picking out an outfit—a summer dress with tiny birds on it—and doing my hair and makeup. Nick probably wouldn't notice or care, but for some reason I wanted to put in a little extra effort. Maybe not so much for him, but for me. It'd been a long time since I'd felt good about myself, but when I was with Nick, I felt strong, different, better.

Aggie had left early to run some errands, even after working half the night at the hospital, so I had the kitchen all to myself. I decided I'd make French toast for Nick and me, using Aggie's special recipe. I never made it as good as she did, but I could get close enough.

I grabbed my iPod, picked a pop music playlist, and stuck in my earbuds. I loved cooking while listening to music. It took less than five minutes to grab all my dishes and ingredients, save for the eggs. Aggie tended to bury the carton in the bottom of the fridge. I rummaged around inside, found the eggs, and grabbed four, coddling them in my arm.

As I straightened, a fast-paced song blaring in my ears, someone tapped my shoulder, and I yelped. The eggs dropped to the floor and splattered across my bare feet, globs of the whites squishing between my toes.

"Sorry," Nick said when I pulled out the earbuds. "I knocked, but..."

My heart hammered in my throat, and I was having a hard time catching my breath. I shoved the refrigerator door shut and collapsed against it, bringing my hand up to my forehead, shielding my eyes.

"It's okay," I said. "I didn't hear you, is all." I held up the earbuds by way of explanation. "I just need a second."

He went to the end of the peninsula and leaned into it, arms folded across his chest as he waited.

I kept telling myself not to freak out. *Do not freak out.*

When my hand fluttered at my mouth as if to quiet the ragged gasps coming out of my throat, I inhaled and caught the scent of my Hope oil mix. I'd dabbed it on my wrists this morning after my shower, and the smell reminded me of my normal life, the life I was desperately trying to have.

It reminded me of Nick, too, and that Nick was here, and I was in my own home, and I was safe.

Nervous chills made my shoulders shake, but my breathing slowed and my heartbeat returned to normal. Another panic attack diverted. Dr. Sedwick would be proud.

"Are you good?" Nick asked, his voice even and husky, but his eyes pinched with concern—an expression I hadn't seen on him before.

I nodded. "I'm good." I grabbed a towel from the cupboard and wetted it as Nick cleaned up the broken eggshells, scooping up as much of the guts as he could. I knelt on the floor next to him.

"I thought you were going to sleep in."

"I was."

"But?"

"But... I couldn't sleep."

I started to ask if something was wrong, but his jaw tensed and he said, so hoarsely I'd have sworn he had a cold, "I don't want to talk about it."

"Okay."

We finished cleaning up the eggs in silence and stood at the kitchen sink together, washing our hands. The daylight pouring through the window accentuated Nick's blue eyes and the shadows spreading beneath them.

"I was going to make French toast," I said. "We can eat here in the house, instead of the carriage house, if you want."

He nodded. "Would you like me to help?"

I thought about it, about cooking with him next to me, watching him crack open an egg, pour in the milk. Seeing him perform such domestic tasks might be amusing. After all, his hands looked more used to making fists than cracking eggs. But I got the feeling he was only asking to be polite.

"I can manage on my own. You can just hang out and relax."

A lock of hair fell across his forehead as he nodded again and settled in at the table.

We ate in silence. The more I got to know Nick, the more I realized the *real* him, the Nick he didn't show often, was the quiet one. I liked silence, too, and it was a rare quality to find in other people. Most can't stand the empty pauses, as if they can't bear to be alone with their own thoughts.

I'd spent six months locked in a single room, but really I'd spent those months locked in my own head. Silence was familiar, like an old friend.

When we finished eating, I cleared our dishes, but decided to put them in the dishwasher later so I could follow Nick into the living room. He took his time circling the room, examining the things on the wall, the pictures on the mantel. He paused at a picture of my mother hanging above one of Aggie's old sideboards.

"Who is that?" he asked. He frowned at the picture, as if he were trying to figure out the identity of the woman without the benefit of my explanation.

"That's my mom."

I wondered if he saw the similarities between us. The dark wavy hair. The big green eyes. The nose that seemed too small for its face.

We were so similar in appearance, but so different on all other levels. My mom was smart, the kind of smart that won awards and titles and memberships in special clubs. She was one of the top doctors at Cosmell Medical Center. She was determined in everything and ambitious, too.

My favorite thing about her, though, was her spontaneity, the way she'd come up with something and act on it moments later, damn the consequences. When I was little, she was always pulling me from one thing to another. Out of ballet, into gymnastics, out of school, to the ice cream shop.

One night, after it'd been raining for two full days, she crept into my room at midnight, shook me awake, and handed me a raincoat and rubber boots that looked like ladybugs.

"Come on," she whispered in the dark, pressing a finger to her lips. "This is our little secret."

It was always like that, secrets between us, adventures kept from my father, the man who was the opposite of spontaneity, devoted as he was to his schedule.

I dressed quickly. I couldn't help but be swept up in her excitement when she was like that, as if we were always on some grand mission.

Mom took my hand and hurried me down the hallway, out the back door, and into the backyard. The night was dark, the stars and moon blotted out by the rain clouds. There was one lone light in the yard—a battery-powered lantern that Mom had hung from the big cherry tree. It cast golden light that glittered on the puddles that had gathered in furrows.

Mom squeezed my hand tighter and twirled me around like a ceramic ballerina in a jewelry box. The rain was warm and slow, as if it wanted to take its time disappearing into the soil beneath our feet. It clung to Mom's hair in fat droplets and ran down her cheeks like sweat.

I giggled in the dark, and Mom pressed her finger to her lips again and said, "Shh. We don't want to wake Daddy! This is only for us, remember?"

I nodded and smiled and clamped my mouth shut.

Only for us.

Rain still felt like that, like a secret.

But now, when I looked at pictures of her, all I saw was the terror in her eyes when her life had been threatened to gain my cooperation. I would have done anything they asked of me if it meant protecting her.

"What's her name?" Nick asked, dragging me from the memories.

"Moira. Moira Creed."

He turned away from the picture and toward me. "Were your parents still together when you went missing?"

I shook my head quickly. "They split up a long time ago. My mom wanted us to have the same last name, so she never changed hers back. Just made things easier, I guess."

He didn't say anything in response and left the living room for the parlor. Aggie and I hardly ever set foot inside it. It was done in the traditional Victorian style, with rose-red wallpaper and dark woodwork. The windows were draped in heavy curtains, and the hardwood floor was covered in threadbare rugs.

The furniture was traditional as well, and Aggie had a complete matching set. There were four chairs and one settee. The wood frames were hand-carved mahogany, and the upholstery rose-colored damask. I respected that they were old, and that someone had taken a lot of time to make the set, but it was ridiculously uncomfortable.

Nick stopped just over the threshold and stared at the baby grand piano in the corner of the room. "Do you play?" he asked me.

"No. Do you?"

His eyes narrowed as he thought. "I don't know."

"You don't know if you can play the piano?"

He went over to it and pulled out the bench. I followed and sat beside him, our legs pressed together. With his index finger, he reached out and touched a key, then gave it a tap. The note vibrated through the room. It'd been forever since I'd heard anyone play. Aggie didn't either. It was her daughter's piano, and Aggie hadn't had the heart to get rid of it after her daughter died.

Nick stretched out his fingers, one after the other, testing the keys beneath, as if the ivory suddenly felt familiar. He pressed a key, then another, and then suddenly he was playing, his fingers running over the keys with quick, decisive precision.

I slid off the bench, stunned, in awe, wanting to see the whole picture, see it from afar.

The more notes he strung together, the more his body loosened, as if whatever strings held him permanently taut had been severed.

The music turned darker, deeper, the rich notes hitting me in the chest until there was nothing but the music and me, until it filled every corner of the room, every hollow of my senses.

I closed my eyes as Nick hit a few higher notes, striking them softly as the deeper ones played beneath with a steady *thrum* and *drum*. The song reminded me of so many things. Of rain and thunder, of bare feet on cool sand, of pomegranate seeds bursting open between your teeth.

And then suddenly the music was gone and Nick's hands—the same hands that had just created something so real that I felt it in my soul—shook me and I opened my eyes.

"You okay?" he asked, and without thinking, without doubting, without waiting, I reached up on tiptoes and kissed him.

He stiffened immediately, and I could almost hear his uncertainty.

But then he was kissing me, too, pressing back until I rammed into the wall and rattled the picture frames. He didn't stop. I didn't stop. He placed one hand at the small of my back, driving me closer. The other he ran behind me, to my neck, and my skull vibrated at his touch.

I felt his tongue graze my lips, and I answered, parting, letting him in. My breath came quickly, my insides quaking.

And then, just as quickly as it began, it ended and Nick pulled away. "Elizabeth," he said, hoarse and wavering, "this can't happen."

"Why?"

"Because I'm not one of the good guys."

The side door banged open and I jumped. Aggie's voice carried through the house. She was talking to someone, but I couldn't tell if she was on the phone, or if someone was with her. Curious, I stepped through the doorway into the living room and caught a glimpse of Dr. Sedwick following Aggie down the hall toward the den.

I turned back to Nick, to say something, *anything*, but he was already gone.

27

NICK

I STUMBLED INTO THE APARTMENT ABOVE the garage, my fingers clenched into fists. When the door slammed shut behind me, I slumped against it and scrubbed at my face.

What the hell just happened?

The piano.

Elizabeth.

Her mouth on mine.

I needed to move. I needed to do something. I needed to get out of here.

I threw the door back open and thundered down the stairs, down the driveway. I wasn't wearing running clothes, but I didn't care. I could run in a snowsuit if I had to.

On the street, I turned left, heading away from town. With my legs moving beneath me, arms at my sides, shoulders loose, lungs pumping, I started to feel more like myself.

I'd hardly ever pushed a girl away. If someone offered a hookup, I almost always took it. And the fact that I'd stopped Elizabeth, even though she was clearly up for it, left me feeling detached from myself—the immoral version of myself I'd grown accustomed to. It was screwed up that I was freaking out over the fact that I'd actually done something right for once, but no one ever said I was a perfect picture of stability.

Add to this whole fucked-up situation the fact that I apparently played the piano, and I felt like I'd just body swapped with someone.

The piano.

The thought pulled me to a stop. Suddenly, as if the memory had never been gone, I knew how I'd learned to play.

Connor. The head of the Altered program. He'd made me take lessons.

"You have no discipline," he'd said. "And you lack focus."

"And learning how to play the piano is supposed to teach me those things?"

Although I seriously wanted to know the answer to that question, my voice had been laced with a heavy dose of sarcasm.

But instead of an explanation, all I'd gotten was a yes.

I didn't admit to it, but I actually liked playing the piano. And I was good at it.

Now that the memory had returned, I couldn't wait to play again. And an irritating voice in the back of my head said, *You can't wait to kiss Elizabeth again, either.*

I told that voice to shut it. I couldn't get close to Elizabeth like that. No matter what.

28

ELIZABETH

THROUGH THE PARLOR WINDOW, I WATCHED Nick take off. I thought about calling after him but decided against it. He'd pushed me away. And in truth, he was right, to some degree. He wasn't one of the good guys, in the sense that he wasn't a normal guy who went to high school and played basketball with his friends in the afternoon and hung out at the lake at night.

Although he hadn't told me his entire story yet, I got the sense that whatever he'd done for the Branch wasn't good. After all, he'd been ordered to kill me that night in the forest.

Regardless, I felt drawn to him, and there was no way I could ignore that. No matter what his past was. It'd been only ten minutes since we'd kissed, and already I couldn't wait another second longer to see him again. It was as if he were a block of iron and I were a magnet drifting closer and closer, waiting for the inevitable moment when our magnetic fields would connect and pull us together.

Once Nick was out of sight, I slumped onto the couch, hugging one of Aggie's homemade throw pillows to my chest, my fingers distractedly tracing the cross-stitch pattern on the front panel.

Without meaning to, I replayed the kiss in my mind, analyzing every move Nick had made, wondering if there was some hint as to his true feelings in the way he'd placed his hand on the small of my back, or in the way he'd drawn his tongue across my lips.

A thrill of butterflies took flight in my stomach, and an unbidden smile spread across my face. I covered my mouth with a hand, as if to stop my grin from spreading too wide, wide enough to escape.

Sometime later—I'd lost track of how many times I relived the kiss—I heard my name muttered from a room down the hall and remembered, vaguely, that Dr. Sedwick was here.

I tossed the pillow to the couch and stood up, straining to hear more. The conversation was only a ghost of a sound, whispered too quietly for me to make out anything important.

On bare feet, I made my way to the hallway and crept along the far side to avoid the squeaky, well-trodden boards in the center. When I reached the hall bathroom, I slipped inside and pressed myself in the corner near the open door.

It was much easier to hear from my new vantage point.

"We've lost track of him," Dr. Sedwick said. "And that makes me nervous."

"He must know this town isn't his anymore," Aggie said.

Dr. Sedwick sighed. "I don't like this, Agatha. I don't like it at all."

"Neither do I, but what else would you have us do?"

There was a moment of silence before Dr. Sedwick went on, avoiding answering the question. It had sounded rhetorical anyway.

"What about our *other* situation?"

A chair squeaked.

"Elizabeth is doing well," Aggie said. "I would say the situation is as good as we can hope for."

At the mention of my name, I held my breath, wanting to hear as much as I could. Unfortunately, the subject changed just as quickly as it'd started, and I wasn't mentioned again.

"Did you send for the boy you spoke of?" Aggie asked.

"I did."

"And?"

"He's here. Another set of eyes is always a good thing."

Aggie murmured something I couldn't make out. The chair squeaked again, louder this time, like someone had left it to stand.

Panic started to form in the base of my throat. Every muscle in my body said to move. I squeezed out of the doorway and hurried into the kitchen. I banged a few dishes around in the sink so it would appear as though I'd been here all along, preoccupied with cleaning.

A moment later, Aggie and Dr. Sedwick emerged, smiling, as if they hadn't just had a cryptic conversation in the den.

"Morning, Elizabeth," Dr. Sedwick said. He was wearing a plain T-shirt, sunglasses hanging from the collar, and a pair of khaki shorts.

"Morning. I didn't know you were here." I grabbed a dish towel and pretended to dry my hands. "I hope you're not here to pester me."

He laughed, and Aggie ambled past him to the coffeepot. "No," he said. "I just needed to talk with Aggie about the fund-raiser coming up."

I tossed the towel over my shoulder. "I see. Can I get you something to drink?"

"No. No. I should be going. But I'll see you on Thursday?"

"I'll be there. It's the highlight of my week."

He laughed again. "I'm sure. Have a good day, ladies."

When the side door clicked closed behind him, I turned to Aggie. "What was he really doing here?"

She rinsed out her coffee cup from earlier that morning. "Just what he said. The fund-raiser." She frowned. The cup dripped water on the floor. "I promise we didn't talk about you, sweetheart."

I rolled my eyes, because I knew that was the proper response. "I hope not. Because that would be a waste of a trip. And a boring conversation."

She chuckled, and her beaded earrings swung back and forth. "Oh, you. What would I do without you?"

Another rhetorical question.

Aggie filled her cup, stirred in some creamer, and left me alone in the kitchen. I didn't feel like cleaning, but syrup was stuck on my hands from the towel I'd just used. I squirted some hand soap out, and the lemony scent filled my nose.

The floors of the building where I'd been held had been scrubbed with lemon-scented cleaner.

Lemons reminded me of that place, of the walls closing in, of secrets kept and secrets shared.

I'd never told Aggie about that particular trigger because she usually bought things that smelled like baked goods.

What were Aggie and Dr. Sedwick talking about, and what did it have to do with me?

Always so many secrets.

Immediately, I knew what my next mixed scent would be.

I would make a bottle and label it SECRETS and fill it with nothing but lemon.

I met up with Chloe at the coffee shop later in the day. Nick hadn't returned to the carriage house, and Aggie had disappeared into her bedroom right after Dr. Sedwick left. I didn't want to be alone. I had called Chloe, but now I worried that the moment she set her eyes on me, she'd know I was keeping something from her.

My cheeks still felt hot from the kiss, the heat of the moment setting my skin aglow. Chloe would take one look at me and see the truth written across my face.

"Hello, you," Chloe said, and hooked her arm in mine as we entered the coffee shop. "How are you?"

The question felt like a trap. How was I? I was many things. Confused. Thrilled. Worried. Anxious.

All I said was, "Good."

We got in line at the counter, and Chloe let go of my arm to dig around inside her purse. She pulled out her cell phone. "I have something to show you. And once I show you, I think you will be more than good."

I frowned. "Okay."

She tapped in a few things and handed the phone to me. It was a text conversation between her and Evan.

The first one on the screen, from Evan, said, *Is Lis seeing that d-bag Nick?*

I looked at Chloe and raised a brow.

"I know," Chloe sang as she stepped up to order her drink.

I kept reading. Chloe had replied, *Why?*

Evan said, *Bcuz he's a creep? Bcuz she deserves better? Bcuz I want to know?*

Interesting, Chloe said.

Just answer the question.

Which one?

UR so fking annoying sometimes.

That was the last one. Chloe hadn't responded to Evan, and he hadn't pressed for more.

When I glanced up from the cell, the barista behind the counter was staring at me expectantly. "Oh, sorry," I said. "Iced latte, please."

Chloe and I scooted down the counter to wait for our drinks at the other end.

"So?" Chloe said after she dropped her phone back in her bag.

"So. I'm not sure what to think of that."

"Should I hire a skywriter for you? Would that make the message clearer?" She sighed and shook her head as she tore the wrapping from a straw. "Evan likes you. And he's jealous of Nick. And we all like a jealous man." She narrowed her eyes thoughtfully and twirled the straw between her fingers. "I don't know what it is about them. Oh wait, yes I do. It's the jealousy. Jealousy gives you power. Everyone wants something. And jealousy makes them want it more."

"You are depraved," I said.

"Yes," she answered simply.

Our drinks were thrust onto the counter. I grabbed mine and made my way to a table in the far corner, near the windows, and Chloe followed.

"So, speaking of Nick," she said, and all my senses went on alert. Did she know about the kiss?

"What about him?"

"Are you with him?"

"No. It's not like that." *Liar*, I thought.

"Well, have you...you know?" Chloe asked with a waggling of her eyebrows.

My mouth dropped open. "Chloe!"

"What? I would. I would do it so hard."

"Stop. Please."

She shrugged. "So clearly you haven't. But it's only a matter of time, I'd say. He can't keep his eyes off you. Next step, it'll be the hands."

My face flushed, as I recalled the feel of those hands on my body, his fingers buried in my hair. And just like I'd predicted, Chloe saw it.

She gasped. "You *are* hiding something."

"No." I looked out the window, wincing at the zealous tone of her voice.

"Have you at least kissed him?"

I didn't say anything.

"You did! Well. Kissing is the foundation of sex, so I guess you're off to a good start."

I lowered my voice. "Can we not talk about this here?" I scanned the shop, feeling as though everyone was staring at me, listening in on the conversation about my sex life. Or what little there was of it.

But no one was looking. The two people closest to us had their headphones on.

"Let me tell you something about guys like Nick, though." She folded her hands around her cup, and all traces of her earlier light-heartedness disappeared. "It's okay to lust after them. It's even okay to sleep with them. But a girl, in a situation like this, has to protect her heart with everything she has.

"If you just want to have a good time with someone so gorgeous it hurts the eyes, then Nick is your guy, but you do not, under any circumstances, give him your heart. A boy like that will break it in a million pieces and leave it on the side of the road for the scavengers to pick at."

I let her warning settle in. In some ways, I believed she was right. Someone as handsome as Nick couldn't possibly settle down. Not that I was looking to settle down with him, or anyone. But I was also convinced that there was more to Nick than what Chloe saw on the outside.

"But," Chloe went on, "if it's love you're looking for, then Evan is the one. Evan is someone you can love."

I took a sip of my latte and tried to think of anything other than boys. Two weeks ago, all I'd wanted was to catch Evan's attention. Now I had two guys and no idea what to do with either one.

I glanced out the window again, watching everyone who passed by the coffee shop. A woman crossed Washington Street heading toward Merv's, her back to me. She was tall and thin, shoulders board straight, feet moving quickly. She carried herself the way my mother had, as if she always had somewhere to be, somewhere important.

The woman had the same dark wavy hair as my mother, too.

When I was first rescued, I used to see my mother everywhere, in every female face. Once, when I was shopping with one of my foster families, I chased after a woman who I thought was my mom. I followed her out of the store and to her car, where I banged on her window screaming for my mom.

When the tinted window rolled down and I saw the woman's face—fearful, and concerned about the hysterical girl at her door—I realized she didn't look anything like my mother. I could see my own hysteria reflected back at me.

That was the first time I truly felt aware of my sanity, or rather the crumbling of it.

Since then, I'd learned that if I saw someone who looked like my mother, it was better to ignore it. If she returned, I'd surely hear about it before spotting her in a grocery store or crossing the street.

"Lissy?" Chloe said.

"What?"

"I said, so which guy are you going to pick?"

I sighed. "Nick is going to leave town eventually anyway. So he's not even a choice."

"Good girl," Chloe said, but there was no hint of humor in her voice.

If only she knew how badly I wished he'd stay.

29

NICK

I RAN FOR MILES AND MILES UNTIL I had no clue where I was. I brought up the GPS on the phone and navigated back toward town. When I was a few blocks from Arrow, the nightclub where I'd met Chloe, Trev called me.

"Where are you?" he asked.

I gave him my location.

"Good, you're close. Can you stop by my hotel room? We need to discuss something."

"Sure," I said, and hung up without saying good-bye.

Fifteen minutes later, I was slumped in one of the chairs in the corner of Trev's room. "I like what you've done with the place."

There were weapons everywhere. Two Glocks on the nightstand, a knife in between them. There were full clips on the table in front of me and more in an open bag on the floor. I saw the unmistakable curve of the mattress that indicated there was something shoved between it and the box spring. Probably more guns.

"Yeah, well, after you blow up the Branch, you realize there's a permanent target on your back."

"Technically Anna blew up the Branch. She was the one who hit DETONATE."

"True, but the Branch doesn't care who did it exactly. Only who was involved, and I was the one who planted the bombs, remember?" He sat in the chair across from me. "Anyway, I have bad news."

I folded my arms on the table. "When do you ever have good news?"

Trev ignored the jab. "My contacts in the Coats lost track of Riley yesterday."

I ran a hand through my hair, pushing it back. It was still damp with sweat. My shirt, too. "Where did they lose him?"

"Near Milwaukee."

I let out a string of curses. "What time?"

"Around five p.m."

He could already be here by now. Milwaukee was only a few hours north of us.

"Is he coming here for me? Have you been able to verify that?"

Trev shook his head. "He's not coming for you. The Coats think he's coming back to reestablish the old program here. He's going to open up the lab."

"Son of a bitch."

"The Branch is broken," Trev went on, "and Riley is scrambling. If that Angel Serum does what we think it does—reanimate the dead—then it's worth a lot of money. And money is what the Branch needs in order to get back up on its feet."

I lurched from the chair. "I have to get Elizabeth out of here."

Trev nodded. "I thought you'd say that. Meet me back here with her in an hour. One of my Coat contacts can help talk her into leaving. I doubt she'll just skip town with you without a good reason."

There was something Trev wasn't telling me about this contact, but at the moment I didn't care.

"I'll get her here," I said. "Make sure your contact is here, too."

"Good luck," Trev called as I raced out the door.

30

ELIZABETH

"WHAT'S TROUBLING YOU?" AGGIE ASKED as she spooned me a serving of Stroganoff. "You have that look on your face."

"What look?"

"Like you're lost in thought."

I tried to shake off whatever that look was, and set my chin in my hand. "I had one of those moments today. Where I thought I saw someone who looked like my mother, and then was immediately filled with despair when I realized there was no way it could be her."

I grabbed a biscuit from the basket on the table. "Are you going to call Dr. Sedwick and tell him I'm having delusions?"

Aggie didn't say anything for the longest time. I looked up. She stood over me, the pan of Stroganoff in one hand, the spoon in the other, both hanging there like she'd been frozen in place.

"Aggie?"

"Your mother?" she finally said. "Where did you see her?"

She said *see her*, as if it was a fact.

I frowned. "Crossing Washington Street."

"Did you see her face?"

"No."

"Was she with anyone?"

"Aggie?" I said. "Why—"

Her eyes were locked on something in the backyard, but when I followed her line of sight, I caught only a flicker of motion beyond the fence.

Aggie set the pan down on the table and raced around the peninsula with a speed I hadn't thought she was capable of at her age, and with her ailing hips. She tore her cell phone from its charger, her fingers racing over the screen.

"Are you calling Dr. Sedwick?" I asked, disgruntled.

"Where's Nick?" she said, ignoring my question, never taking her eyes from the phone.

"I don't know. Why?"

The back door opened.

I expected it to be Nick, as if he'd been summoned by Aggie's inquiry.

But it wasn't.

Aggie dropped the phone to the counter with a clatter.

I lost all feeling in my body. I couldn't even feel the beating of my heart in my chest, though I could hear it drumming loudly in my ears.

The person standing in the doorway was my mother.

The kitchen went eerily quiet. My heart slowed to a staccato beat.

"Elizabeth," Aggie said sharply. "You should leave."

I heard Aggie's words, but I couldn't make sense of them. It was as if she'd spoken in a language I did not understand.

Chair legs scraped against the floor. I looked down, realizing it was *my* chair, realizing I was now on my feet. My hands trembled at my sides.

"Elizabeth," Mom said, and took a step toward me.

It was startling, how little she had changed. The wrinkles around her eyes were cut deeper with age, but that was the only visible sign that six years had passed since the last time I'd seen her. Her hair was the same dark auburn, the same length it had been, cut just below her shoulders.

Her lips were tinted with the same lipstick—her favorite shade, Vintage Rose. She'd bought it in bulk, afraid that it would be discontinued. All these details came together, forming a picture I didn't want to see.

Nothing had changed in my mother's life except that I'd been absent from it.

I'd thought she'd died.

"Don't come any closer." Aggie's voice was pitched low and throaty.

"Elizabeth," Mom repeated, and locked her eyes on me, eyes that were watery and tinged red. "Honey, I—"

Aggie came around the peninsula and put herself between me and my mother. "No," she said, as if she were reprimanding a dog for digging in the garbage. "Don't you dare."

"Mom," I whispered. "Where— How—"

A tear streamed down her face, and she swiped it away with hands that were dry and cracked. Whenever she'd worked long shifts at the hospital, her hands looked like that from too much washing. It was a detail so familiar, it was almost as if the years between us had evaporated and I was a little girl again, happy to see my mother home from work.

But I wasn't that girl. And six years was a long time to go without the one person you needed most.

"Listen to me, honey," she started. "We have to leave. Now. It's not safe here."

"Don't listen to her, Elizabeth," Aggie said. Her shoulders were rigid, her back pulled up in a straight line. "You are not welcome here, Moira."

"Aggie!" I said. None of this made sense. I needed more time to process. I'd dreamed of this moment every day since I'd escaped. I was not going to force my mom right back out the door.

Mom looked past Aggie at me. "Please, honey."

Where had she been? Why hadn't she been *here*?

"Please, baby," she said. "You have to listen. Nick is not who he says he is. He's dangerous. He was sent here to kill you six years ago, and he's here to finish the job."

"Do *not* listen to her," Aggie said.

With a swiftness that Aggie could not match, Mom stepped around her and took my hands in hers. Hers were cold and shaking.

"You have to come with me. I know someone who can help us."

Aggie was suddenly beside me. She whacked my mom's hand with a wooden spoon. Mom's face hardened as she pulled back.

"Get out," Aggie said.

"Aggie!" I shouted again.

The back door opened. And this time it *was* Nick.

He looked from me to Aggie to my mother holding her hand close to her chest, and back to me.

"Elizabeth—" he started, narrowing his eyes, his hand sliding behind his back, as if he were reaching for something. But whatever it was he was looking for wasn't there, and he grimaced, his blue eyes flashing with regret.

Mom got in close to my side, winding her arm around my waist. "We have to go," she whispered. "Now."

Something crashed through the front door. The door blew back and slammed into the wall. The stained glass in the window shattered. Aggie yelped. Mom grabbed my hand and pulled me toward the den.

Several men and a woman flooded into the kitchen, guns in their hands. Nick tore one of Aggie's vintage rolling pins from the wall and hurled it at the first person he saw. The man, clothed in black, hit the floor hard, his eyes fluttering shut.

I shrieked.

Another man swung at Nick, but Nick had already moved, ducking, and then kicking the man in the knee. Something cracked. The man crumpled with a howl. Nick went down with him and yanked the man's gun from his hands. He brought it up to his line of sight and aimed.

"Elizabeth!" Mom shouted, but I couldn't move. I couldn't feel my feet beneath me. There was only the throbbing of my pulse in my neck and the air stuck helplessly in my throat.

Nick shot, and a bullet lodged itself in yet another man's head. I backpedaled and slammed into the counter, the edge digging into my hip.

Another body hit the floor with a sickening *thud*, and Nick stole his gun, too.

He started shooting both guns at once, and the *pop-pop* of the shots, followed by the cries of the men, filled the room until it was deafening, until I couldn't take it any longer.

I slammed my hands over my ears, slammed my eyes shut, as old images flashed in my head. Of men, dressed in black, hunting me in a lab where I'd been held captive for months.

Guns in hands, barrels aiming for anything that moved, and one person standing at my side, ferrying me to safety.

Six years ago, in that lab, I knew who I could trust. I might not have known the person's name, or even what they looked like, but the line in the sand had been drawn in black, so stark that I knew exactly which side I was on.

But now, in Aggie's kitchen, with the Stroganoff cooling on the table and the air punctuated with the smell of blood and fired bullets, I couldn't find the line.

I didn't know which side I was on.

The window behind Nick shattered. Glass plinked against the table. My eyes snapped open in time to see Aggie stagger back against the table, to see my glass of iced tea tip over and puddle on the floor.

Aggie's mouth widened into an O and her apron turned black with her blood.

"Aggie!" I shrieked, moving toward her, but my mother yanked me back. "We have to—"

Aggie's knees gave out. She turned her eyes to me as she fell, the deep-set wrinkles around her mouth hardening as she said, *"Run."*

Mom wrapped her arms around my waist and pulled. I flailed, digging my nails into her hands. She let me go, and I raced across the kitchen.

"Grab her!" Mom yelled, and two men scooped me up before I could reach Aggie, pinning my arms in their grip.

Another black-clad man went after Nick and kicked the gun from his hands. The gun flew back, bounced off the table, and thudded to the floor. The man threw a punch, but Nick was quick to dodge and came back up with a blow to the man's stomach. When the man bent over, gasping for air, Nick rammed his knee into the man's head, knocking him unconscious.

"Nick!" I screamed.

He looked up, and I realized too late that my saying his name was the wrong thing to do at a time like this.

It was the distraction his assailants needed.

A punch landed in Nick's stomach, and he doubled over. The attacker slammed his elbow into Nick's kidney, and Nick hit the ground.

"No!" I screamed.

But no one was listening to me.

"Follow me!" Mom yelled above the cacophony, and my captors raced to obey her.

I was dragged into the den. Mom flipped the lock on the French doors and shoved them open. We clambered out.

Once on the deck, I wrestled out of the men's grip. "I'm not leaving Aggie!"

Mom shoved aside the men and came to my side, taking my face in her rough, dry hands. "Listen to me, honey. We cannot stay here. Aggie is not your friend."

I batted her hands away. "You act like Aggie is the bad guy."

"That's because she is. She and Nick both. They work for the Branch. They have been waiting for the right time to hurt you."

"But—"

More shots rang out in the house. Someone shouted an order.

"We have to go before you're the one who's shot," Mom said. "No more arguing. I won't lose you now that I finally have you back."

She nodded at the men, and they grabbed me again, tugging me across the deck and down the stairs. We wound our way through the garden, and through the gate to the alley where a black sedan sat idling.

Sirens blared in the distance.

The man on my right opened the car's back door. I was pushed inside, and the door slammed shut a second later, sealing off the sounds of the sirens and of the gunshots still being fired in the house. Mom climbed into the passenger seat. The locks thunked closed.

The man behind the wheel turned around. "I'm glad you got out safe and sound," he said to me. "Everything is going to be fine now."

"Who are you?" I asked.

He smiled briefly, and the smile was so wrong for a time like this. "My name is Tom Riley," he said. "But you can just call me Riley."

31

NICK

I LIMPED OUT THE BACK DOOR AND hurried to the garden, my shoulder and abdomen on fire. I'd been sliced twice with a kitchen knife, and though I didn't think anything vital had been hit, the pain still slowed me down.

The gate leading from the backyard hung open. I powered through, gasping, and stopped.

I made a circle. Nothing moved. No one was there.

Elizabeth was gone.

I growled out a curse as sirens wailed up the street. I couldn't stay there.

Cop cars screeched to a halt out front. I'd left enough of the Branch agents alive to keep the police busy for a while.

With blood running down my face and from a wound on my

leg, walking on the streets would draw too much attention, so I cut through a few neighboring yards until I reached the line of woods that would eventually thin out to a church.

I'd made this same trek two days before. It was always good to have an escape plan. But I wasn't so sure I'd make it this time. My leg kept folding beneath me, and I had to rest for a second until the feeling came back to it.

I was leaving obvious tracks in the woods, too, but I didn't have time to cover them.

A half mile from the church, I leaned against a tree and strained to listen. No sirens here. No dogs barking. That was a good sign.

I bent over and sucked in air. It never seemed like enough. My chest was burning, my leg was pounding, and my vision kept winking out.

The church parking lot was empty save for a small white car and a truck. I found an unlocked back door that led to the church's basement and stumbled inside, blinking against the dusky light.

There were kids' toys everywhere, spilling from toy boxes and piled in baskets along the wall. The carpet was dark green, thankfully, so it hid the blood still dripping from my wounds.

I followed a hallway to a lounge, and then another to a storage room and plopped down on an old wingback chair shoved between stacks of boxes.

I dug out the cell phone to call Trev, but he didn't pick up. Trev was closest, but I needed more help than one guy could give. Looked like Sam was going to get his wish. I needed the others right now. I hated to admit it—I liked to think I could manage just fine on my own—but I was clearly in over my head.

The Branch was here. And I bet Riley wasn't far behind.

With a blood-crusted finger, I pounded in Sam's number. Anna picked up. "Where's the dog?" she said, opening with our code.

I inhaled, biting down the urge to cry. I did not cry. I wasn't going to start now.

"Nick?" she said.

My voice wavered as I managed to get out, "I need your help."

She immediately went on alert. "What's wrong?"

"The Branch... they have Elizabeth and I might have been shot. I'm not sure yet."

"Where are you now?"

"In a church about two miles from Elizabeth's house."

"Are you safe for now?"

"For now."

"I'm calling Trev—"

"I just did. He didn't pick up."

"Then I'll keep trying him until he does." She shouted for Sam, then Cas, before coming back on the line. "We're on our way, okay? Sit tight."

"Hurry. Please."

"We'll be there in a few hours, if we have to speed the whole way there." Her voice hardened. "And then I'm going to kill whoever hurt you."

I heard the back door open sometime later and realized I wasn't hidden very well. I didn't have enough energy to burrow in somewhere now, so if it was Riley here to finish me off, he wouldn't have a hard time finding me.

There had been a total of eight Branch agents in Aggie's house, and I'd taken them all out. But not without some major damage. After looking at my leg, I was confident I had only been grazed by a bullet, not shot, but the longer I sat there, the worse I felt. My wounds were growing hotter by the second and pounded in time with my heart.

"Nick?" Trev called.

Not Riley then.

"In here," I replied.

The door opened, and light washed through. I shielded my eyes.

"Jesus Christ," he said.

"I don't think you're supposed to say that in a church."

He chuckled and came closer. "I'm pretty sure I'm going to hell for a dozen other things already."

"Like turning on us?"

" 'Failure is not fatal, but failure to change might be.' "

"I'm sorry I brought it up."

"Can you walk?"

"I think so."

He helped me to my feet and put my arm around his shoulders. He was a few inches shorter than I was, which made it a lot easier to walk using him for support.

"We got a problem," I said.

"What's that?"

"I think Elizabeth's mother is working with Riley."

"Really?"

"She was at the house when I got there, right when the Branch agents swept in." I winced, and held my breath for a beat as a new twinge of pain subsided. "And when I saw a picture of her at Elizabeth's house earlier today, I thought she looked familiar, but the memory was one that just appeared, you know? Not a flashback, just a memory that resurfaced, like it'd never been gone. I knew I'd seen her before, I just couldn't place where until now."

"So where did you see her?"

"At the lab beneath the barn, which makes sense, because she was kidnapped with Elizabeth, except I don't think she was a prisoner."

"Well, we can sort all this out after I clean you up."

We hobbled out of the church together. Trev's car was waiting nearby. "Looks like you'll be getting blood all over your pretty Jag."

"I brought plastic."

"You what?"

"Anna told me you were injured, so I brought plastic."

"I can't believe you right now."

"I can't believe you're surprised."

The plastic crinkled as I sat down. It stuck to my arms, covered in sweat and blood. I needed a shower. And a shot of tequila.

"Got any booze at your place?"

Trev slid in behind the wheel and started up the car. "What do you think?"

I grumbled as he took off.

"We're a half hour out," Anna said through the line. "You're okay?"

"For now," I said. "Bring booze."

She relayed the message to Sam, who grunted in the background.

"Hey," I said. "I'm going to need it. I'm banged up, remember? We can use it to numb the pain and clean the wound."

"I can buy rubbing alcohol for that," Anna said. "I think there's some in the first-aid kit already."

"Bring me booze," I said again, and she finally relented.

I lay back on the bed in Trev's hotel room and slammed my eyes shut. The room was spinning. And not because I was drunk this time.

"We have to go after them," I said to Trev as he handed me a glass of water.

"I know."

"They have Elizabeth."

"I know."

How had I lost her? She'd been so close. And then she was just gone.

Probably that had been their plan all along. Send in a bunch of Branch agents to distract me so they could nab Elizabeth without a problem.

Of course, I couldn't compete with her mother. Elizabeth would probably have followed her anyway.

I took a gulp of water and set the cup down.

Trev stood at the end of the bed staring at me. "We should probably check out your wounds."

"Are you trying to get me naked?"

He sighed. "You're a lot more like Cas than you care to admit."

I snorted. "Bullshit."

"You've got the sarcasm down pat."

I tugged off my shirt and tossed it aside. Trev had to help me with my jeans, which were almost glued to the wound in my leg, and I had to bite back a string of curse words while he doused the area with water to loosen some of the old blood. Then he quickly and none too gently ripped the material away.

"Fuck!"

"Sorry."

The jeans met the shirt on the floor.

Trev pulled on a pair of black-framed glasses.

"Since when do you wear glasses?"

He shrugged. "About a month, I guess. It's been getting worse lately. I think I might have worn glasses before the Branch, but the alterations, and all the shit they had us on, changed my sight for the better. Now that I'm not receiving treatments..." He gestured to the glasses. "Sight's going again."

He crouched beside the bed to examine my leg. "Didn't go straight through, so that's good. Seems to be a superficial wound."

He stood up and came to the head of the bed to check out the wound in my shoulder.

"Knife wound," I explained. "But just a slice."

"Deep, though," Trev said. "It'll need stitches." There was a second slice on my abdomen, on the lower right side. "That one, too, probably."

"You got any pain meds?" I asked.

"Ibuprofen."

"That'll work."

A half hour later, as promised, Anna, Sam, and Cas showed up. Cas whistled when he saw me lying in bed with hardly any clothes on. I told him to screw off.

Anna came straight over and wrapped her arms around me. I groaned from the pain, and she pulled back. "Sorry," she said. "I'm just glad you're okay."

"We have to get Elizabeth."

She nodded. "We will."

"How bad is it?" Sam asked Trev.

"Not bad at all. He should be fine in a week or two."

I sat upright and winced when the wound in my side pulled open. "I'll be fine by tonight. When we go get Elizabeth."

The longer she was out there, the farther away she'd be. And not just in physical distance. If she was with Riley right now, they could have already wiped her memories. Or brainwashed her into thinking I was the bad guy. Or worse... killed her. And I still didn't know the answer to the question that'd been nagging me since I arrived here: Why Elizabeth? What had the Branch done to her?

And then it all clicked into place.

The Angel Serum.

The other night, when Elizabeth was cut by a shard of glass from the broken rum bottle. The cut was gone minutes later.

"Hey," I said, the realization becoming clear. But my call was drowned out by Cas and Trev arguing. I yelled again, "Guys!"

They all turned to me. "Elizabeth was treated with the Angel Serum."

"Yeah, we already figured that out," Anna said.

I groaned. Sometimes I hated how smart she was.

"But," she went on, "that doesn't explain why they'd take her now, instead of killing her. Why do they want her back? If they created the Angel Serum once, they could do it again. They don't need her."

"And based on the audio logs for Patient 2124," Trev said, "she was more trouble than she was worth."

I shook my head. "I don't think Elizabeth was Patient 2124."

Trev frowned. "No?"

I got a flash of the girl in the cell in the lab, the one who'd whipped me with a bedsheet. I closed my eyes, tried to recall the whole memory. The girl had been skinny. Her eyes were narrow, pinched at the corners, as if there was a drop of Asian heritage somewhere in her past. Definitely not Elizabeth's big, round eyes. I was such an idiot for not seeing it sooner.

Even though it wasn't Elizabeth, I still felt like I knew that girl—I just couldn't place her. The answer was right there, but my head was pounding and nothing made sense.

I lay back down, feeling like I might puke.

"Here." Anna handed me a plastic cup.

I gave it a sniff. Vodka. I grinned at her and emptied it in one gulp.

"We can debate all this later," she said. "Right now we need to patch you up."

Anna, Sam, and Trev got to work while Cas flipped through the TV channels and settled on one of those *Real Housewives* shows. "This bitch is crazy," he said, right before he stuffed his face with a handful of popcorn.

Once the wounds were cleaned up, and I'd downed two more shots of vodka, Trev came at me with a needle and suture thread. "Ready?"

"As I'll ever be."

The bullet wound wasn't too bad, and had been deemed safe for patching up. The knife wounds were another story. Trev started on the one on my shoulder. The pain was searing, like a hot poker in my skin, over and over again.

Fifteen seconds in, I couldn't wait for it to be over. I gritted my teeth. Tried to internalize the pain and swallow it down before I ripped someone's head off.

Trev was quick and efficient and had the first wound closed up in less than ten minutes. The cut on my abdomen was bigger, though, and would require more stitches. Twelve, it turned out.

"You really should stay off your feet for a few days," Sam said as Anna bandaged up the last wound with gauze and tape.

I sat up when she finished, swallowed a grimace, and got to my feet. "I can rest once Elizabeth is safe."

I had a sudden, driving need to find her, a need to protect her. It wasn't like what I'd felt with Anna, when the Branch had programmed me to defend her at any cost. This felt different.

It wasn't an automatic reaction, it was a conscious decision.

I didn't *have* to protect her, I *wanted* to, and that was something I hadn't felt, ever.

"You barely know this girl," Sam said as he moved in front of me, blocking my way from around the bed.

"I know her enough."

The room grew quiet.

"Is she worth risking your life for?"

Was she? I'd been with her less than a week, but it felt like forever.

I couldn't stop replaying that kiss over and over in my head, and the wounded look on her face when I pulled back. I'd never felt any lingering attachment to any girl in the past, but Elizabeth was different.

She saw through all my bullshit and accepted me for who I was, broken pieces and all.

I couldn't leave her in the hands of the Branch so they could wipe her clean.

I knew jackshit about relationships, but deep down, in the darkest part of me, I knew I needed a girl like Elizabeth. I needed *her* to save *me.*

"If it was Anna," I said to Sam, "would you go?"

"That's different."

"No, it's not."

"Sam," Anna said. He flinched.

"Whatever reason the Branch had for wanting Elizabeth in the past is still a reason to worry about in the present." I shoved around him. "So I'm going. With or without you."

32

ELIZABETH

MOM AND RILEY TOOK ME TO A TWO-story house on the outskirts of town, crammed onto a small lot on the corner of Apple Street and Sherman Avenue. Children were outside playing in the front yard of the brick house next door when we pulled up. A girl blew bubbles through a wand while her younger brother chased after them, giggling. Their mom sat nearby watching, a magazine open in her lap.

It all seemed so normal, so unlike my life.

Riley hit the garage door opener clipped to his visor and pulled inside a moment later.

"Come on, sweetie," Mom said, coaxing me out of the car.

Reluctantly, I climbed out, and let Mom lead me through a

mudroom and into the kitchen. Two men in plain clothes, with guns at their waists, stood around discussing a recent sports game.

Riley interrupted the conversation and introduced them to me, but I couldn't be bothered to remember their names. Everything everyone said seemed hollow and distant, as if I were underwater and drowning.

I blinked.

I was in the living room now. Sitting. Mom was sitting next to me, her hand threaded with mine.

"Would you like some tea?" she asked.

I nodded. *Yes.*

"Do you need anything else?" she asked.

I shook my head. *No.*

"Pills," I said, a second later, changing my mind. "My anxiety meds."

Currently, I was numb inside, but it would only be a matter of time before everything caught up to me, and when it did...

"I'll have Riley look into it," she promised.

Riley.

Riley.

That name was familiar. His voice was familiar. Everything about him was familiar except his face.

I blinked again. Tears clouded my vision. I glanced down at the mug of tea that had somehow appeared before me. I hadn't even heard or seen Mom go out or come back in. I took the cup between my hands, soaking in the warmth because inside I was cold to the core.

Aggie had been shot. Aggie was dead. I was dead.

Drowning.

The old gunshot wound in my chest flared, and my hands started to tingle.

"Pills," I repeated, but when I looked around the room, I was alone.

I brought the mug up to my mouth, the steam leaving behind a sheen of warmth. I blew across it and inhaled. Earl Grey with a squirt of lemon.

Lemons.

Secrets.

Shh, Mom had said. *This is our little secret.*

Voices murmured from the kitchen.

Something was wrong.

Something was wrong.

I pulled my cell from my pocket and texted Chloe. *Where are you?* I wrote. *I need you.*

My hands trembled as I typed.

The phone buzzed less than a minute later. I quickly navigated to my settings and shut off the vibrate. For some reason, I didn't want my mom to know I was talking to anyone. Which was crazy, I realized. It was *my* phone—I wasn't a prisoner here. Was I?

Just got coffee. At the park, Chloe replied. *Come over if you want. Something happen with Nick?*

More than something.

I texted, *Can you come pick me up? Meet me on the corner of Bryant and Saxton?*

What are you doing way out there?

Please. Can you be here in ten minutes?

I'm leaving now. I'll be there soon.

"Mom?" I called.

She poked her head through the doorway leading to the kitchen. "Yes, honey?"

I saw her face all those years ago, etched with panic, her life threatened, her daughter held captive. There were no mirrors in the building where I'd been kept, but I'd seen my face reflected in glass and steel enough times to know I had looked like a person held captive. Hollow, haunted eyes rimmed in shadows, face washed out, lips dry and cracked, hair disheveled and limp.

And looking at her now I realized one important detail I'd missed back then. Mom had looked the same way she'd always looked. Shoulders level, head held high, complexion perfect, hair perfect, everything perfect.

She hadn't looked as fraught as I had. She hadn't looked like a prisoner.

"Can I use the bathroom?" I asked.

"Third door on the left down the hall."

I nodded. I got up. The walk to the bathroom seemed to take forever. One foot in front of the other. One inch, two inches, *hurry up*.

As soon as I was inside the bathroom, door shut and locked, I was a flurry of movement. *Hurry.*

Hurry.

Hurry.

I turned on the faucet and went to the window. The latch came undone easily enough. There was no screen.

Though the window was small compared to the other windows in the house, I was sure I could fit through.

And I did.

I hit the ground on my shoulder and rolled. My head swam.

Up on my feet.

Run, Aggie had said. I ran.

Lungs burning. Someone yelling. A kid yelling.

Just a kid.

Go. Go. Keep going.

I made it to Jefferson Street and turned left. I didn't dare look over my shoulder. I was running from my mother. My mother who had been gone for six years and shown up out of nowhere. Who had shown up in my kitchen ten minutes before Aggie was dead. Shot by people ambushing the house. People Nick had fought and shot and killed.

Who were those men and woman dressed all in black like they were ready for combat? They couldn't have been the Branch, otherwise they wouldn't have attacked Nick, who my mother had said was working for the Branch.

The Branch.

Riley.

And then I realized how I knew that name. Where I knew that voice from.

In the woods.

The night Nick saved me.

Take care of it, the voice had said. *It* being me.

Riley was the Branch.

And my mother was a part of it.

Chloe picked me up within ten minutes, as promised. She handed me an iced coffee as soon as I slid in beside her.

"You sounded like you needed one," she said as she pulled away from the curb.

I took a drink. Even though my stomach swam, my throat was raw, and my tongue was like sandpaper in my mouth. Something cold felt good.

Chloe eyed me. "So what happened? You feel like talking about it?"

I didn't. I wasn't even sure how to put it into words. Aggie was dead. My mom was back. And she was working for someone who'd ordered Nick to kill me. Unless... I'd been mistaken?

Nothing made sense. Maybe I'd overreacted. Maybe I had been safe with my mom.

"Not yet," was what I told Chloe. "I just needed to get out of there."

"Where was 'there,' exactly?"

"It was a friend of my mom's."

Chloe went silent for a moment as she turned a corner back toward town. "You never talk about your mom."

"That's because there hasn't ever been anything to say."

I took another sip of my coffee. The liquid ran cold down my throat.

"So anywhere you want to go?" Chloe asked. "Back home?"

My stomach churned. I couldn't go back there ever again. It had been the only place where I'd ever felt safe after what had happened six years ago. Now it was painted with Aggie's blood.

"No. Do you feel like just driving?"

"Sure. Whatever you want." She glanced at me. "Drink some more coffee. You'll feel better with some caffeine in your system."

I took another long gulp. Then another, and set the cup in the holder. I curled into the seat and rested my head against the passenger-side window.

My vision thinned and grew fuzzy on the edges. I shot upright. I really was exhausted.

Another sip.

Chloe stopped for a red light, and the traffic passing through the intersection blurred.

My eyelids grew heavy and winked closed. I shook myself awake again.

"If you want to sleep, go ahead," Chloe said. "I'll wake you up in a bit."

"Yeah, maybe I will." I scrubbed at my eyes. Maybe when I woke, everything would be right again.

I slumped in the seat, propped my head in my hands, my elbow on the armrest.

"Thanks, Chloe," I mumbled as I let my eyelids win over and slip shut.

"No need to thank me." She reached over and patted my shoulder. "Get some rest."

And then I was out.

33

NICK

MY CELL RANG.

"Who is it?" Anna asked.

"It's Elizabeth."

We all looked at each other as the phone continued to ring.

"Answer it," Sam said.

"Hello?"

"Hey, it's Chloe."

I let out a breath. "I thought you were Elizabeth."

"She's here. With me."

"She is?" I started to pace and then thought better of it when a shot of pain ran up my side. "Is she okay?"

"Yeah. A little tired. She's sleeping right now. But..." She trailed off, and I clutched the phone harder.

"But what?"

"She texted me, all hysterical. And then when I picked her up, she didn't want to talk about it. Did something happen?"

I glanced at Sam, then Anna. Cas and Trev were silent on the couch.

"Can you meet me somewhere?" I asked. "I just want to see her. Make sure she's okay."

"What happened, Nick?" There was an edge of suspicion in her voice.

"Something... with her mom. She's back."

"Her mom is here? Where?"

"I'll explain it all later. Where can I meet you?"

She ran off an address for a park in a residential area. I hadn't been there yet, but I had an idea of how to get there.

"Give me fifteen minutes," I said.

"We'll wait here for you."

"Thanks, Chloe."

"No worries."

We hung up, and I relayed the conversation to the group as I tugged on some clothes Sam had given me.

I checked the bullets in my gun and slid it behind my back. "We should go. Now."

"Wait." Sam held up his hand. "You sure this isn't a trap?"

"No. No way. Chloe is a friend of Elizabeth's. They work together at a restaurant in town. She's just some girl."

Sam and Anna shared a look.

"Stop it, you two. I'm going. And I'd like it if you came with. If you don't want to, fine."

I started for the door.

"Obviously we're coming, Nick," Anna said. "We just want to be sure we're smart about this."

I hated it when they ganged up on me.

I didn't want to wait as we hashed out a plan or dissected all the ways this could go south. I wanted to get to Elizabeth, and I didn't want to wait another second.

We found Chloe parked along the curb in front of the park. An iron fence surrounded it, with an arched gate on each of the four sides. This park was quieter and smaller than the town's main park. There was no playground here. No fountain. Just a lot of flowers, bushes, and picnic tables. A couple was spread out on a blanket in a patch of sunlight.

I could make out Elizabeth in the backseat, pressed against the door on the passenger side, her face buried in her hands.

Chloe met me halfway to the car. "She's really upset right now. When she woke up, she started bawling. She keeps asking for you."

I pushed past Chloe.

"Wait," she said, and caught up to me. "Please, just be gentle with her."

"I've never been anything but gentle with her," I said. "I need to see her."

I opened the back door and slid inside. It was silent. Elizabeth was folded in on herself, her hand covering her eyes. Her head lay against the door.

"Elizabeth? Talk to me."

Nothing.

She didn't even move.

I inhaled. I'd already proven to her that I sucked at consoling, but I had to try something. Otherwise I'd just look like a jackass.

I reached out to her, slid my fingers around hers, and pulled her hand away from her face.

Her eyes were closed. Her arm was limp in my hand.

"Elizabeth?"

Chloe opened the driver's door, pinned herself in the crook of it, and pulled something from the seat.

I saw the flash of silver too late, heard the gunshot next. Heard Anna scream to Sam. Heard the *pop* of a tire.

"What the—" I started, but I wasn't quick enough.

Chloe reached over the seat and pistol-whipped me in the face.

Everything went black.

"You are the worst bad guy in the history of bad guys."

I blinked.

"You had her in your grasp and she got away. Slipped out a bathroom window? Isn't that the oldest trick in the book?"

I didn't make a sound.

The car was moving, but not speeding. If Sam and the others had come after us, Chloe had lost them.

"Yeah. Yeah. I know. My absolute, perpetual freedom for theirs. I got it. I'm on my way."

Chloe hung up the phone and cursed. I moved just enough to glance over at Elizabeth. Still out.

How long had I been unconscious?

Did I still have my gun?

I slowly reached behind me. Nothing there.

I'd apparently been out long enough for Chloe to escape Sam and the others, and for her to stop to retrieve my weapons.

The car lurched as the tires left pavement and hit gravel.

Stalks of corn turned into a blur outside the window as Chloe pressed into the gas pedal.

We were on our way to the barn lab.

Shit.

I looked on the floorboards for something I could use as a weapon. Empty coffee cups. A tube of lip gloss. A notebook.

Nothing that would hurt.

What was the surest way to take her out?

Gun.

I didn't have a gun.

Knock her out.

I could punch her, but from this angle, it'd be iffy.

Choke her. I could put her in a choke hold, but if she had a gun close by, she could shoot me in the goddamn face.

Seat belt.

And Chloe wasn't wearing hers.

I charged upright, grabbed the belt, and gave it a yank so I had as much slack as I needed.

Chloe saw me in the rearview mirror and reached for her gun. I wrapped the belt around her neck, pushed my foot against the seat for added strength, and crouched.

My weight was too much for her to fight. The air left her lungs in one ragged gasp. She came up off the seat, lost her footing on the pedal, and the car slowed.

Chloe let go of the wheel. The front end swerved.

I tugged harder on the belt and felt my stitches pop. I bit down a cry of pain.

Chloe reached up and cut the belt with one swipe of a knife. I dropped to the floorboard. She slammed on the brakes, and I rammed against the seat.

With the car in park, she got out, came to the back door, and just as she opened it, I slammed a foot into it. She staggered back from the hit.

I hurried from the vehicle, feeling the hot welling of blood in my wounds.

Chloe had a gun trained on me.

The barn rose out of the cornfields in the distance.

"I'm out on the road," she said, and it took me a minute to realize she was on her phone. "Nick tried to get away." She narrowed her eyes at me but smiled. It was a real smile, too, as if she was amused at my daring play for escape. As if she was impressed.

"Get out here now before I shoot him."

I put my hands up as she ended the call.

"Why are you doing this?" I asked.

If I couldn't fight my way out of this, maybe I could talk my way out. Doubtful. I sucked at talking.

"You don't remember, do you?" She sniffed. "The Branch and their memory wipes."

"Remember what?"

I took a step toward her. She lowered the gun and shot me in the leg.

I went down. Dirt gritted between my teeth. A sharp pain raced up my leg.

"Son of a bitch. What was that for?"

"For being an idiot."

Chloe walked over, the gravel crunching beneath her flip-flops. She was in a dress. Flowers all over it. Her blond hair hung forward in a loose braid. Her lips were pink and glossy.

She looked like any other teenage girl dropped into the middle of an Illinois summer.

But she wasn't.

Obviously.

She was obviously someone else entirely.

"Six years ago," she said, staring down at me as I blinked up at her, "you didn't come here to kill Elizabeth. You came here to kill me."

34

NICK

MY FREEDOM FOR THEIRS.

That's what she'd said on the phone.

She was using Elizabeth and me to bargain for her own freedom.

Chloe sat beside me in the dirt, propped herself up on an outstretched arm, and used her knee as a rest to keep the gun pointed at my face.

She stared down the road, squinting into the sunlight.

Chloe was involved with the Branch? Chloe was a part of my old mission here?

"You knew exactly who I was when we met up at Arrow, didn't you?" I said.

Chloe nodded, but didn't look at me. "Imagine my surprise. I had to know what you were doing here again."

"So you got me drunk."

"Is there any other way to get information out of a guy like you?"

I didn't answer her. She was right.

"You shot me that night you saved Elizabeth," she said. "When I first came over to you at Arrow, I thought for sure you'd recognize me. Then when you didn't, I realized you must have had your memory altered. So then I started wondering why."

"Would you have hooked up if I hadn't had that flashback?"

She finally turned to me, her eyes running up and down my body. "Maybe."

We sat in silence for a beat.

"Why was I sent here to kill you?"

"Do you remember what Riley's instructions were? From that night?"

That night was still vague in my head. I was fuzzy on the details. There were a few that stood out. Elizabeth staring up at me from the forest floor. Me with a gun in my hand. Elizabeth crying.

I had known Riley was there, but I couldn't remember what he'd said.

What I did know was that Target E was supposed to be decapitated—and then suddenly all the pieces I'd gathered over the past few days added up.

The Angel Serum. Decapitation, incinerating the body. The mystery girl from the barn lab. The one who kicked my ass with a bedsheet.

That girl had had dark brown hair and...

Chloe tilted her head, and I cursed my lame-ass observation skills. Her roots were dark brown.

"Target E," I said, and she nodded.

I filed through my flashbacks, trying to see where she fit.

Two stood out: the one of a girl in a white room, and the one I'd had that night when Chloe and I had stumbled back to my hotel room after meeting at Arrow. They were the same memory, I realized, just different parts.

It made sense, though, that if the flashback was of Chloe, it had come racing out when I was with her. Memories are always easier to access when you have a physical anchor in the present.

The only flashback of Elizabeth I was absolutely certain of was the one in the forest. It was possible that was actually the first time I met her.

"My real name is Emily. Emily Chloe Noelle," Chloe said. "I was known as Patient 2124 in the lab."

For a brief second, I forgot that we were enemies, and instead I was just in awe of her. "You shot yourself in the head."

She laughed. "Oh yeah, I did do that. Hurt like a bitch when I came to."

"Weren't you afraid you wouldn't survive a hit like that?"

"No. Side effect of the Angel Serum—probably why they wanted me gone—I don't feel fear anymore." She snapped her fingers. "Just like that. Like a light switch. It's just gone."

So not only could she survive blowing off her own head, she didn't fear anything. Which made her the most badass opponent the Branch had ever seen. No wonder they'd wanted her eliminated.

"So that night, in the forest," I said, "I *did* shoot you, and then you healed while I took Elizabeth to the hospital."

"I'd already died fifteen times by then. Healing from a bullet wound took less than three minutes."

"Why would you stick around here, though?" I asked. "With the lab so close. Why didn't you run?"

"I did run the first time I escaped." She must have seen the confusion on my face, because she said, "That's why you were sent here? To hunt me? Do me bodily harm? Ringing any bells?"

I scowled. "But you were in the lab that night, the night Elizabeth got out. You're in my flashbacks."

She blinked and looked away. "Let me tell you a story. It's a short one. I think we have time. There once was a girl who broke free of the Branch, but her escape was scarred with regret. There was another girl, a girl she'd left behind, someone who needed saving.

"So the first girl hatched a plan, and when she returned a few days later, she broke back in and freed the girl with big green eyes because it was the right thing to do.

"But not just that. You see, the green-eyed girl was—" She stopped abruptly. "Well, I don't want to ruin the ending."

I buried a grunt of annoyance. "But you could have left after that. After Elizabeth was free."

"No. I had to know if they returned. I had to know if they took her again."

My scowl deepened. "So you could use her to save your own ass, you mean."

She sent me a cutting look. "It's not as simple as that. You of all people know how deep this game is we're playing. This story is stitched with revenge, Nick, and we all have a seam to make, even Elizabeth. And besides," she added, "the game has changed. Now I have you."

I wasn't sure what that meant, and even if I asked, I doubted she'd explain.

I shifted my leg, trying to take as much pressure off the wound as I could. "They'll kill you, you know. Riley isn't a man of his word."

She grinned. This girl could change emotions quicker than anyone I'd ever met. "Oh, I know. And I'm not a woman of mine."

An SUV skidded to a stop twenty feet away. Branch agents spilled from the vehicle and formed a line on either side of us, semiautos up and ready.

Before Chloe got to her feet, she muttered to me, through clenched teeth, "Don't screw this one up."

Riley slid out of the passenger side of the SUV and walked over to us.

Clearly, he was in charge now. Awesome.

"You did good," he told Chloe.

Chloe grabbed the hem of her skirt and curtsied, with a sly grin on her lips.

Riley scowled.

If the girl wasn't so damn psychotic, I might actually like her as a fighting partner. She knew how to piss people off, and how to make herself look innocent while doing it.

"Get them in the car," Riley said, and the agents swooped in, grabbing me beneath the arms and dragging me to the SUV. I was tossed in the backseat, and sandwiched between two agents. Zip ties were tightened on my wrists.

"Am I free to go now?" I heard Chloe ask.

Riley didn't say anything at first, and I thought for sure he'd make her come. Instead, he nodded, and Chloe climbed back into her car.

Elizabeth was gently sprung from the backseat and put in the trunk of the SUV, still passed out.

As Chloe stomped on the gas and barreled past us, she looked at the back window of the SUV, even though the glass was tinted and there was no possible way she could see me.

She grinned again and winked.

The short ride to the barn lab was a bumpy one, and my leg throbbed with each hit. The pain had lessened, though, so it was only a dull ache in the bone. Two gunshot wounds in less than twenty-four hours. That must have been a record.

Riley didn't say anything to me as we made our way back. Which was fine, because I wasn't sure what I'd say in return. Probably something smart and civil, like, *Fuck off.*

The SUV was pulled inside the barn, and the door closed behind us. A lock slammed into place.

"Carry them down," Riley ordered, and I was lugged from the SUV and dragged down the winding stairs and through the lab.

The agents at either side of me seemed to know exactly where they were going through the maze. I was deposited in the room from my flashback.

I still didn't know the details from the past, though it was easy to figure it out. I'd come to kill Chloe. I'd had to chase her through the woods where I finally shot her. That's when I'd stumbled on Elizabeth, who'd been trying to escape on her own.

That still didn't explain Elizabeth's role in all of this. Was she just another test subject? Or was she somehow more involved?

There were two agents stationed outside my locked cell. I could see them through the window that looked out over the maze. I sat, slumped, on the bed, cursing my injuries, though slightly dumbstruck by how much the wound didn't hurt. The pain grew less and less with each passing minute.

If my pain had lessened, then my agitation had grown, and I cracked every joint I had as I waited.

I needed a plan. I needed to find Elizabeth. I could fight off a lot of guys, but even my abilities had limits. I couldn't fight everyone inside, while injured, and while trying to save Elizabeth, too.

Finally, after what seemed like hours, the lock clicked, and the door opened. Riley came in first.

"I'm glad it ended this way," he said, his face blank, emotionless. Riley had always been even-keeled.

It hasn't ended, I thought. *Sam and the others are coming. We're going to break out of here. We're going to survive like we always do.*

"Kill him," Riley said.

Three agents stepped into the room, their semiautos trained on me.

My heart pounded against my skull.

I had to get out of here. This was not how this would end. No way in hell.

I charged toward them. I could fight my way out of this room. I had to.

They opened fire, and the force of the gunshots sent me staggering back.

I looked down at the bullet holes peppering my chest. Blood poured from the wounds like water from a spigot.

I dropped to my knees. My line of sight skittered sideways, then narrowed.

The room grew dark and sticky and cold.

My body went numb, and I keeled over on an exhale. My heart slowed to a *thump-thump* in my ears. I had a flash of an old memory, of a time before the Branch, when I lay on dingy carpet that smelled of stubbed-out cigarettes and spilled beer as my dad glowered over me, blood smeared across his knuckles.

Back then, I'd thought I was dying. This time I really was.

"Get in a few more for good measure," Riley said. "Then bury him out back."

The agents blasted me again.

35

ELIZABETH

I SQUINTED AGAINST THE GLARE OF overhead fluorescent lights. I sat up. My body protested, as if it'd been in the same position for too long, my muscles cramped from disuse.

"Chloe?" I mumbled, finding my tongue too dry, too thick.

Beneath me was a thinly padded mattress covered in stark white sheets. The bed creaked when I shifted. I tried to recall what had happened before I'd fallen asleep. I was with Chloe, that much I knew, but everything else was a haze.

Using my hand to block out the blinding light from above, I examined the room. The walls were as white as the sheets, the floor gray tile. There were two doors, both closed. No windows.

I took in a breath and caught the old scent of lemon floor cleaner.

I jerked to my feet and opened the door on my right—bathroom.

I tried the door on my left—locked.

My heart rammed against the back of my throat. Panic burned through the air in my lungs, and I staggered against the wall, gasping.

It was a mistake. I wasn't back here. *I wasn't here.*

Maybe I was hallucinating. It wasn't so far-fetched, was it? I was mentally unsound, officially diagnosed, even. It wasn't such a leap to think I'd transitioned from panic attacks to full-blown delusions.

I closed my eyes and counted to four, over and over again until my breathing was regulated. I wasn't going to fix whatever this was if I was having a panic attack on top of it.

When my heart slowed, when I could no longer hear it hammering in my ears, I opened my eyes, but the room hadn't changed and the artificial-lemon smell was as present as it had been five minutes ago.

I tried the door again, tugging on the handle with everything I had. When it didn't budge, I beat against it and screamed until my ears hurt.

I couldn't go through this again. I wouldn't survive this time.

Defeated, I sat on the bed and propped my head in my hands, tears pricking my eyes. I recalled Dr. Sedwick assuring me months ago that I was safe, that I was home now and that I was never going back to the place where I'd been held.

But here I was. *Here* again.

And somehow, in some twisted way, I wasn't surprised. I might have been free for the past six years, but the memory of captivity had haunted me every single day. I had never truly been free of the lab, and maybe now I never would be.

Footsteps approached outside, and a lock on the door slid open. I scrambled back on the bed, drawing my legs up, as if they were a shield between me and them, but when the person walked in, the tension in my body immediately faded.

"Mom," I said.

Her hair was tied back in a tight bun. She wore a white lab coat, silent lab sneakers. A stethoscope wound around her neck.

"Hi, sweetie," she said.

Somehow, her being here didn't surprise me, either. Even so, despite what that implied, I was relieved to see a familiar face.

"What's going on?" I asked.

"Shh." *This is our little secret.*

She came to the bedside and sat next to me, running a cold hand across my forehead, pushing the hair from my face. "It's all right. You're safe."

I shrank away from her, away from her touch. "Am I?"

The corners of her mouth turned down. "Of course."

"This is the lab, Mom. The lab where I was held captive, where your *life* was threatened."

She shook her head, and a lock of hair fell from her bun. "We are not in danger here. I promise."

"Even if that is true, this place... everything here..." A growing lump in my throat threatened to choke me. I swallowed hard against it. Just being in this room was setting me on edge. Surely she must understand that, considering she had been as much a prisoner here six years ago as I had.

I turned to her. While I could hardly breathe, as if the walls were pressing in around me, her shoulders were loose, her mouth relaxed. Being here didn't faze her at all. She was almost comfortable.

As if this place had never been her prison.

She reached out for my hand, but stopped when I flinched.

"You aren't in danger here, are you?" I said.

"And neither are you."

I looked away from her and stared at the tile floor, trying to make sense of the nagging feeling in my chest that I was missing something. Something important.

"This is a medical lab. Everything I was subjected to here was medically based and"—I flicked my gaze back to her—"you're a doctor. And a good one at that."

Realization dawned, and I felt like the biggest fool ever. "You're part of their medical team. You"—I jumped from the bed—"you've *always* been a part of their medical team, haven't you? You were *never* in danger here. Not now, not six years ago."

"Elizabeth—" she started, but I surged on.

"Why was I taken? Why was I part of this whole thing? I don't"—I swiped at my cheeks as tears escaped out the corners of my eyes—"I don't understand why you kept me here. Why would you do that to me?"

"Honey—"

"Tell me!"

She stood up and straightened, pulling that familiar steel back into her shoulders. "I needed you. You were the most important part of this whole program."

When she paused, I wanted to urge her on, but I couldn't seem to find the words, so I waited several long seconds as she put her thoughts in order.

"When your father and I were trying to have kids, I miscarried several times, and then when I finally carried a baby to full term, it died within minutes of birth."

My mouth clamped shut with surprise, my teeth clacking together. She'd never told me this. I'd always thought she and Dad had wanted only one child, because they were both so busy with work.

"I knew how to fix it. I *knew.*" Her eyes turned bloodshot with unshed tears. "All I had to do was modify the genetic makeup at the embryonic stage. The goal was to strengthen the embryo to the point that it was indestructible."

She reached over, taking my hand in hers. "The first successful baby was you."

"Me?" I whispered.

"I made you stronger, Elizabeth."

"But—what does that even mean?"

"Think about it. Have you ever been sick?"

I tried to recall being sick. Aggie suffered from frequent sinus infections, and last winter she caught the flu and lay in bed for six days. I'd thought for sure I'd catch it, since I'd taken care of her.

But I hadn't. In fact, now that I thought about it, I couldn't recall ever lying in bed with an illness, other than a mental illness.

Mom went on. "Remember that car accident we were in when you were nine?" I nodded weakly. "You had a broken arm and a deep gash on your forehead, and I suspected you had a cracked rib as well, but by the time the ambulance arrived—"

"I was fine," I said, my voice so low I wondered if she'd heard me.

"The EMTs said it was a miracle you weren't injured, considering the wreck, and considering the injuries I'd sustained. They said you were left untouched, but that wasn't true. You just healed before they reached us."

I tried to make sense of the questions crowding my head, and the memories of my childhood, wondering if perhaps they held more clues to my mother's unbelievable story. Skinned knees that disappeared by the time I ran to my mother's arms. Mosquito bites that were swollen, itchy, and then gone in seconds.

I had thought, when I left this lab six years ago, that my captors had changed me irrevocably, that they'd poked and prodded me to make me invincible. But I was wrong.

I had been invincible when I arrived.

"So why did they bring me here in the first place?" I asked.

"I published an article years ago, only theorizing the practice of genetic modification at the embryonic stage to immunize future generations against cancer and diabetes and other diseases. Someone at the Branch read the article and approached me with an offer I couldn't turn down.

"They wanted to create a serum, something that could be administered at the adolescent stage, or even well into adulthood. But... I couldn't replicate what I'd done with you. Every attempt failed. I didn't understand it, and we were running out of time and money. The only other course of action was to use you as our map."

"You had me kidnapped on purpose so you could study me?"

"I knew I would need you for an extended period of time, without you fully knowing and—"

Rage burned in my chest till my vision was tinted red with it. I reached over and slapped her across the face.

Her head snapped aside, and she brought her hand to her cheek where the skin was already an angry shade of pink.

"How dare you!"

She clenched her hands into fists at her side. "Do you have any idea what this kind of medical breakthrough could mean? We can cure diseases! We can save lives!"

"Are you working for the Branch? Is that who's in charge of this program?"

She pursed her mouth and said nothing.

"The Branch is not the kind of organization that works to cure cancer." I recalled the things Nick had told me about his past, and the Branch. Terrible, terrible things. "They kill people, Mom."

"You can't believe everything Nick has told you."

"Well, I do. I trust him more than I trust you."

The look she gave me was almost as if I'd slapped her again.

"Why am I here now?" I asked.

"We need to make more serum, and make it better. We need to finish what we were prevented from finishing."

Because I escaped, she meant.

I backed up toward the door, wondering if she'd left it unlocked, if I could perform the miracle of escaping a second time. "I won't be a part of this. You can't seriously think I'll cooperate."

"No harm will come to you. No harm came to you six years ago. You were always treated with respect and the utmost care."

I narrowed my eyes, feeling the hard edge of my teeth as I bit into my lip. She had no idea what she'd done to me, what the whole ordeal had done to me. The nightmares. The anxiety. The panic attacks.

I might have been indestructible on the outside, but inside I was broken, and it was all my mother's fault.

"Get out," I shouted. "Out!"

"Elizabeth."

"Out!"

She lurched backward.

The door opened, and Riley strolled in. "Move forward?"

Mom discreetly wiped the tears from her face. "Yes."

Without another look, she turned and left the room.

Two lab technicians swept into the room, carting a massive machine, wires spilling from several ports.

"What is that?"

Once the machine was parked near the door, two more men entered the room. They were different from the technicians in that they were larger, colder, unflinching. They strode over to me and grabbed me by the arms, tossing me onto the bed.

"Let me go!"

Straps were tugged from beneath the bed, and my wrists were pinned down at my sides, my ankles secured at the end of the bed.

"Mom!" I screamed, until my voice broke.

Riley checked his phone briefly before looking over at me. "Don't worry, Elizabeth. When you wake up, everything will be fine again."

"What does that mean? What are you doing to me?" I tried the straps, yanking my arms up, hoping for some slack.

Riley murmured instructions to the technicians, ignoring me. The two large men exited the room once I was secure on the bed. I flailed again as adrenaline took over. I needed to get out of here. I needed to escape. Instinct told me that if I didn't get out of here right now, then there'd be nothing left to fight for.

"Call me when it's finished," Riley said. "I'll see you in the morning, Elizabeth." He left.

The technicians placed several electrodes on my head, then attached the wires. When they switched on the machine, it started up with a whine and a rushing of noise.

“Relax,” the male technician said. “Everything will be fine.”

“What is it? The machine?”

The female technician, a short, blond woman with wide-set eyes, attached a final probe to the center of my forehead. “It’s a memory alteration system.”

36

NICK

SOMEONE HELD MY HEAD IN THEIR LAP. Something wet kept plinking against my face.

"We have to go," a voice said from somewhere far away, like I was underwater. "We'll come back for him. I promise."

"I can't leave him." Anna. "We never should have let him go off on his own."

"Anna," Trev said. "We can't sit here any longer. Either we save the girl or we go."

Hair fell in my face as Anna bent over to kiss my forehead.

I gulped for air, and the expanding of my lungs, pressed against my ribs, felt like a balloon about to pop.

Anna shrieked.

"Holy shit," Cas said. "He's a zombie!"

Trev knelt beside me and pulled my eyes open. "Nick?"

I slapped his hand away and rolled over, my insides pinwheeling. On all fours, hands splayed in the dirt, I vomited until there was nothing left to get out.

When I was done, I collapsed on my stomach, the ground cold against my face. I didn't know where I was, or how I'd gotten outside, but if I was no longer in the lab, then Elizabeth was in danger and I had to return to save her.

I rolled over again, onto my back. With a voice on the edge of fading out, raw, my throat too dry, I croaked, "They shot me. So many times I lost count."

When I opened my eyes, treetops shook above me as the wind picked up speed. Anna, Cas, Sam, and Trev were all staring at me. Sam nodded at my chest. I looked down. There were multiple bullet holes in my shirt, and my shirt was caked with old blood and dirt.

I patted my chest. I should have been in pain. I should have been dead.

But when I ripped my shirt open, my chest was untouched. Not a single bullet hole in sight.

"What the hell?"

"Should we kill him?" Cas said. "Before he starts lurching around and eating our brains?"

"Cas!" Anna said.

"What? Too soon?"

"What happened?" I asked, and lurched to my feet. When I stumbled back on unsteady legs, Sam jerked forward and caught me. I used a tree to keep me upright and waved Sam back.

Now that I had a better view of where I was, and what surrounded us, I noticed two Branch agents either dead or knocked out ten feet away. And beside them was a half-dug hole. The perfect size for a body. Probably mine.

"Chloe," Trev said. "She called us about an hour after she took you. Said she had done what she had to do, but that if everything went according to plan, you'd be safe. She gave us the location of an air vent about a hundred yards away from the barn, an unmarked entrance to the lab, but on our way, we stumbled on these guys"—Trev gestured at the agents—"and then we saw you."

Anna covered her mouth with a hand and looked away.

"I'm not dead, Anna," I said. "See." I patted myself down. "Don't start crying again."

"I'm not," she snapped as a tear streamed down her cheek. She gave us her back as she swiped at her face.

Sam frowned at me, but I ignored it.

"That still doesn't explain why I'm alive."

"She must have used the serum on you," Trev said. "It's the only explanation."

Chloe was the one who'd broken out of the lab six years ago, and she must have known where the serum was kept. It wasn't too crazy to think she'd swiped some of it for herself.

She'd also had enough time on the way to the barn to stop the car and retrieve my gun. She'd had enough time to shoot me up with the serum, too.

By giving me the drug, she'd saved my ass, but still came through on her end of the bargain she'd made with Riley.

"We have to get back into the lab." I shoved away from the tree and was relieved I didn't fall flat on my face.

"Slow down," Sam said. "We don't know what sort of effect this serum will have on you. And furthermore, we don't know what we're running into. With you inside, it was different. Now that you're out, and you're safe—"

"What, you're just going to leave Elizabeth in there?"

Sam crossed his arms over his chest. "That's not what I'm saying. What I *am* saying is we have some time to think about this. There's a reason they wanted Elizabeth. They won't kill her."

"Yeah, I know that." I started pacing, leaves from last fall crunching beneath my boots. "That doesn't mean she's safe."

When I first heard Elizabeth's mother speak, I'd thought her voice sounded familiar. And now that I knew she was working with Riley, it all made sense.

"The audio files," I said to Trev. "The doctor? Dr. Turrow?"

"Yeah? What about her?"

"She's Elizabeth's mother."

"Son of a bitch," Trev muttered.

Anna sighed and scrubbed at her face. She of all people understood the complications of mixing family with the Branch. Her uncle was the guy who'd created the organization after all.

"They might not kill Elizabeth if she has family on the inside," I said, "but if we know anything about the Branch, it's this: if they can't kill you—"

"Then they'll alter your memories," Anna said.

I nodded. "We all know what it's like to have our memories gone, and then to suffer the pain of them when they return. I can't let them do that to her."

I grabbed a gun from one of the fallen agents and stuffed it beneath my shirt. "I'm going—with or without you guys."

I started off through the woods and was relieved when they all followed.

37

ELIZABETH

DARKENED GLASSES WERE PUT OVER MY eyes. The female tech flipped a switch on the frame, and several green lines flickered on the lenses.

"This won't hurt," she said. "In fact, you won't feel a thing. It'll be over before you know it."

They'd inserted a rubber guard into my mouth so I could no longer talk. There was no point in trying anyway. My mother was gone. And there was no one here who would save me.

Nick had told me he suffered from partial amnesia. I could still recall the pain of the emptiness in his eyes. How not knowing, while freeing in some ways, was also damaging. And I would be just like him when I awoke.

My eyes clouded with tears.

"Ready?" the male tech said.

"Ready," the woman confirmed.

"Here we go." He pushed a button. The machine clicked. The glasses lit up, images flashing in quick succession. A house. An ant. A woman. A tree. A dying tree. A tree falling down. A woman again.

"Listen to my voice," she said, but the words didn't match the movement of her lips.

A needle pricked the back of my neck. I flinched and bit down hard on the mouth guard. My toes curled in my shoes. Whatever came out of the needle was warm at first, then turned biting hot, like melted wax running down my neck.

I flailed. Trying to wipe the burning away.

Ants. Ants again. Ants on my arms.

I arched my back.

The ants tore the flesh away from my bones, piece by piece.

The burning in my neck faded, and my body relaxed until I felt like I was floating.

The mouth guard was pulled from my mouth, and my teeth clicked together.

"Listen to my voice," the woman said again. "Your name is Elizabeth. Your name is Bethany. Your name is Tiffany. Your name is blank. You live in Trademarr. You live in Illinois. You live nowhere.

"What is your name?"

"Eliz..." I murmured.

"What is your name?" she said again. "Your name is..." Static filled my ears. Then a sharp rapping. A clap. *Clap. Clap. Beep.*

My mind grew fuzzy, as if my thoughts were clouds burned off by the sun.

"You live nowhere," she continued.

An image of a forest flashed in front of my eyes, and then the same forest shed its leaves and the branches fell to the ground and a great inferno filled my vision with a blaze of blinding orange light.

When the light faded, the forest was gone.

"Listen to my voice," the woman said. "What is your name?"

"My name is blank," I answered.

"Where do you live?"

"Nowhere."

38

NICK

"CHLOE SAID THE VENT WAS A HUNDRED yards from the back of the barn," Trev whispered.

We were crouched in the woods, the barn a dusky shadow in the distance. "Is it hidden?"

"Didn't sound like it."

"Once we get in, then what?" Anna asked. She was on my left and Trev was on my right. Sam and Cas were behind us. "We don't know the layout, so anything you can give us will help."

"I'm not sure where the vent runs to." I shifted, dropping onto one knee. "But the layout is a maze of office partition walls, and they're tall enough that even I can't see over the top. If Elizabeth isn't in an exam room, then she'll be in one of the holding cells along the back wall."

"And if she is in an exam room?" Sam asked over my shoulder.

Then we might be screwed, I thought. No way would I tell him that, though. If there was any chance at failure, Sam would call off the rescue mission, and I needed him at my back.

Trev dropped out the clip in his gun and filled the empty slots with new bullets. "We'll find her, Nick. We're not leaving without her."

I nodded at him in the half dark, happy he was here. Then disturbed that I was happy he was here.

Sam came up alongside Trev. "Looks like they have at least six men patrolling the grounds."

There was a man at each back corner of the barn, two more in the field farther out, and one on each side of the barn. We also had to assume there were probably two more in the front.

"How do you want to do this?" I asked. As much as I wanted to run in there and start shooting people, Sam was the better strategist.

"We could probably get inside the vent by taking out the two agents at the rear, but we risk being discovered when the others patrolling the grounds realize they're missing two men. It might be better to take them all out now."

"I agree," Trev said. "It'll take the guys inside longer to realize the outside patrols are gone than it'll take the outside patrols to realize they're missing someone."

"Nick and I should go in first and take out the men closest to the woods. Trev and Cas go in wide and take out the men at the back of the barn. When Nick and I have taken care of our targets, Nick will go right and I'll go left for the last two."

"What about me?" Anna asked.

"You watch our backs."

She scowled at her inferior placement in the attack plan, but didn't argue.

"Ready?" I asked. They all nodded.

My gun in my hand, I crept through the trees with Sam on my left. We had about twenty feet of woods for coverage before the trees broke up and the field took over. When we reached the edge of the field, Sam raised his fist, pulling me to a stop. He held up two fingers and pointed to the north, where two more men had appeared.

Shit.

Sam waved me forward, though, so apparently we were still going through with the plan.

We divided at the perimeter of the woods. I edged forward, dropping to my stomach in the tall grass when my target made a circle, scanning the area. When his back was to me again, I shot ahead silently, putting a bullet in him before he knew what hit him.

Twenty feet to my left, Sam's guy hit the ground as Trev and Cas blazed past us, knocking out their targets before any of them realized they were under attack.

I went in for my second target—a short, solid guy who was patrolling the north side of the barn. My gun was up, ready to take the shot, when someone shouted from my right.

"Carson! Behind you!"

My guy—Carson—turned just in time to get a bullet in the chest. When his knees buckled beneath him, I yanked him toward me, using him as a shield as a round of bullets was sent my way. Several thudded into the wood siding of the barn. Two hit Carson. I dropped him and ran, ducking behind a rusted-out trailer as another wave of bullets whizzed overhead.

I crawled to a better vantage point, where I could make out the agents' legs from the underbelly of the trailer. They were at least thirty feet out, with nothing but open field between us. There was a handful of trees at their back, giving them coverage if they needed it. All I had was this damn trailer.

Fighting broke out in front of the barn. I took the opening, hoping the guys to the north would be distracted, but as soon as I popped up over the edge of the trailer, several gunshots rang out and I had to drop to my stomach again.

This battle was over before I'd even entered the barn.

I'd have to wait until they came for me.

From my spot, I could see only their legs as they raced toward me. And then, suddenly, there was another set of legs—shorter, skinnier legs. Something cracked. A gun went off. A body hit the dirt with a wet, sloppy lurch. A man shouted, then choked. Then nothing.

I chanced a look. Anna was the only one left standing.

She jogged over to me, a smile stretched wide across her face. "You're welcome."

"I had them," I said.

"Uh-huh," she countered.

"Come on. Let's see if the men in front are down."

When we rounded the front corner of the barn, Cas was stuffing an agent in the trunk of a car. Trev and Sam were there, pulling guns from the dead agents at their feet.

"Let's go find that vent," Sam said. "Before someone realizes these guys are missing."

With the area secure, finding the vent was easy. It was a circular port in the middle of the field, recently cleaned of the topsoil and vegetation that had most likely hidden it from view. I wondered if Chloe had cleaned it off days ago, knowing we might need it.

Once inside, I nearly choked on the cold, sterile air. It reminded me of the lab back at the farmhouse, and the cell I'd spent five years locked inside. The walls of the vent closed in around me, and my heart raced in my chest.

I couldn't wait to get out of there.

Trev had offered to take the lead, but now I was glad I'd shoved him aside, because it meant I was the first one out.

The vent led us to a storage closet, big enough that we could all stand inside once we'd climbed down from the vent.

The air was stuffier here, hot and pressing. With Sam at my left, a gun in his hand, I popped the door open a crack. We were at the back wall, the maze in front of us. Which meant the holding cells were to our left. There were no Branch agents in sight. If I had to guess, Riley had used up a lot of his manpower to guard the outside.

I signaled to Sam which direction we should go, and he nodded in the half dark. The others filed in behind us. I was the first one out of the closet, the need to find Elizabeth fueling me. If she was in a holding cell, she was within my reach, and escape was not far behind.

The first cell was empty. And the second. And the third. The last was open, the floor still painted red with my blood.

I cursed beneath my breath.

Elizabeth was somewhere in the maze, and if she was in the maze then she was in an exam room, and I didn't want to think about what that might mean.

I wanted the group to divide to cover more ground, but Sam vetoed that, so we all crept through the maze like an army of ants with guns in our hands.

We crossed paths with only two agents, and both were on the floor in seconds, then tucked into offices, out of sight.

The farther we got into the lab, the more I panicked, worried that Elizabeth wasn't here, that this was some kind of decoy. I could sense Sam growing edgier behind me, but I couldn't give up yet. Not until I'd searched every corner of this lab.

And finally, somewhere in the middle of the maze, at a window that looked in on an exam room, I froze.

Elizabeth was strapped down on a bed, her dark hair spread across a pillow. A pair of dark-tinted glasses covered her eyes, and electrodes were plastered all over her head.

My gut twisted on itself, and my free hand tightened into a fist at my side.

We were too late.

Too fucking late.

39

ELIZABETH

THE GLASSES WENT DARK.

Something thumped beneath me, and I had the distinct feeling that I was floating, the world carrying on below me, far, far away.

Hands shook my shoulders, and I came crashing back to my body. Sounds floated in and out of my hearing like river currents, and the sounds formed into words that seemed suddenly foreign. So I just stared. Stared and stared at the face looming above me, wondering when it was I'd opened my eyes.

The face belonged to a boy. Black hair curled around his ears and down his neck, and his eyes were two orbs of glowing blue staring back at me.

"Elizabeth," he said, and the word felt familiar in my head. I repeated it without a sound, forming the word with my lips, testing it out.

"Elizabeth," he said again, more urgently.

My body trembled in his arms. He tightened his hold around me, and the heat from his touch spread through me, fiery and immediately recognizable.

"We have to run," he whispered in my ear, and his voice hitched with an emotion I thought might be misery. "Can you?"

I nodded, only because I knew it was what he wanted, and if I was sure of nothing else, I was sure of this: pleasing him pleased me.

So I ran.

He pulled me alongside him, his arm at my waist.

"Keep going," he said.

There were others with us. A girl. Three other guys. They were young, and I wondered, fleetingly, how old I was.

"Pulling her out like that was wrong," another dark-haired guy said. He was shorter than the one who'd grabbed me first, less imposing. "I'm afraid of what the consequences will be."

"We can worry about that later," my boy said. Not knowing his name, I'd started to think of him as mine. He seemed to know me, anyway. "Right now we just need to get her out of here."

Noises, not far off, pulled us to a stop. We huddled in an empty office and waited until it seemed safe.

"What is my name?" I asked the blond guy on my right.

"Elizabeth," he said. He pointed at all the others, rattling off their names before his own, which he said was Cas.

I had thought my name was Blank. But that sounded less familiar than *Elizabeth*, so I believed this Cas, and decided Blank was a terrible name anyway.

"We are your friends," Nick said. "Everyone else is an enemy. Remember that."

"I will."

We twisted and turned through walls that reached above my head, but did not reach the ceiling. They were all the same.

Somewhere in the distance someone yelled, "Find them!"

It was a woman's voice. A voice that sounded familiar.

Shh. It's our little secret.

"Don't stop," the boy said.

My legs ached and my shoulders burned and my head wouldn't stop pounding, but slowing down didn't seem like an option. So I kept moving.

When we rounded a corner, a man dressed in black charged toward us, and the girl in our group—Anna—brought up her gun. But she wasn't quick enough. Someone else took out the man for us.

A group of men and women emerged from the hallway. I

remembered what Nick had said, that everyone else was an enemy, and immediately stiffened in his protective hold.

Trev noticed and put a reassuring hand on my shoulder. "These people are here to help. They are not our enemies."

Our group of friends was growing too fast, and there were too many people to keep track of.

The new arrivals were dressed in nondescript clothing—jeans, flannel shirts, boots—but they all carried weapons and had matching looks of determination and desire for revenge etched across their faces.

"I'm glad you made it," Trev said. "We can use the help." He nodded at the tall man in front. "This is Dr. Sedwick, Elizabeth's therapist."

Nick's expression turned to one of surprise, so I tried to look surprised, too.

"Elizabeth's therapist is one of the Turncoats?" Anna said.

"Aggie was, too," Trev added. "Just so we're clear."

"Talk about being well insulated."

The therapist stepped forward and examined me with a quick sweep of his brown eyes. He had kind eyes. "Thank God you're okay."

"Yes," I said simply.

The line of his thick brow furrowed deeply. He glanced at Trev. "Tell me you got here in time. Tell me they haven't wiped her."

Trev frowned. "We found her when she was halfway through the memory alteration."

The therapist cursed, and tried to hide the wobbling of his bottom lip by clamping his mouth closed. He pulled in a breath through his nose. "I'm so sorry, Elizabeth. I will fix this. I swear it. They will pay for what they've done to you and Aggie."

Voices picked up some twenty feet away, followed by the quick pounding of feet.

"We have to go," Nick said.

"We'll cover you." The therapist waved his group ahead. "Good luck."

Our groups separated. I glanced over my shoulder at the man as he retreated, something nagging at me as he disappeared behind a wall.

We wound our way through several more hallways, but were ambushed before long. The dark-haired boy with the green eyes killed a man with his bare hands. I sucked in a breath.

Anna shot another man, and he crumpled to the floor.

Another man barreled out of a hallway. This one was bigger than any of the others, with a scowl on his face and several scars running along his jaw.

Anna ran, dropped to her knees, and slid across the floor, whacking the man in the kneecap with the butt of her gun. He howled. Cas punched him in the face, then shot him in the foot.

Another down.

The walls that all looked the same, that had trapped us in their maze, disappeared. We turned to the left and went through an open door. Once inside, I realized it was a storage room, with mops and brooms and stuffed filing cabinets. The room—not the contents—felt vaguely familiar, like it was a place I'd dreamed about.

"I'll go first," Sam said. Sam, the one with the green eyes and the impenetrable expression. "I'll pull the girls up."

He jumped on top of a filing cabinet and pulled himself inside a hole in the ceiling. He shimmied around until he was able to poke his head back through.

"Elizabeth next," Nick said, and he ushered me to the filing cabinet.

A shadow crossed the doorway. Anna shouted.

A gun went off.

The boy in the ceiling cursed beneath his breath, lost his hold, and fell through the opening, crashing into me and taking me down with him.

More bodies filled the room. More enemies dressed in black. Fighting broke out.

"No shooting," a woman called. "Do not hurt Elizabeth!"

Sam grunted and rolled off me, leaving behind a stain of something red on my chest.

A gun fell to the floor, skidded across the concrete, and stopped only inches away from me.

I reached for it, pulled it into my hand, and rose to my feet.

Everyone else is an enemy.

I put my finger where a finger should go and squeezed.

40

NICK

AGENTS LAY AT MY FEET, A TANGLE OF arms and legs, blood running in rivers on the stained concrete.

A gun went off behind me. I could almost feel the air part as the bullet left the chamber, sailing past me, hitting Dr. Turrow in the chest.

Another bullet. Then another.

"Everyone else is an enemy," Elizabeth whispered, and then she began to shake.

Dr. Turrow's knees buckled. She stared at her daughter, her eyes wide and bloodshot.

"Elizabeth." Her voice cracked as blood turned her white lab coat black. Tears ran down her face. She collapsed against the door frame, and frowned. "I am not your enemy."

One final shot took the doctor out, and she fell over, just another body on the concrete floor.

"Go! Go," Trev said as he cleared the door of bodies and slammed it shut, propping it closed with a shop broom.

"I'll go first," I said, since Sam had been shot in the arm and could barely keep himself upright.

I leapt onto the filing cabinet and into the air vent, and then twisted around to hang back down into the closet. I took Elizabeth first. Trev told her which way to go, and she started crawling on her hands and knees in the direction of our freedom.

Anna came up next. "I'll help her along," she said to me. "Don't worry."

"Thanks."

With Trev's and Cas's help, we managed to get Sam inside.

Cas came up next. Trev came up last. I closed the vent behind me.

The sound of our shuffling echoed through the vent, but the farther we got, the more the vent smelled of fresh air and pine trees. When the access panel was opened at ground level, colder air rushed in, and my fingers went numb.

When I climbed out, dirt jamming beneath my fingernails, I sucked in a breath. Trev offered me a hand for a boost up. There was some weird symbolic shit going on there, some bridges mended and all that.

I took his hand and set my feet on solid ground.

The sky had darkened in the hours we'd been inside the lab. There was no moon, only the silver of stars, and the swaying of the treetops.

Cas shut the vent behind us. "Which way is out?"

Trev pointed to the left. "To the east."

Elizabeth wrapped her arms around herself, and looked lost. I'd had to keep myself together inside the lab, but now, out in the open, freedom so close, everything that had happened came rushing in.

We hadn't reached her in time, and they'd wiped her memories. Or at least, partially. She'd shot her own mother. She hadn't even recognized her. That would be a memory so volatile that when it returned it would ruin her.

"Hey," I said. "You okay?"

She frowned and ran her teeth over her bottom lip. "I don't know. I'm so... confused."

I reached for her hand. At first, she stiffened, but then she relaxed. I threaded my fingers with hers. "I'm right here. I'm not going anywhere."

She nodded.

We started walking east, keeping our steps light, but quick. If there were any agents left in the lab, they'd be after us soon. As soon as Riley got his shit together.

Ten minutes into the walk, a twig snapped to the left. We all froze. Sam waved us to the trees, and I dragged Elizabeth beneath a massive oak, shielding her body with mine. She trembled beside me.

Footsteps came heavy and quick. But only one set.

I met Sam's eyes across the ten feet or so separating us. He motioned to me with three fingers.

On the count of three.

We stepped out into the path of the runner, and the man collided with us, bouncing back.

It was Riley.

Sweat poured down his forehead despite the bite in the night air. His shirt was unbuttoned at the top, untucked from his pants. There were dark circles beneath his eyes.

He staggered back. Brought a gun up. His hand shook.

He was only one man, and there were six of us.

"No. No no no," he said, and turned around and ran.

"Get him," Sam said.

"Stay with Elizabeth!" I shouted to Anna, and she nodded as I took off.

Sam, Cas, and Trev fell in step behind me. No way were we letting Riley go this time. No way in hell.

Out of all of us, Sam had the best endurance, but he was lagging because of the bullet wound, and anyway, I was the fastest runner.

And I wanted Riley. He was mine.

My lungs opened wide. My arms pumped at my sides. I was gaining on him.

Riley wove through the trees, trying to lose me. But I felt better than I'd felt in a long time, like I could run for days.

The trees thinned out. The barn came into view again. I had a split second to wonder if this was another trap, but Riley veered away from the barn, toward the road. Where an SUV sat, waiting.

I picked up speed.

When Riley reached the end of the cornfield, he cut right, disappearing from view. I blasted around the corner three, maybe four seconds later, just in time to see him reach the SUV and slide in behind the wheel.

He slammed the door shut, flipped the locks, and started up the vehicle.

I pulled the gun out from behind my shirt. Shot. Missed.

In the center of the road, watching the SUV spin dirt as it took off, I squared my shoulders, held the gun with both hands, and pulled the trigger. The back window shattered, glass plinking against the bumper.

But Riley kept going, and drove out of sight.

41

ELIZABETH

THE BOY NAMED CAS DROVE ALL OF US to a motel on the outside of town. It was stuck beneath a sign shaped like a horseshoe that glowed neon orange in the dark.

We rented three rooms. Sam and Anna in one room, Cas and Trev in another, and Nick and me in the third.

Once we were inside, Nick locked the door, slid in the dead bolt, and shut the curtains. He set his gun on the nightstand.

There was only one bed.

"Elizabeth," he said.

I looked over at him. In the hour or so since we'd left the barn, I'd been having these flashes, like déjà vu, laced with a rush of knowing and understanding. And then it would disappear again, leaving me with an emptiness that settled in my heart.

Nick had explained to me what had happened. That the Branch had tried to wipe my memories, and that he'd stopped the process before it had been completed. He didn't know what that meant for me.

The more he used my name, the more it felt right.

My name was Elizabeth, and I lived in Trademarr, Illinois.

And the way my heart jumped every time he looked at me said all that needed to be said about how I felt about Nick.

I liked him. More than liked him. Just as my name felt right, so did he.

"Yes?" I said.

He sighed and scrubbed at his face. "I wish I could make it better."

There was something else he wanted to say, but didn't.

I sat on the edge of the bed. He sat next to me. Our knees bumped together. He reached over and took my hand in his. His fingers were long, and covered in scars. They were thick at the knuckles, knuckles threaded with veins. I liked his hands.

"Will I ever not feel empty like this?" I asked.

He squeezed my hand. "Yes. I promise."

42

NICK

WE HUNG AROUND TRADEMARR FOR A FEW days, long enough for Trev, Sam, Cas, and I to break back into the barn lab and steal whatever information we could. The place had been cleared of people and bodies, but there were still computers intact and filing cabinets stuffed with old logs.

We were still unclear as to what exactly Elizabeth's mother had done to herself, and therefore to Elizabeth, to change her genetic makeup. And we needed to know everything.

Could Elizabeth die and come back to life like Chloe and I had? So far, we had found zero record of the Branch killing Elizabeth as part of their testing.

I didn't want to find out the hard way.

Anna also wanted to know what we could expect from me now that I'd been given a dose of the serum. Would I become fearless, too? Would I no longer feel anything?

Anna was good at the research bit, and now that Trev had been accepted back into the group (on probation, though, maybe with a hazing or two), she had a study partner who was good at the whole memorizing-and-compiling-facts crap.

Those two were set for months.

Later, before we left Trademarr, Trev and I broke into Aggie's house to grab some of Elizabeth's things. She'd wanted to come with, but I quickly shot her down, knowing it'd do more damage than good.

Anna helped me talk her out of it. Anna was better at talking than I was.

The attack at Aggie's had made national news, and the house was boarded up now, sectioned off with crime scene tape.

It was easy to get in, though.

Trev and I stared at the bloodstain on the hardwood floor where Aggie had lain before the coroner took her away.

I regretted not having talked to Aggie more. She must have known a lot of incriminating things about Riley and the Branch, having worked for them in the past, and later becoming a Turncoat. Trev said we'd ask the Coats for info on the Angel Serum once we settled in somewhere.

In Elizabeth's room, I stood in the center, wondering what she'd want. Realizing that I didn't know her well enough to know. Wishing like hell I did.

I found a bag in the bottom of her closet, and tore a few things from the hangers. Tossed them inside the bag. I went to her dresser, grabbed a fantasy book that had been marked off with a bookmark, and threw that in, too.

I went to the desk, picked a few things that seemed important. I glanced up. The blue glass bottles looked black in the dark. When Elizabeth had explained them to me, she'd said scent was a strong trigger, tied to memories. Maybe it was true for her.

I grabbed the CARNIVALS, AGGIE, MERV'S, and NICK bottles. Last, I decided to grab two newer bottles—I could tell they were newer because the labels weren't faded. One was marked HOPE and the other SECRETS. I wrapped all of them in a few pillowcases and packed them in the bag, too.

Back in the kitchen, where Trev was on lookout, I stepped over the bloodstain on the floor again, feeling something old stir in my gut.

I hadn't really known Aggie, but I knew what she meant to Elizabeth, and I couldn't help but wonder what the loss would do to her once she remembered it.

Because she would. No matter how good the Branch technology was, the memories always came back.

I had a flash of my dad, angry and drunk, and quickly pushed it away. Turns out, I'm nothing like him, and no way was I wasting another second thinking about the man.

"Ready?" Trev whispered.

I nodded.

We made our way out the back door, around the carriage house, and through the gate to the alley.

No one ever knew we were there.

43

ELIZABETH

IN A DARKENED HALLWAY, NICK PICKED at a locked door with furrowed-brow concentration. A second later, the lock clicked, and Nick pushed the door open.

I stepped inside Chloe's apartment.

Only a few days had passed since we'd escaped the barn lab. Certainly not enough time for Chloe to pack everything.

Except her apartment was empty. Only dust remained, swirling in the filtered sunlight. I took a step inside, an eerie sense of déjà vu washing over me. Her bed had sat against the far wall, her dresser directly across from it. A couch had been pushed into the corner where a little TV had sat on a rickety stand. Now there was nothing.

I wasn't sure how I remembered those things when I had a hard time remembering the girl who'd lived here. But there it was: some random, unimportant detail burbling up from the locked rooms inside my head.

Nick had told me who Chloe was. She was the mysterious girl who broke me out of the barn lab six years ago. She was the whole reason I'd been in the forest that night when Nick saved me.

But she'd also double-crossed us, delivering us to Riley so she could secure her own freedom.

I wasn't sure how I felt about that. In some ways, I owed Chloe so much. But she owed me, too. We'd been friends for so long, and she'd never breathed a word of the secrets between us.

"Have you heard anything from her?" I asked Nick.

He took a few tentative steps inside. "Nothing. Trev's looking into it. Maybe find out where she's hiding."

"No," I said quickly. "Let her stay hidden."

I walked to the far window. The glass was frosted and glowed silver in the light. I pulled a cobalt bottle from my sweater pocket and turned it over in my hand. The label on the front read SECRETS. A word scrawled carefully in my own cursive handwriting. A label I didn't remember making.

The oil inside was pure lemon, and whenever I uncorked the bottle and took in a deep breath, I was overwhelmed with the feeling of being trapped, of things being buried and lost.

I set the bottle on the windowsill. "No more secrets," I whispered, and wondered if Chloe would ever return here, and if she did, what she'd think of the message I'd left her.

"We should go," Nick said.

I nodded at no one and gave the bottle one last look before walking out the door.

44

ELIZABETH

FIVE WEEKS. IT'D BEEN FIVE WEEKS since I'd gone through a memory alteration. But it felt like months.

Pieces were coming back, little by little. I remembered Evan, and Merv's. I remembered Aggie and Dr. Sedwick and the Victorian house.

But mostly, I remembered my mother, and what she'd done to me, and what I'd done to her, and I wondered if, in a cosmic sense, we were somehow even. Or if my actions far outweighed hers, and if I'd be repaying that debt for an eternity.

I took a sip from the Pumpkin Spice Latte in my hands and stared out at Lake Michigan in front of me, the wind from the lake biting and crisp. It smelled like nothing I'd ever smelled before. Something I needed to chronicle as soon as I bought some new oils and cobalt glass bottles.

A strand of hair came loose from my messy bun and fluttered in front of my face. A hand reached over and tucked the strand behind my ear, and I smiled before I looked at him.

"Thanks," I said.

"You're welcome," Nick said.

The others, Sam, Cas, Trev, and Anna, had gone in search of dinner. I just wanted to stare at Lake Michigan a little while longer.

Fall was coming, and the trees lining the sidewalk of the park by the lake had started bleeding with the colors of autumn. Away from the lake, the world smelled like the eventual death of the seasons, and the promise of rebirth.

It was fitting, considering my *own* rebirth.

No longer was I Elizabeth, the frightened girl, the crazy girl. I wasn't her, but I didn't know *who* I was yet, and I wouldn't until all of the pieces came together.

I began to shiver from the cold, and Nick moved closer, winding his arm around me. In the weeks since we'd left Trademarr, he'd been kind and gentle, keeping his distance when he thought I needed it, but there right after, when the trauma came rushing back and being alone seemed to crush my ribs until I felt like I couldn't breathe.

He'd kissed me a handful of times. And every time it left me dizzy and grinning like a fool. Anna said she'd never seen Nick so happy. I didn't know the difference between happy Nick and unhappy Nick. But I hoped he'd stay just the way he was.

As if he'd read my thoughts, Nick leaned over and kissed the top of my head. I went up on tiptoes and brought my lips to his. One kiss. Two kisses. "Much better," I said.

He smiled. "You taste like pumpkin pie."

I grinned and hoisted my coffee cup. " 'Tis the season."

"I guess so. Coffee is best black, if you ask me."

I let my mouth drop open. "Take back those words. They're practically blasphemy during Pumpkin Spice Latte season."

His smile grew wider.

Suddenly, all I could think about was returning to the house where Nick and the others lived, and curling beneath the blankets with him and feeling his body pressed against mine. Who needed dinner? I didn't.

Nick shifted and grabbed my hand, tucking both of our hands into the pocket of his coat. "How are you today? I just realized I hadn't asked yet."

He asked every day.

I shrugged. "Better than yesterday. Every day is better than the last."

He nodded. "Good."

"I just wish things had been different. I wish there'd been a bit more closure."

Nick's expression hardened. He knew I was talking about Riley. The man was a cockroach (Cas's word); no matter how many times the group went up against him, he always seemed to get away.

And if he'd dragged my mother and me into the Branch's fold once, he could do it again. To me or someone else.

I had this constant fear in the back of my mind, like I could never relax until Riley was gone for good. Anna said that was normal. They all felt that way.

"There's something I've been meaning to ask you," I started, turning back to the lake. Asking what I wanted to ask seemed somehow easier if I wasn't looking at Nick, at his unsettlingly blue eyes.

"Yeah?" he coaxed.

"Why did you save me that night in the woods?"

I'd thought about that night a lot. Nick had later told me he'd been in the woods chasing Chloe, since his order had been to kill her. He could have easily left me in the woods and continued with his mission. Or he could have given up my hiding spot, and the Branch would have taken me back.

Nick thought for several beats, and I waited impatiently for him to answer.

"I saved you," he said, "because you needed saving." His jaw clenched and his eyes grew watery. I could tell there was more he wanted to say, things left unsaid about who he was, and who his father was, and whether or not they were the same.

He'd told me only scant details about his life before the Branch, about his family, and Anna had filled in some of the missing information. But I could tell that always, every day, he was fighting to be a better man than his father had been.

Without warning, tears burned my eyes, too. "Thank you," I said quietly. He pulled me in closer. "So now what?" I asked.

"Now we go home," Nick said. "And we..." He tried to read my face. "We watch TV?"

I shook my head.

"We eat dinner?"

Another shake.

"We... read a book?"

"Think cozier."

He ran his free hand through my hair, drew me in, and kissed me, long and eager. His lips were warm, gentle. So good.

"We go to bed," he said finally, with a glint in his blue eyes.

I nodded. "You lead, and I will follow."

ACKNOWLEDGMENTS

There are always a gazillion people I want to thank when it comes to completing a book.

My husband, JV, for putting up with me.

My agent, Joanna Volpe, for putting up with me.

My editor, Pam Gruber, for putting up with me.

All my friends and family—for putting up with me.

In all seriousness, these books would not be written without these people.

JV takes care of me when I'm an emotionally crippled mess.

Jo has all the answers, and tons of patience.

Pam has the wisdom to make these books better (and trust me, she helps me make them TONS better).

And my friends and family have always supported me, with encouraging words, home-cooked meals, cookies (thanks, Mom!), and good humor.

Writing a book is not a solitary experience. It takes a village to make it happen.

And lastly, thanks to all the readers—for buying the books, for reading the books, and for spreading the love! Anna, Sam, Nick, Cas, and Trev would not be where they are without you.

DON'T HATE THE PLAYER.

Turn the page for "Played," a sexy and suspenseful Altered saga novella.

LOUD ROCK MUSIC PLAYED OVERHEAD, but the heavy bass *thumps* did nothing to cover up the incessant buzzing of the tattoo machine at my back. I'd decided to go big for my first tattoo, and this was my third and final sitting.

"Almost done," my tattoo artist said. "How you feeling?"

"Feeling fine," I answered. "Thankfully, I have a high pain tolerance."

Tony was the kind of artist who focused more on his work than on his conversation, so I'd filled in the silences during our sessions. I liked to talk. One of my friends, Evan, said I liked to hear the sound of my own voice.

Tony surprised me, though, by pushing the conversation further. "What's the worst pain you've experienced?"

"Getting shot in the head."

The tattoo gun let out a short *buzz* and then cut off abruptly. "Seriously?" he asked.

"Seriously."

The needle returned to my back with a sharp bite. "How'd you survive something like that?"

"I was a test subject in a clandestine government experiment that made me invincible."

The tattoo machine went quiet again. The radio switched from hard rock to pop and the front desk girl sang along with the lyrics.

Tony still said nothing.

I glanced at him over my shoulder and put on my liar's smile. "I'm totally kidding, Tony. Do I look like someone the government would turn into a science experiment? I mean, with this sweet, innocent face?"

He exhaled with a shaky laugh. "Dude, I was going to say."

I chuckled with him. If only he knew.

The truth was, I really *had* been a volunteer test subject for a program that had made me invincible. The organization behind the program was known as the Branch, and they'd pumped me full of something they'd named the Angel Serum. I had, in fact, died when I'd been shot in the head.

But I came back.

Which was why I'd decided to get the tattoo Tony was currently finishing up.

Fifteen minutes later, he said, "All right, Chloe. All done. Wanna take a look?"

He cleaned off the excess ink, my skin still burning and tender from the needlework. When he was done, he hurried over to his floor-to-ceiling mirror and crossed his arms, waiting excitedly. I held the flimsy sheet to my naked front as I turned my back to my reflection.

The tattoo started at the nape of my neck and ran down the length of my spine, all the way to the small of my back. In swirling, vibrant reds, yellows, and oranges, the phoenix was a symbol of my own resurrection, rising from an inferno of embers and ash.

"It's beautiful," I breathed, and twisted left, then right, to get a good look at every angle. "Thank you, Tony."

He smiled, big and dopey. "You had the vision."

That I did.

Seven years ago, my family and I had been on our way to see a movie when a semitruck lost control on the icy roads and sent our car through a guardrail, plummeting us into the frigid East River.

The only reason I made it out of the car was because my brother sawed through my seat belt with a pocketknife, then smashed his feet through my window.

That was the last time I saw him. He'd managed to cut through half his seat belt, and the police suspected it was the river current that finally freed him, sending his body so far down the river that he disappeared into Lake Michigan. His body wasn't recovered with my mom's and dad's.

Emerging from the frigid water was my first resurrection. I'd had many more since then.

After Tony taped up his work with plastic and skin tape, I paid the last of what I owed, promising to return once the tattoo had healed so everyone could see how it looked. I'd never been good at keeping promises, though, so I considered my good-bye a final farewell. Chances were, I'd be leaving town soon anyway.

I went straight home to the apartment I'd rented above a bookstore in this small Ohio town. It was a studio with boring beige walls and rough oak flooring. I'd only been there a little over a month, and tonight I planned on packing what few possessions I had so I could leave first thing in the morning.

Every day I felt like I was getting closer to my goal: tracking down Tom Riley and killing him.

Back when I first volunteered to work with the Branch, Riley had been second-in-command of the program that had changed me. A man named Connor had been the program leader, but he'd been killed less than a year ago. Killed in action. So if I was going to get revenge, it had to be on Riley. He was always the bigger asshole anyway. All things considered, I'd actually liked Connor.

Last time I'd seen Riley with my own eyes, he'd been in Trademarr, Illinois, the headquarters of my Branch program. I'd elaborately planned my revenge, but the people involved—Nick, Elizabeth, a few others—royally screwed it up and Riley got away.

I was trying not to get my hands dirty, but you know what they say: "If you want something done right, don't send a bunch of idiots to do it for you."

So here I was, getting shit done.

I'd tracked Riley here, to northwestern Ohio, where he and a few of his remaining men had acquired a new SUV from someone government affiliated. I didn't so much care about the government contacts as I did the Branch agents. The government people were the financiers, the fringe interest group, and not directly involved with turning people into bio-weapons.

I needed to take the Branch down first. I would worry about the government entanglements later.

From Ohio, it seemed Riley had headed south, to Virginia, and I suspected he'd gone there to be closer to his government contacts.

I'd also found out that some members of the Turncoats—an opposition group founded by ex-Branch employees—were tracking Riley, too. Which meant if I wanted to dish Riley a plate of sweet, hot revenge, I had to get to him first.

The next morning, I showered, grabbed my bag, and headed out for Virginia. I managed to make the trip in just over eight hours. It would have been less had I not had to stop every hundred miles to give my freshly tattooed back a break. While I was technically invincible, and therefore nearly impossible to kill, I still needed time to heal. Thankfully, it didn't take as long for me as it did for normal people.

When I turned off the freeway and headed into the city, I passed a wood sign on the side of the road that said ROCKWELL in big golden letters. The bottom of the sign proudly proclaimed NUTCRACKER CAPITAL OF THE WORLD.

I wasn't sure if that was something worth bragging over. I'd Googled the place this morning, while I had breakfast in a little roadside diner, and found out that a famous jazz musician from the '20s had been born here, too. It was rumored he'd sold his soul to the devil in exchange for his talent. Now that was something I'd carve a sign for.

ROCKWELL: THE DEVIL WAS HERE.

The outskirts of Rockwell were residential, with coffee shops, drugstores and gift shops threaded throughout. Cookie-cutter suburbia always gave me hives, so I headed straight toward downtown using my phone's GPS to navigate.

As the cookie-cutter houses faded away, and the turn-of-the-century buildings took over, I started to feel a little more relaxed. The streets were narrow and stained with a hundred years' worth of dirt. The buildings were built with brick—red and white and rusty-red—and fronted by wrought-iron balconies that reminded me of intricate henna tattoos.

I liked this place more already.

Since I'd left for Rockwell in a hurry, I didn't have an apartment lined up. I stopped at the first hotel I could find. Its sign hung from the roof like an icicle trimmed in neon lighting.

I parked out front along the curb and grabbed my bag. The warmer southern weather breathed a sigh down my neck. I'd never been a fan of the Illinois autumn and winter, and I silently thanked Riley for coming this way.

Maybe once I'd put a bullet in him, I'd do some sunbathing. I could use a little bit of a tan.

Inside the hotel, I gave the desk clerk my fake driver's license—Phoebe McDonald was my new, temporary name—and the credit card I'd acquired with it.

"All set," the clerk said a few minutes later, and handed me a room key. "You're paid up through the week. Let me know if there's anything else we can help with."

"Sure thing," I said.

Once settled in my room, I dropped onto the bed, on my stomach, and pulled in a deep, settling breath. The bedding smelled like bleach and lavender, but it was thick and clean and that's really all that mattered.

I always plotted murder better on good sheets.

After tending to my still-sore tattoo, I went out in search of food. Less than a mile from my hotel, I found a pizza place that hadn't yet filled with dinnertime customers.

Inside, I took a booth along the south wall that afforded me a view of the front door and the street I'd just come in from. My server came over a few minutes later. I couldn't help but watch him navigate the dining room with a quickness and grace that seemed at odds with his tall, muscular frame.

He smiled when he reached me, and I smiled back, glad to have him instead of the harried middle-aged waitress who clearly thought her customers were there to annoy her rather than help pay her wages.

I'd been a server at a restaurant in Trademarr before I'd ditched town. I knew how stressful the job was, but rule number one was, you didn't take it out on your customers. Unless they deserved it, of course.

My friend Elizabeth, who'd been a server with me, had had a hard time knowing when to be a dick. She was almost annoyingly kind.

"Evening," the waiter said. "Can I get you anything to drink to start with?"

"Whatever you have that has the most caffeine."

"Long night?" he asked. "Or early morning?"

I looked up at him through my lashes, and let my mouth spread into a crooked grin. "Every night is a long night." I was, of course, referring to the fact that I usually only slept four hours a night. But he didn't have to know that.

"I see. Well, we have some kind of energy drink here. Not sure what the brand is, and it probably tastes like shit, but the caffeine content is practically illegal."

"I'll have that, then."

He nodded. "I'll be right back."

"Hey?" I called, and he twisted half-around. "What's your name?"

"What's yours?"

"Phoebe."

"You don't look like a Phoebe."

No shit.

"Family name," I explained.

"Uh-huh."

I frowned. "You don't believe me?"

"Never said that."

"So?" I nodded at him. "Your turn."

"You'll have to work harder than that, *Phoebe*." He started off and then said, his back to me, "Don't go anywhere."

I definitely liked this guy. Maybe I'd invite him to my hotel room after his shift. No one ever said you couldn't have fun *and* plot murder.

As I waited for my drink, an older couple dropped a few coins in the jukebox and Elvis Presley crooned from the speakers a second later. In the far corner, two kids animatedly played a game of foosball. From the kitchen, a cook called out an order and the harried waitress scurried to retrieve it.

My waiter returned. He set the drink down on the table.

"What time do you get off?" I asked.

He glanced at the clock over his shoulder. "Well, now, actually. You're my last table."

"What do you say we go back to my hotel for a drink?"

He frowned. "You haven't even ordered food yet."

"Then we'll order in."

A smile spread across his face. He was considering it. Of course he was considering it. It wasn't like I was ugly.

"All right," he finally answered. "A drink sounds nice."

So I paid for the energy drink that I hadn't touched and followed mystery boy out the door.

Back in my hotel room, I mixed two drinks and gave mystery boy the one with more alcohol. Mine probably wouldn't even be considered alcoholic, since I'd gone light on the rum. I wanted this guy to loosen up, but since I was technically on a mission, I needed to keep a clearer head.

"So," I started as I handed him the glass. "When are you going to tell me your name?"

He took a sip of the drink and winced. "Are you trying to get me drunk, Phoebe?"

I gave him an innocent grin. "Not at all."

He set the glass on the dresser and came over to me, fetching my own glass. That, too, went on the dresser. "We didn't really come back here to drink, did we?" he said.

God, this guy was smooth. I wondered how many times he'd hooked up with random girls from the restaurant. I had a flash of myself getting Nick drunk in a club back in Trademarr, and following him back to his hotel. The hookup hadn't really gone as planned, what with his violent, sudden flashback, but I probably would have gone through with it, all things considered.

Nick was hot. Can you blame a girl?

Mystery guy ran his fingers back through my hair, his short nails grazing my scalp. I suppressed a shiver.

"What do you think we came back here for, then?" I asked, trying to sound coy. Instead I sounded sleepy and somehow hungry.

His grip on me tightened, and he brought his mouth down on mine, and I thought, well, at least he's hungry, too.

We ended up on the bed within seconds. My lips parted beneath his, and a tingle went down my entire body. All of the Branch shit melted away, and there was only the press of our bodies against each other, and the feeling in my limbs like I was on the edge of a never-ending tremor.

Mystery guy's hand came down to the hem of my shirt and his fingers slipped beneath it. His mouth pulled away from mine and trailed along my jaw, then my neck and lower, following the deep V-neck of my shirt.

I reached down, grabbed his shirt, and pulled it off in one quick motion. He had the kind of body I knew he'd have—muscled, corded, and tight. I couldn't help but run my hands over his abs.

My shirt came off next and, impatiently, I fumbled with his belt. He smiled down at me.

"You still don't know my name," he said, voice husky and teasing.

"I don't need to know your name," I said. What I wanted was to know every inch of his body.

When I woke late the next morning, still naked beneath the sheets, mystery guy was gone. He'd left nothing behind to prove that he'd been there at all. Well, except for that near-constant shivery feeling in my gut and the silly smile that looked back at me in the mirror.

Sometimes a girl just needs to blow off some steam.

I took a shower and dressed. I felt more rested than I had in a long time. Surprisingly, I'd slept more than my usual four hours.

After a cup of black coffee, I walked over to the pizza place where I'd met mystery guy intending to thank him for last night, and to figure out his identity.

He'd made finding out his name a challenge, and I intended to win.

Inside the restaurant, the dining room wasn't as packed as it had been last night. Of course, the lunch hour hadn't struck yet. I found the harried waitress from last night filling shakers of Parmesan cheese.

"Hi," I said.

"You can take any table you want, darling," she said without looking at me.

"Thanks, but I'm actually here for a friend. He works here. Worked a shift last night? Tall, blond, eighteen or nineteen, maybe. Super-hot."

She side-eyed me with a frown. "Kitchen staff or waitstaff?"

"Waitstaff."

She shook her head. "There's only me and two other girls on the waitstaff." With a grumble she added, "We're extremely short handed right now."

"Okay, so maybe he's kitchen staff but helped out waiting tables last night?"

"No one here by that description, actually."

"Excuse me?"

She set the canister of cheese on the counter and turned on the bar stool to face me. "There is no one here by that description," she said slowly.

Anger, and a growing sense of panic, ran through me. "Then why did you ask whether he was waitstaff or kitchen staff? You could have just said no from the beginning instead of wasting my fucking time."

She scowled and went back to her work. "I need to quit this godforsaken place."

I took two steps away from her, disoriented and unsure. What now? I found myself heading toward the back door, out into the late-morning sunshine.

A sliver of annoyance burrowed into my side. Mystery guy had played me, and I prided myself on being unplayable. And I couldn't help but wonder, was he Branch affiliated?

I'd been counting on the element of surprise in my attack on Riley. If the guy was Branch, then they already knew I was here.

I started walking, hyperaware of my surroundings, but with no destination in mind. I just needed to clear my head, think through every conversation I'd had with the mystery guy and see if I could glean any clues.

I slipped around a small crowd of hipsters on the sidewalk, then dodged a mom pushing a stroller. Near a line of newspaper boxes, I wedged myself between the last one and a lamppost, to pause and get my bearings.

I needed to identify whether there was any sign of the Branch nearby. If you knew the signs, you could spot their presence easily enough.

They liked their black Suburbans, and usually several of them in a procession. But that was the easiest evidence to spot, and I didn't think Riley would be stupid enough to follow such a pattern when he needed to keep a low profile.

I studied the faces of the passing pedestrians. Typical Branch agents either wore business suits or black tactical gear. The latter would be too conspicuous in a place like this, so that was definitely out.

Clover Hill was the site of some long-ago battle and there were hotels and B&Bs all over that claimed one historically significant attraction or another. A lot of the pedestrians had the marks of tourists—sun visors, baseball hats, khaki shorts, shopping bags from tourist traps. Most traveled in packs, or at least in twos and threes.

A guy across the street, baseball hat tugged down low, shopping bag hanging from his left hand, caught my attention. He was alone, for one, and there was a cell phone glued to his ear, held in place by a shrugged shoulder. Except he wasn't speaking to whoever was on the other end, only listening, and he wasn't using his free hand like someone usually would when using their shoulder to hold their phone in place, which gave me the impression he was trying to keep both hands free.

As a truck rumbled past, I crossed the street and fell in behind a group of rowdy tourists. Ten feet from cell-phone guy, I straightened my back, keeping my weight well distributed between both feet. That way I could move quickly if I had to.

But just as I was about to pounce on him, consequences be damned, someone grabbed my wrist, whirled me around, and shoved me into an alley. I brought my elbow up, intending to clock the attacker on the jaw, but my tall adversary caught it with his open palm, deftly swatting me away.

I jackknifed a knee to his groin, but he blocked that, too, one second before he slammed me into the brick wall of the alley. All my breath rushed out of me, emptying my lungs and I gulped to get it back.

It took me too long to reorient myself, giving him the opportunity to establish an inescapable hold on me. He leaned his weight in to me and pinned my wrists between us.

I could probably escape, but it'd take a lot of energy to fight his strength, and I wanted to preserve what I had until I absolutely needed it.

The guy shifted, chuckling.

It was mystery guy.

"You son of a bitch!" I said. "Who are you?"

"Calm down, Chloe."

He knew my real name. *He knew my real name.*

"What do you want?" I bit out, silently castigating myself for the sharp tone of my voice. Anything other than cool and even would give away an emotion I didn't want him reading.

"I was wondering if you could point me in the direction of Harbor Drive."

"You know, they have tourist maps for that." I tested his hold on my arms and his grip tightened.

He chuckled. "When they told me you were fearless, I didn't believe them." He shifted as I wiggled beneath him, and pressed a bony hip into my stomach. "But wouldn't you know, your heart rate isn't even escalated."

I realized his thumb was pressed against the underside of my wrist.

"Who are *'they'*, exactly?" I asked, although I had a pretty good idea. "And who are you?"

There were only a few people in the world who knew what I really was, who knew it was possible to be truly, biologically, psychologically, fearless. It was a side effect of the Angel Serum the Branch had given me. Fear had left me a long time ago, about the third time the Branch killed me just to see if I'd rise from the dead.

The absence of fear was a side effect the Branch hadn't counted on, but it was one I embraced. Fear made people weak. It made them doubt their gut instincts, cower from those stronger than them, and avoid doing what needed to be done.

A lot of the people I'd met in the last few years thought of me as a cold-hearted bitch. I liked to think it was because I was capable of doing and saying the things they couldn't. But my fearlessness also affected other emotions. For instance, it was hard to feel guilt when you didn't fear the consequences of your actions.

So yeah, maybe I was a cold-hearted bitch. But it wasn't my fault. And the list of people who knew why was short.

1. The Branch: I could deal with the Branch, and with Riley, because after all my time with them I knew how they thought. *Know thy enemy*, and all that garbage.
2. Nick and Elizabeth, and their little kumbaya group: Nick had been a Branch test subject for a different program, as had the rest of his ragtag group. Elizabeth had been the origin test subject for the Angel Serum. It was her blood that was used to create it.
3. The Turncoats: They were the wild card. I didn't know them, and I didn't know their leader, which meant I couldn't predict their movements. It was like playing chess blind.

The Coats and I did have the same goals—kill Riley and destroy the Branch.

But while I obviously supported the mission, I wasn't into team sports.

The question was, which group did this guy belong to? I felt fairly certain I could eliminate group number two from the list. It didn't seem like he and Nick would get along. Call it a hunch.

"Who are you with?" I asked. "Branch or Turncoats?"

"Do I look like Branch to you?"

"You move like them."

"That's because I've trained. But I have a proposition for you," he went on, and leaned in closer. His breath spidered down my neck.

"I have a predisposition to rejecting propositions," I said before he could continue.

"Join the Coats."

So there was my answer. He was with the group behind door number three.

"Why? What do I get out of it? Besides dead."

It was a trick question, and part of me wanted him to get the right answer. I wasn't sure why.

"Come on," he said, and canted his head. His mouth wasn't smirking, but his eyes were. He'd given me the same look last night, like he knew a secret. If only I'd read between the lines then.

"You and I both know dying isn't really your thing, Chloe."

Vague answer, but answer enough. He knew I couldn't be easily killed.

"Yeah, but it hurts like hell," I said.

"We know how to reverse it."

My breath stopped short, and I froze.

I'd died twenty-six times, in twenty-six different ways. And I always came back. I was beginning to wonder if I had the ability to survive a bomb, or a beheading. If the apocalypse came, I was in for a long, solitary life. Sometimes, when I let myself really think about it, about my immunity to death, my ability to quickly heal, I felt achingly, irritatingly, alone. I'd long ago learned to be self-reliant, but there was something about touching another human being, the nearness of skin, even if only sexually. It made me feel alive in a way I hadn't felt in a long time—long before the Branch and the Angel Serum.

I would never admit it, but deep down, I was afraid of being alone. I'd been by myself for too long, and being invincible seemed to stretch the aloneness out for an eternity.

It left me empty inside. Not just fearless, but vacant of that thing that made someone human.

I'd never given much thought to being cured of the effects of the Angel Serum, because I didn't think I could be. But if it were possible, would I feel whole again? Would I suddenly start caring?

Deep down inside, I worried that the fearlessness was an excuse: Maybe I was just a bitch. A product of my environment and my history and the absence of anything even remotely close to family.

Maybe the cure would do nothing other than make me vulnerable.

Of course, it was possible he was lying just to hook me.

"Say I believe you, then what?" I asked. "What would I have to do?"

He grinned and eased off, giving me some breathing room. I could knee him between the legs now and escape if I wanted to.

"Help us kill Riley."

He released his grip and straightened. The sunlight caught his face, highlighting his cheekbones and perfect nose. I watched him lick his lips and wondered if he'd done it on purpose, trying to draw my attention to his mouth, reminding me of last night.

"Maybe I don't want to be cured," I countered. "And I can kill Riley on my own."

"That's not all I have to offer."

"I'm listening."

I couldn't think of anything else he'd have that I'd want. I'd never been big on material possessions anyway. I wasn't sentimental, and I needed to be able to grab my things and bolt as quickly as I could, at any given moment.

"You can find us at the warehouse on the corner of 7th and Hart," he said, ignoring my question. "You might find what you've been searching a long time for, *Emily.*"

Emily was my real name, my first name, and I cringed whenever I heard it. I usually went by Chloe, my middle name.

I scowled at him and he laughed.

I hated that he knew I hated being called Emily. I hated that he knew more about me than I did about him, which was virtually nothing.

"If I come," I said, as he turned away, "who do I say sent me?"

"Ask for the Rook."

He rounded the corner onto the street. I jogged out of the alley and looked left, the way he'd turned, but he was already gone.

Despite the soft, clean sheets of my hotel room bed, I didn't sleep well that night. I was too keyed up, too anxious about the mystery guy—or the Rook—and Riley, and the decision I had to make.

After waking for the third time in less than two hours, I realized it was pointless to try to sleep. I crawled from bed and made a cup of coffee on the one-cup maker on the desk. It was weak, but it'd do.

I flicked on a desk lamp and dug inside my bag for the journal I'd kept over the last few years. I'd been involved with the Branch long enough to know that memories aren't always reliable, and not always permanent. They'd experimented with the art of erasing memories over six years ago, and had even developed a way to implant fake ones in the void. By now, they were probably certifiable pros at it.

Just in case they ever got to me, I liked to document what I thought was important at the end of each day.

I flipped toward the back of the journal, looking for a blank page, but the book opened on a picture I'd taped in. It was of Elizabeth and me, taken at Merv's Bar & Grill, where we'd worked together as servers.

In it, she was smiling, genuinely happy. It was such a rarity to see her like that, I'd stolen the picture from the mirror behind the bar and added it to my journal before I left town. I might not be sentimental, but I could appreciate the beauty of a moment like that.

Elizabeth's mother, Dr. Turrow, had been the lead doctor on the project dedicated to developing the Angel Serum. She'd used Elizabeth's altered genetic makeup to create the serum.

The whole thing was beyond fucked up. If my own mother had done something like that to me, I would have killed her a long time ago.

I flipped to the beginning of the book, to the second page, where I'd glued in a picture of my family. My mother, my father, and my older brother, Lukas.

We were never perfect, but we were happy.

I'd gotten more of my father's looks. His dark brown hair, his blue eyes pinched in a feline point. My brother had gotten more of our mother. Black hair, and gold-flecked brown eyes.

After the funeral, I'd started seeing a therapist regularly. It was recommended I talk to someone about the trauma in my past, to get it all out. I didn't know it then, but my therapist happened to be on the Branch payroll. She was screening her clients looking for someone for a new program. They'd wanted an orphan who was so dead inside that killing her repeatedly wouldn't affect her overall state of mind.

My brother had been my best friend. Losing him had felt like losing all of myself. I'd definitely been a fit for what the Branch was looking for.

Sometimes I wondered if I still had Lukas, if I'd be who I was today, if any of this would have happened. My brother had kept me grounded, and he'd always looked out for me. He never would have let me get involved with the Branch. Of course, if he'd been alive, I wouldn't have been what the Branch needed in the first place.

I tried to imagine what he'd tell me to do now. He'd probably tell me to work with the Coats, because they were the good guys. He'd tell me that the cure would bring me closer to the girl I used to be, and that that was more important than revenge.

I guess my dead brother was now my conscience.

At the very least, I decided, I could hear what the Coats had to say, and what else they had to offer me. The Rook hadn't given me a time to show up at the warehouse, so I left the hotel just after six AM. It'd give me enough time to grab a proper cup of coffee and to stake out the warehouse for a while before going in.

The corner of 7th and Hart Street was in the business district, three miles from my current location. A lot of the surrounding buildings had been converted either to boutique hotels, or apartment buildings. The place belonging to the Coats was still under construction, and metal scaffolding covered most of the front.

Across the street was the Revived Arts Hotel, so I paid for a room that afforded me a clear view of the warehouse, both its roof and its front door. Since I was technically paying with a stolen credit card, I didn't mind the extra expense, considering I'd only use the place for a few hours. It'd be worth it in the long run.

In my room, I pulled a cushy gray leather chair up to the windows, made sure all the lights were off, and grabbed my trusty binoculars. I kicked my feet up and began the stakeout, shoveling crackers in my mouth as I scanned the warehouse.

For the first hour, there was zero movement outside the building, or within. I'd thought perhaps I'd see the Rook holding up a welcome sign somewhere.

What kind of code name was that anyway? I wondered. And was he the chess piece, the bird, or the swindler? I hoped he was the chess piece. I was pretty good at playing games.

Traffic picked up over the next hour as people headed out for work.

By 11:00 AM my crackers were gone, and the Coke I'd bought from a vending machine down the hall was lukewarm.

"Screw it," I muttered, and tossed the binoculars in my bag.

Outside the hotel, I slid big, dark sunglasses over my eyes, let my long hair fall forward over my face, and crossed the street. Music played from the Mexican restaurant just around the corner. Traffic was comprised mostly of yellow taxicabs and small sports cars.

I entered the warehouse using a side door that was partially obstructed by scaffolding and loose plastic sheeting. The plastic gusted in the breeze.

The door creaked when I opened it, and inwardly I winced. I'd expected to come in on a stairwell, or maybe some faraway hallway, so I could sneak in unannounced, but the ground floor of the warehouse was one wide-open space, with only support columns to break it up. The lighting was murky, and green-cast from the plastic covering the windows. The whole place had an underwater feel.

My footsteps echoed as I walked. It was the only sound in the entire place.

I was beginning to wonder if this had been some kind of joke when a figure silently stepped away from a support column twenty yards to my left. The man was at least ten years older than me, and two hundred pounds heavier. He had the stocky, bald-headed look of a bouncer. Despite the warmer weather, he wore a black leather jacket. Perhaps to hide the gun at his hip.

The guy held up his hands. "I'm unarmed."

"Except for the gun at your side?"

"I meant I'm not immediately armed."

"Semantics," I said.

"Are you Chloe?"

"Presently." I grinned. "I was told to ask for the Rook?"

"This way." The guy hitched a thumb over his shoulder, indicating the stairwell in the far corner.

I'd purposefully left my bag in my stakeout hotel room, but I'd made sure to bring weapons. There was a gun at my back and a knife in each boot. I'd also clipped a few barrettes into my hair that could double as picks. I hadn't ever had to use them—I preferred the efficiency of a gun—but it was always good to have backup.

Big guy went up the stairs first. I'd expected him to be winded after the first flight, but he kept a quick pace.

"So what's your name?" I asked.

"Sasha," he said.

"Are you the Rook's bodyguard?"

"No. I'm his hairdresser."

His back was to me and I couldn't see his face, but the even tone of his voice made me pause. I couldn't tell if he was joking or not. "You think when we're done here, you could touch up my roots?"

His massive shoulders shook when he laughed. "I could probably fit you in."

We went up three flights of stairs before Sasha finally led me out of the stairwell. The fourth floor's renovation was complete, so all I could see was the hallway that stretched before us. Sasha started down it.

"So what's the Rook's real name?" I asked.

Sasha shrugged. "Can't tell you. I don't even know his real name."

"Are you serious?"

"As serious as burnt popcorn."

"Oh, Sasha, I like you."

He shot me another wolfish grin before stopping at a set of double doors. He grabbed both handles and turned, pushing the doors in with a rather exaggerated spread of his arms, as if he were revealing the inner sanctum of some important holy figure.

When I stepped around him to get a better look at the room, I realized it wasn't an office so much as a penthouse suite. Two walls were constructed entirely of glass, giving the space a fishbowl feel.

In the corner opposite the door was an L-shaped couch, upholstered in caramel-colored leather. A massive glass coffee table sat in the center, a stack of books perched on the edge.

Sasha led me in farther, and the suite opened up to a state-of-the-art kitchen. In the kitchen stood the Rook.

"Hey," he said, and smiled at me. There was a beer in his hand. "Want something to drink?"

"Sure. A Coke will do, if you have one."

He nodded. To Sasha he said, "Alert the others. We'll be ready in an hour."

Sasha saluted the Rook and left, closing the doors behind him.

"You came," the Rook said. He turned away from me and dug inside the fridge.

"I was curious. You said you had something more for me and I couldn't help myself. Apparently you know the way to my cold, undying heart."

He straightened and closed the fridge behind him with the sole of his boot. He came over and handed me a can of soda.

"Thanks." I popped the tab. "So tell me what else you have to offer."

He took a swig of his beer, still eyeing me. Although he wore a simple white T-shirt and jeans, he somehow managed to look incredibly hot. He tapped a finger against the beer bottle, the silver ring on his middle finger clinking against the glass.

“Right,” he said. “Straight to business, then?”

“Always.”

“It’s better if I show you.”

“Then do.”

“You’re not going to like it.”

“If this is your selling strategy, it isn’t a very good one.”

He shifted just an inch or two, catching a slant of sunlight. It turned his green eyes so pale, they almost looked white. “One thing you should know about me,” he said, “is that I prefer honesty above all else.”

“Show me,” I said again, letting the smile drop from my face.

“This way.” He led me into an office at the back of the suite.

He set his beer down on a console table and went to the desk in the center of the room. With his boot, he nudged the chair away and bent over the computer keyboard, typing in a few commands, then clicking a few times.

“All right,” he said, and stepped away from the monitor. “Come see.”

I wasn’t sure what I expected to find when I made my way around the desk. Maybe logs from the old Angel Serum program, something we could use against Riley as leverage. Maybe photos or something that could incriminate the Branch.

Instead, I saw a video playing, the volume down low. I recognized the voice a split second before the image came into full view, and something close to fear ran down my spine.

There, on the monitor, staring back at me, was my brother. And just behind him, arms crossed over his chest, was Riley.

"What the hell is this?" I breathed, anger turning my voice gravelly.

"They took him after the car crash that killed your parents," the Rook said. "They found him in the river and pulled him out."

I whirled on him. "Who took him?"

"The Branch."

"How is that even possible? How did they know—?"

"Where to find him? Your dad was ex-Branch. He helped create the Turncoats. The car accident wasn't an accident, Chloe."

My hands tightened into fists at my sides. "This is a ruse. It's been Photoshopped or—"

He shook his head.

"How did you get this?"

"I have a good source within the Branch. They've been supplying me with info, particularly on your brother and Riley, for a few months now."

I turned back to the monitor and nudged the volume higher. My brother was describing the symptoms he was experiencing. Headaches, insomnia, muscle aches. The person asking the questions, behind the camera, was Connor.

He knew. The whole time, Connor knew my brother was alive and he never told me.

"Where is he now?" I asked.

"Still within the Branch. He's—"

"I have to get him out. I've gotten people out before."

"Chloe—"

I started for the door.

"Chloe, you have to listen to me. Your brother is not the same person you knew before the car crash. He's been with the Branch so long that he's—"

I twisted around again and the Rook nearly slammed into me. "He's what?"

"He's pretty high up."

"How high?"

"Second-in-command now that Connor's gone and Riley took his place at the top."

I frowned, rage and desperation building inside me. "How does something like that happen? I know my brother, and he would never work for a smarmy asshole like Riley."

"No," the Rook said. "You *knew* your brother. His memories have likely been altered. He probably doesn't even know himself anymore, let alone you."

"I don't care." I surged forward again. "I'll do whatever it takes to get him out."

I left the penthouse and the Rook followed me into the hall.

"Chloe, listen to me."

"I don't need your help."

"I know where Riley will be."

"I can find him on my own."

Before I could reach the stairwell, the Rook grabbed my wrist and spun me around. I yanked my arm back, reaching for my gun.

"Too slow," the Rook said, my gun in his hands.

How the hell did he lift my gun without my noticing?

He dropped out the magazine, letting it hit the floor with a *clack*. He emptied out the chambered round, too.

"You are really starting to piss me off, you know that?" I took a step toward him. "You don't need me on your mission. Clearly you're capable enough, so why the hell are you even bothering with any of this?"

"I do need you," he said. "And you need me."

"Maybe you don't know this, but a personal vendetta isn't very personal when you work with a group."

"I can get you your brother back by dinnertime."

I paused, waiting for the rush of blood in my ears to subside. As good as I was at tracking, even I couldn't find Riley that fast. It'd take me a few days, at least, and now that I knew my brother was alive, I wanted him back, and I wanted him back right now.

I set my hands on my hips. "What the hell can I do that you can't?"

He smiled, obviously pleased with the slight uptick of interest in my voice. I silently cursed myself for letting on.

"You can get inside," he answered. "You're the one person who Riley will want to see with his own eyes. He'll want to watch you die."

"Problem number one: I don't actually want to die."

"It won't get that far."

"Go on."

"The plan is to get you close enough to gas them all. Then we'll come in."

"They're going to be suspicious when I waltz in with gas canisters."

The Rook smirked. "Do you really think so little of my strategizing?"

I shrugged.

"I have a plan," he reassured me. "Are you game?"

There was really only one answer to that question. "Get me inside with the gas and I'll be game for just about anything."

The smile on his face shone all the way to his eyes. Apparently plotting murder and revenge put him in a good mood. I could relate.

"Come on," he said, and strode away. "Let me introduce you to the team."

The team was a large group of Turncoats, thirteen including the Rook. Sasha the hairdresser, I learned, was actually the Rook's tech guy and would be facilitating the mission from a surveillance van two miles away.

The Rook's inside source had said Riley and his team would be meeting a few business contacts at a house just outside the city. By the time we'd arrived and settled into our places, the sun was starting to set, sending a diffused, pale blue glow across the landscape.

The house where Riley was holding his meeting was, thankfully, far removed from its neighbors, with at least twenty acres of land on all sides. The Rook's team had spread out upon arrival, waiting for the signal.

After the Rook and I left Sasha in his van, we ran the few miles to our entry point—a small grove of trees to the east. Hidden in some underbrush, we surveyed the property.

There were two Branch agents at the back of the house, and two more at the front. Through a gap in the curtain, I counted four more agents, and the Rook counted an additional three. His source had said there'd be at least eighteen agents present, plus Riley and my brother, Lukas, and three other business associates. That was a lot of people, and Riley was notorious for slipping through the cracks in the middle of a fight.

But he wasn't getting away this time.

"You ready?" the Rook whispered.

I nodded.

"Double-check the setup," he ordered.

I sighed, but drew my thumbs inside my shirtsleeves, feeling for the two buttons sewn to the cuffs. "Check," I said.

"Good." He leaned closer and pressed his lips to my ear. "Any sign of trouble, you get out of there ASAP."

"Copy that," I said through gritted teeth. This was exactly why I hated team sports. The coach always drove me crazy.

"You're a go," Sasha said through my earpiece. "Team is in place."

"Copy that," the Rook said. He put a hand on my shoulder and squeezed. "Be careful. Think clearly."

"You think just because my brother's in there I'll lose focus? Getting to Riley has always been my mission. I won't let it go now."

He smiled and laughed low. "Go get 'em, tiger."

With a grumble, I slipped through the trees, keeping my steps light, silent. Although I meant to be captured, I still had to pretend I'd tried for stealth.

When I broke from the trees, I pulled my gun from the borrowed holster at my side and shot the Branch agent on my right. He dropped where he stood, rustling the bushes as he rolled out of them and to the ground.

I swung around, aiming for the agent to my left. He'd already pulled his gun and had it pointed at me. I went flat on the ground as a bullet whizzed by overhead. I fired another shot, purposefully missing.

The agent barreled toward me and I leapt to my feet, raising the gun to eye level. He clocked me across the jaw with one hand as the other disarmed me.

In less than two seconds, I was lying on the dew-soaked grass, looking up at the darkening sky.

The man peered down at me, my own gun pointed at my face. The man blinked, and his eyebrows drew together as realization set in. He recognized me. We'd hoped for that.

Riley had a lot of enemies, but only a few worthy of concern.

Nick and his group were high on the list, and I suspected I ranked pretty close to the top, too. Which meant most of Riley's men probably knew us—knew me—by face.

A surprised laugh escaped him, painting the darkness with a cloud of glittering breath. "Well, look who it is," he said. With a flick of his wrist, a zip tie appeared and was quickly tightened around my wrists.

I played at wriggling beneath his hold, grunting and cussing as he hoisted me to my feet.

"Riley will be pleased to see you," the man said as he hauled me toward the back door.

And just like that, I was in.

I was dragged in through a massive kitchen, down a hallway, and into a library on the south side of the house. I was confident the Rook and Sasha were tracking my movement through the house and knew exactly where I was.

"Look who I found outside," the agent behind me said as he shoved me to the floor. With my hands tied behind my back, I had nothing to brace my fall and slammed against the Oriental rug shoulder first. Pain jolted through me.

"Get her up," Riley said.

The agent grumbled, but hoisted me back to my feet. Now I had a chance to scan the faces in the room. There were three men in business suits near the wet bar, and three agents holding defensive positions near Riley and his associates.

And four paces to Riley's right was my brother.

I nearly choked on a breath at the sight of his face. Part of me had worried it had been some kind of nightmare, seeing his face beside Riley's on the Rook's computer screen. That I had imagined it. A flash of a memory came rushing back, of my brother shoving me out the car window as the East River swallowed him up, and for the first time in a long time the burning of tears swelled in my eyes.

My brother really was alive.

He'd obviously aged since I'd seen him last, but like a lot of Branch pawns, it hadn't happened at a normal rate. And that realization registered another fact: the Branch had used Lukas in one of their programs. That was the only reason he would have been given the anti-aging alteration.

What else did they do to him? I wondered. Was the Rook right? Was Lukas no longer the brother I knew and loved?

He wore loose black jeans, a white T-shirt, and a quilted black leather jacket. The Lukas I'd known had always been more of a polo-shirts-and-designer-jeans type of guy. He hated leather.

On his face, I was sad to see not a thread of recognition. He was staring right at me as if I were a stranger.

"Gentlemen," Riley said, "allow me to introduce you to one of our runaway test subjects."

The business-suit-clad men appraised me. Riley motioned to an agent for a gun.

"This one here can't die," Riley said, and shot me in the shoulder.

A cry of pain escaped me, and I staggered back, falling to one knee. I sucked in a breath and glanced at my brother. He hadn't even flinched.

"Interesting," one of the men said. "Is that alteration available?"

Riley curled his upper lip. "Unfortunately, no. This one and her friends killed the doctor responsible for the science behind it."

"Pity," another man said. "The things we could do with something like that."

"Can we see her up close?" the third man asked.

"Of course." Riley motioned them forward, and my brother followed.

The men, and the agents in the room, closed in. My brother hung back, but as the men inspected me, I caught his eye over Riley's shoulder.

Over his years with the Branch, he'd grown into his face, the baby fat disappearing to reveal a hard jawline, and hollow cheekbones. His eyes were the same, though, the same as our mother's—caramel colored and fringed in long lashes.

The girls must love him.

"*Now*, Chloe," the Rook said through my earpiece.

My heart leapt in my chest, not from fear, but from heady anticipation and the thrill of getting exactly what I came here to get.

I drew my thumbs inside my shirtsleeves.

I noticed Lukas take a step back as the library plunged into a murky darkness. The power lines had been severed by a member of the Rook's team.

Riley shouted orders.

I hit the buttons sewn into my sleeves and the bitter smell of sleeping gas filled the room as two clouds of white smoke hissed from the thick soles of my boots.

Everyone immediately started coughing.

My vision teetered and the rapid beating of my heart slowed to a dull drum in my head. My body felt sluggish, like it was weighed down with bricks. Moving one foot felt like moving a mountain.

Somehow, though, I stepped through my arms, bringing my tied-off hands in front of me, and swung. The double-fisted punch caught Riley at the temple and he backpedaled, bumping into a coffee table and slamming to the floor.

Somewhere far off, a window shattered.

"Welcome to the party," I said to Riley as I slumped next to him. Everything went black.

The world came back to me in broken sounds. Shouting. Silence. Gunfire. Silence. I took a breath and felt the hot press of it fall back against my face.

There was something heavy and dark covering my head. My eyes took considerable effort just to open.

Gas mask, I realized, and dragged myself to an upright position. The zip ties on my wrists had been cut. Through the cloudy lenses of the gas mask, flashes of light lit the darkened room. People fighting. The spark of gunfire.

I felt along the floor next to me but didn't find Riley.

His absence brought me to my feet.

I teetered, unsteady, for a second, but the world quickly righted itself.

I needed to find a gun. I needed to find Riley.

"I'm up," I said, hoping the Rook heard me. "Riley's gone."

No answer.

I started for the hallway when something hit me from behind. I dropped to the floor again, rolled to my back, and swept a leg out, catching the guy off guard. He fell and I climbed on top of him, landing a punch to his temple. It would have connected better had the guy not been wearing a gas mask, too.

Only Rook's team had gas masks.

The guy hooked his long leg around my midsection and pushed me backward, rolling with the move to give him the dominant position. A knife gleamed in his hand.

I reached up and tore the mask from his face.

"Lukas?" I said. I pulled my own mask off. "Stop! It's me! Chloe. Your sister. Do you remember?"

The knife came down. I blocked him with both my arms, but he was far stronger than me. The blade came uncomfortably close to my neck.

"Lukas, please. Listen to me."

He gritted his teeth. The veins in his forearms bulged with the strain.

"Your name is Lukas Monroe Tacktor. Your parents were Margaret and John. You had a sister once, named Chloe, remember? We lived in a white house on Cherry Hill Drive and we always fought over the bathroom every morning and you hated the smell of my hair spray and the sound of my laugh but you loved my grilled cheeses."

Tears blurred my vision. I blinked, felt the trace of wetness down into my hairline.

"Lukas."

The point of the knife grazed my skin.

"Lukas!"

The strain in his face faded, replaced by a deep-rooted frown and an expelled breath. He pulled away and tossed the knife to the side.

"You're... my sister?" he said right before the Rook appeared out of the murky darkness and whacked my brother on the back of the head.

Lukas slumped over, his eyelids fluttering closed.

"Why did you do that?" I shouted.

The Rook knelt beside my brother and secured his hands behind his back. "We have Riley," he said, his mouth twisted into a smile so wide, I worried it'd eat his face. "We have what we came for, Chloe. Time to move out."

Two more men appeared out of the haze and hoisted my brother up between them.

The Rook offered me his hand. "Come on. Time to get your brother back."

I took his hand and let him lead me out the door.

The Rook and his team retreated to the warehouse. It was well after midnight when we arrived, and the streets were dead. Riley and what remained of his team were locked inside windowless rooms on the second floor of the warehouse. My brother was among them.

"I don't understand why he has to be locked away," I said to the Rook as we watched my brother through a two-way mirror in the door. Overhead, the lighting was dim, while my brother's room was brightly lit to allow us to remain unseen on our side. It gave the hallway a hushed feel.

"Because we don't know how much he remembers, or who he's loyal to. This is just a precaution until we can clear his head."

I shifted my weight from one foot to the other. My entire body was one massive ache inside another massive ache, but I was anxious to do something other than stand here.

"Something dislodged inside his head," I said. "He could have killed me. He didn't. And I think he remembers that I'm his sister."

The Rook frowned and crossed his arms over his chest. All things considered, he'd escaped the mission pretty much unscathed. There was a fresh cut, a crescent swipe of the blade, across his forehead, and blood from the wound had dried along the side of his face. A few bruises were blooming along his jaw, and on his knuckles.

At least he hadn't been shot. Thankfully, my bullet wound was already healing.

"Just give him the night, okay?" the Rook said. "Let him rest. Let me talk to him first. And then, tomorrow, you can start poking at him."

"I hate it when people give me orders."

He laughed and ran a hand through my hair, messing it up. "I know you do. It's why I do it."

With an exaggerated salute, he disappeared from the hall. I walked three doors down and peered into the two-way mirror of another cell.

Riley sat on a bed, his elbows propped on his knees, his hands folded on the back of his bowed head.

Riley had been captured. Damn, it was a good feeling.

The Rook hadn't said what would happen to Riley, but I hoped someone somewhere along the line would put a bullet in him.

My stomach grumbled, forcing me to give up my post outside my brother's room for an hour or so. I found pizza, beer, and a cake in a conference room. Pounding rock music vibrated through me.

I guess if there was anything worth celebrating, this was definitely it.

I grabbed a piece of pizza and parked myself in front of the floor-to-ceiling windows as the rest of the Rook's team reveled behind me. Outside, the city glittered in winks of light. The moon hung half full in the sky.

As the party raged on, I watched the Rook's team down beer after beer, pizza slice after pizza slice, and wished I could join in the fun. Usually, I was the consummate party girl, but how could I party now, when my brother had risen from the dead only to have any memory of his family wiped clean from his skull?

After my second slice, and a lot of stewing in my own frustrated juices, I grabbed a third slice and a beer and slipped from the party.

I headed back to where my brother was being kept, intent on spending as much time with him as I could. I'd make him remember, goddamn it.

But as I rounded the corner into the hallway and saw the three guards lying facedown on the floor, a cold sweep of dread ran down my spine.

I tossed the pizza and the can of beer aside and raced to Riley's cell. He lay on his bed, staring at the ceiling, the door still locked from the outside.

I heaved a relieved breath.

If it hadn't been Riley…

A thousand thoughts raced through my head as I ran for my

brother's room. But if my brother was loyal to Riley, why would he escape without him? And if my brother had started to remember me, why escape at all?

At his door, I peered inside to find the place empty. I yanked the door open and stepped in, my boots crunching on something metal. I bent down and found two twisted paper clips.

"Lukas, you son of a bitch."

When I straightened, I noticed a folded piece of paper on the table beside the bed. I snatched it up. Inside was a note. For me.

> Chloe,
> Remember that night when Mom + Dad got into a fight over whether you should take ballet or martial arts? Mom + Dad's fights were always profoundly epic, but that night, it was about you and you felt so bad. Where did I take you that night, Chlo? Do you remember?
>
> —L

I did remember. The question was, how did he?

The Rook would probably kill me when he found out I'd left the warehouse without alerting him to my brother's escape, or to the three unconscious men lying facedown in the hallway, but I'd take my chances.

The night my mother and father fought, Lukas had taken me downtown to the carousel in the city square, and from that night on, whenever I was upset over something, it didn't matter where we were, he'd find me a carousel.

It was a memory that I had swept under the bed, and tried so hard to forget. When my brother died, I swore I'd never visit another carousel in my entire life.

Now I drove through the darkened city streets as fast as I could go. It took only fifteen minutes to reach Louis Miller Park. It wasn't where Lukas had taken me that night, when our parents fought, but Google told me it was the closest carousel in the area. I hoped that's what Lukas had meant when he'd left the note.

I parked near the entrance and jogged inside, my gun in my hand.

I wasn't sure what I'd find.

The carousel came into view when I crested a hill. The horses were frozen in mid-stride, their black eyes gleaming in the moonlight.

"Lukas?" I called.

His answer came instantly. "You showed up."

I whirled around. "What is this about? Why did you escape?"

"Do you remember that night?" he asked.

"Of course I do. I'm here, aren't I?"

"That night, I promised you things wouldn't always be so fucked up."

"Yeah, well, you didn't exactly keep that promise."

He smiled a lopsided smile and spread his arms out. "I'm here now to make it up to you."

I took a step closer and narrowed my eyes. "How much do you remember?"

He leaned closer, as if we were conspiring siblings. "All of it."

The confession nearly knocked the wind from me. "Did you . . . I mean . . . did you just start to remember? Did it all come flooding back tonight?"

Even after I asked it, I knew what the answer must be. Memories didn't come back all at once like that. They came back in pieces over months and months. Putting them back together was like putting together a jigsaw puzzle when you didn't have the box as a reference.

"I never went through a memory alteration," he said, confirming my suspicions.

I rushed toward him. "You tried to kill me tonight!"

He laughed and grabbed my wrists as I swung at him. "It was all in good fun, Chlo!"

"How could you?"

"I've missed you."

I yanked away from him. "But why go to all this trouble? Why keep up the ruse when we saved you?"

He shoved his hands in the pockets of his leather jacket. "My goals were threefold. One, get Riley out of the picture without incriminating myself. Two, allow Riley's enemies to feel as though they've had their revenge. Three, reconnect with you."

"Me?"

"I knew family was the one thing that would motivate you to finally take action. So I made sure you knew you had some left."

Realization crept in. "You were the Rook's inside informant? You fed him all of that information. About you, about where Riley would be and when."

Lukas nodded. "Your friends, the Turncoats, they did my dirty work for me. It's the way I prefer to operate," he added with a grin. "Of course, they didn't know I was the informant."

The way Lukas talked, the way he acted, it reminded me too much of Connor. Clever and dangerous and charismatic. Maybe he did have his memories, after all, but the Branch had changed him.

"What's the point of all this?" I asked.

He shrugged. "With Riley gone, guess who's in charge?"

I sighed. "You."

"Me."

"Then what do you want me for?"

"I want you to join me."

"In doing what?"

He smiled again, and the light in his eyes burned like the heart of a fire. "Remaking the Branch."

I shook my head. "I hate that fucking place. I don't want to hear that name ever again."

"Then we'll rename it. I'll even let you pick."

Somewhere in the distance, I could hear the chopping of helicopter blades. I scanned the sky and saw the blinking of its lights. It looked as though it were headed our way.

"What'll it be, sister?"

Lukas had been right about one thing—the best way to motivate me was with family. Family was more tantalizing than a cure for the Angel Serum. The truth was, I didn't want to be cured. I didn't want to be vulnerable, weak. What I wanted was to not be alone, and being normal again—being without the Angel Serum's effects—had seemed like the easiest route to that.

Lukas was promising me a different solution. With my brother by my side, I wouldn't be alone anymore.

And my problem had never been with the Branch so much as it'd been with the people running it. If Lukas were in charge, maybe it wouldn't be so bad. Maybe we could do great things.

"What do you say?" he asked again as the chopper descended from the sky behind him, landing near the riverbank a hundred yards away.

I brought an arm up to shield my eyes as debris blew in every direction.

I had to shout to be heard over the roar of the wind. "I'll come with you," I said, "under one condition."

"What's that?"

"Riley will never be in charge, of anything, ever again."

"Chloe," he said. "If Riley comes anywhere near us, I'll let you be the one to put a bullet in his head."

I hooked my arm in his. "Then let us go remake the monster in our own image."

"There she is," he said. "My devilish little sister."

"Race you there," I said over a shoulder, and ran for the chopper.

Lukas took off after me, but he didn't stand a chance.

I would win. I always did.

© Joseph VonDrak

JENNIFER RUSH

began telling lies at the age of five and was immediately hooked. Fiction was far better than reality, and she spent most of her teen years writing (about vampires, naturally). She currently lives in Michigan with her husband and two children and enjoys eating ice cream in her spare time. *Reborn* is the third book in the Altered Saga. Her website is jennrush.com.